C000030543

NORTH SEA RISING

NORTH SEA RISING

Book 2 in the North Sea Noir series

by

R.M.Cartmel

NORTH SEA RISING © R.M. Cartmel
ISBN 978-1-9997652-8-6
eISBN 978-1-9997652-9-3

Published in 2018 by Crime Scene Books

The right of R.M. Cartmel to be identified as the author
of this work has been asserted by him in accordance with the
Copyright, Designs and Patents Act 1988.

Cover design by blacksheep-uk.com

Printed by CPI (UK) Ltd Croydon CR0 4YY

This is for Harry, my son, who thought my retirement would see me settling down into a 'lean and slipper'd pantaloon' phase (me? lean?) and maybe pulling the occasional cork. He has tolerated my gadding about the world doing 'research' with remarkable equanimity!

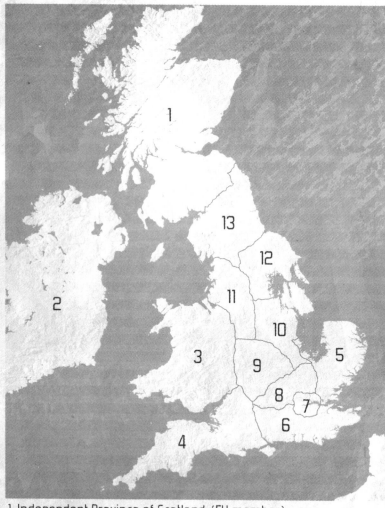

1. Independent Province of Scotland (EU member)
2. Independent Province of Eire (EU member)
3. Independent Province of Cymru (EU membership pending)
4. Independent Province of Wessex (EU membership pending)
5. Independent Province of Anglia (EU membership pending)
6. Province of Home Counties
7. London
8. South Mercia
9. Arden
10. North Mercia
11. Duchy of Lancaster
12. Ridings of Yorkshire
13. Northumbria

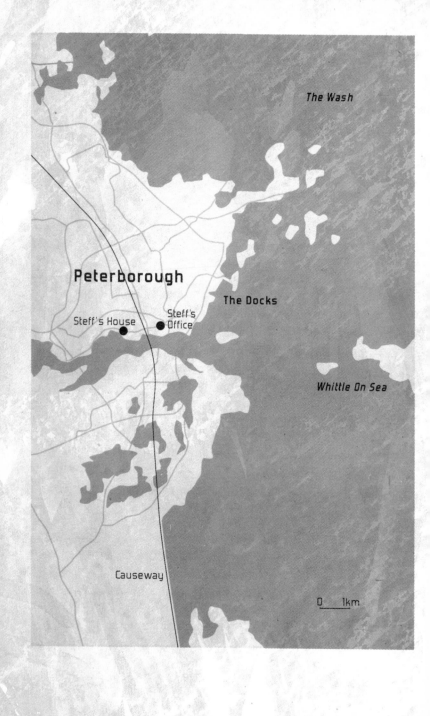

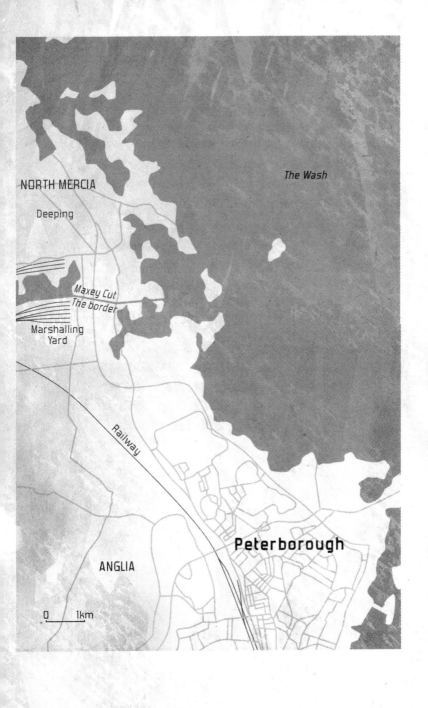

Prelude

She was a dead weight, a great lump of drunken lard. If she hadn't been doing anything whatever to keep herself moving, it would have been impossible, and if he had stepped away and dropped her, that would have been it, he would never have got her up onto her feet again. Propping her up on the wall, and praying that no one would come past, he fumbled in her bag. At least she didn't have a lot in there; pepper spray, check, phone, check, ah here it was, no it wasn't, it was a credit card. Who the hell carries credit cards still? Especially with their name and the name of their bank, now that was just asking for trouble. Here it was, identical in size, shape and feel to the credit card, but it had the name of the hotel emblazoned on the front. He waved it at the lock on the door, and the light on the front of the lock obligingly turned green.

'Are you having any problems there?' came a female voice of uncertain age from behind them. Damn, he thought, he knew he would run into trouble. He painted on an embarrassed smile and without letting the tub of lard fall, he half turned in the doorway.

'Silly old thing had too much to drink, and I'm just trying to get her into bed.'

'D'you want a hand?' came the friendly Glaswegian burr.

'Would you mind?'

It was considerably easier two people moving an insensible body to the bed than it had been for one to get her into the lift, up in the lift and along the corridor to her room. On the bed and flat on her back, she started to snore. Oh dear God, that noise!

'I think we ought to roll her over into the recovery position,' she said, 'I think she's in some danger of swallowing her tongue.' So that's what they did. They rolled her onto her side with the upside knee folded at ninety degrees.

'And she's bound to throw up, and that's a nice wee jacket she's wearing, shall we help her out of it and hang it up?'

Why not? By the time they had finished they had rescued most of the clothes that would matter if they were covered in vomitus, and her tights.

'I know her,' said the Scottish woman, he guessed she might be fifty or so. 'She writes books or something doesn't she?'

He explained she's famous for writing mystery novels based on her day-to-day work, and that she's a forensic psychologist.

'What's that exactly?'

'I suppose it means she looks into the state of mind of killers.'

'And you're her husband?'

'Good God no, I'm her secretary, personal assistant, her jobsworth who discreetly helps her to bed when she's had a skinful, anything useful to her really. It's a living,' he added drily.

She looked him up and down, and added, 'Aye she would need a strong wee lad like you to do all those things. Anyway, are we all sorted here?'

'Yes. I've got one or two bits of paper she will have expect me to have checked for tomorrow, and then I'm off to bed too.'

'Tomorrow?'

'She's doing a book signing in the city library. It's her latest book. It's probably the only reason they still print physical books; so that writers can sign them. It's good for their egos you know. I'll make sure she knows you helped if you come along.'

She chuckles and said, 'I'll see, I'm supposed to be back in Glesca tomorrow afternoon.'

'Ah well, there you go,' he said and she pottered out with a finger wave and pulled the door to behind her.

He looked back at the snoring form on the bed for a moment, and then his hand dived into his pocket. He pulled out an insulin cartridge and stuck a fine needle on one end. A plunger to screw into the top of the cartridge was the next thing that emerged from his pocket. She didn't make any further noise when he stuck the needle into the web space between the big toe and second toe of her right foot, and pushed the plunger down. He carefully removed the needle from the web space, and checked that there was no bleeding. There didn't appear to be any. He put the cap back onto the needle, and dropped the whole thing back into his pocket. Three hundred units of soluble as a single hit should do the trick, he thought as he took one final look at her, smiled grimly, and left the room.

Chapter 1
Snow? In August?

I opened my eyes but it didn't seem to make a lot of difference. It was still dark. What time was it, for heaven's sake? I felt as though I had slept pretty well, so why was it still so dark? I looked at the clock on my bedside table. It was eight o'clock already, so who had put the sun out? I hopped out of bed and went to the window. The sky was overall a grim leaden grey, and what was that coming down? Was it snowing? I hadn't seen it snow for the best part of twenty years, so where was this lot coming from now, and in the middle of August? Mind you, it wasn't settling. As soon as it came into contact with something static it melted instantly and was lost.

Well, it being eight o'clock, I didn't need to be wasting any more time. I hadn't got any early morning appointments as far as I knew but that was no excuse for not being there on the off chance. I hopped into the shower and gave myself a good lathering. When I felt comfortably clean, I grabbed the towel and dried myself all over, including my hair. My hair is straw-coloured and I have had it in a pixie-cut since forever, so when it's wet I don't need a hair drier. There are times when my hairdresser hopefully suggests I might like a change but I have a very good reason for keeping it short and simple. I'm a private investigator, and sometimes PIs need to be invisible. Short and simple means I can wear all sorts of wigs as disguises without it being obvious that I am wearing one. Added to that, I have been in a number of difficulties in the past, presumably because, at the moment I ran into trouble, I stood out. I looked at the midline scar on my lower abdomen for a moment. It may have faded over time but it was still as obvious to me as when I first saw it.

So that morning, the private eye who went downstairs was clean and dressed in jeans and a 'Ramones' sweatshirt. That shirt first went on the market years before I was born and it's still available now. I'm told that the band made far more money out of selling the sweatshirt than they ever did out of the album they made at the same time. And no, I haven't the faintest idea what the record sounds like, it's not in the old vinyl collection that came with my housemate, I just like the shirt.

I couldn't resist looking out of the window halfway down the stairs, as I re-sited my earpiece. Yes, that felt more comfortable; and that was definitely snow coming down and not sleet. Snow floated gently to the ground and was rather fun, sleet fell fast and was sharp and not in the least bit fun.

As usual, I was first down to breakfast, apart from Mrs. Grubbs of course. She and her husband, 'Our 'Enery', occupied the 'granny-flat' at the back of the house. No matter what time I chose to come down, Mrs. Grubbs was already there, and the coffee was just ready, and she always offered it as a request, 'Coffee, Steff?', as if I might not accept. I thought that one day I might decline just to see what happened, but today was not that day. Today I really needed that caffeine hit, especially as one of my regular clients had recently brought us that coffee from wherever it was he had recently been, and it was just wonderful.

'When did it start snowing?' I asked.

'During the night,' she replied, 'Our 'Enery got up to do his business, and told me about it when he came back. It's his prostate gland, you see.'

'I wonder when the last time was that it snowed in August,' I mused.

'Our 'Enery was wondering when the last time was that it snowed in Peterborough, even in winter. You must have been quite a little girl then.'

Henry Grubbs walked in from the kitchen. His wavy shock of white hair was wet, but he had already shed his raincoat. 'Bloody stuff,' he said. 'T'isn't like the old snow.'

'How do you mean?'

'T'is all gritty, this stuff. Don't let it get in your eyes, our Steff, t'will smart like buggery, t'will. Still, I suppose the chickens will like it, they like a bit o' rough stuff, do our chickens. Incidentally, they've laid a few today so if you want an egg for breakfast I'm sure Mrs. Grubbs will fix you one.'

'Not today,' I said sipping my coffee. Oh! I quietly shivered with bliss inside; Mrs. Grubbs' skills blended with the raw materials of

Kenya Peaberry beans were such a good partnership. 'I think I'll just have some toast.'

'With all those scrambled eggs on that uniform,' 'Enery chuckled, 'I don't think our Shove will be needing any of the real variety either!' That was the cue for the second upstairs member of the house to make her entry.

'I think someone looking as smart as that shouldn't be addressed simply as Shove,' I replied. 'I think at the very least she merits the full Siobhan.'

'Dressed up like this, I think Detective Chief Superintendent Flynn would be even more appropriate,' replied the lady in question with a grin.

Siobhan Flynn was in full dress uniform that morning and, bearing in mind her rank, there was a great deal of flash and filigree on that jacket. 'Why are you dressed up like that?' I asked, curiosity getting the better of me. Well, I'm a detective aren't I, so you would expect me to be inquisitive.

'The Senior Lecturer himself has summoned me to a meeting at the Witenagemot.' You could hear those capital letters all over the sentence just by the way she spoke them.

'Why, what have you done wrong?' It had to be something fairly serious for the Senior Lecturer to want to talk to one of his police chiefs without just using a videolink. Generally speaking, the video-links are considered secure enough for most purposes but the Senior Lecturer feels that it's always possible hackers can get into them so, for more sensitive conversations, he thinks it's still best to meet face to face.

'Nothing, as far as I know.'

'So what's it about then? The snow?'

'I've no idea,' she replied, and thought for a moment. At that time in the morning, before the first caffeine hit, even brains as sharp as Shove's require a moment to warm up. 'Do you happen to know where the King is at the moment?' she asked, as her eyes began to light up.

'Not offhand, I don't follow the Royal Family much, unless the King's brother is in on the act. He can be a bit of a giggle.'

'Well, last time the King and his family went to Sandringham to stay, they landed at Huntingdon Airport and were deposited into a number of different pods, as there was no way they were going suffer the indignity of all being piled into a single shuttle bus. Security thought it would be less public than going by train. The King got fairly umpty that they wouldn't let his royal limo out on the open roads but really, the King should know better, as if that was ever going to be likely. It isn't as if those things have sensors or a self-drive chip. Anyway, they left Alconbury in convoy but that's not how they arrived at the other end. The security detail got there first, followed ten minutes later by the King and Queen themselves. They then had a very stressful forty minutes' wait before the pod with the Prince and Princess of Wales on board rolled up. I think it was simply traffic that got in the way but I understand that Her Madge gave the Senior Lecturer quite an earful while they were waiting. The Prince of Wales thought it was a right royal hoot and described seeing all sorts of road features that couldn't possibly have been on any route in less than an hour, like the various views of Helm Crag at Grasmere and, of course, Stonehenge. His mother was even less amused as a result.'

'Helm Crag?' I asked. I didn't remember ever going to Grasmere.

'Yes, it's a peculiar rock formation at the top of a hill on the left as you go north on the old road from Grasmere to Keswick. At one moment it looks like an old man playing an upright piano, then it looks like a lion lying down and finally, as you look back over your shoulder as you go north, it looks like a howitzer.'

'How odd,' I replied. 'No doubt there is an explanation for that.'

'Volffy explained it to me once, when we went up there on holiday together. I can't remember what he said at the time, but everything he said was always interesting.' Back in the day, Volffy, short for Wolfgang, owned the house where we currently sat and shared it with his live-in girlfriend. When the ravages of time took him away, I bought the house from Volffy's kids before they even had the opportunity to put it on the market. Shove, being that live-in girlfriend, was already on site, of course, and I moved in to join her. As the Anglian regulations stated that a house of such a size and location should have a minimum of four adult residents, following the refugee crisis caused by the flooding of The Wash, the Grubbs from Wisbech found themselves a home from home and the four of us have all got along famously ever since.

'Ah, young love,' I grinned at her, and changed the subject. 'Anyway, the government shouldn't have let the royals have their number on speed dial, should they? It's not as if the King would find our government below his dignity or anything – after all, the systems we have in place pretty much guarantee that our leaders won't be thick or stupid or anything. It's about as far as it can be from our beloved city council, when any old prawn can stand for election, and the rest of the crustacean family will vote for him out of crunchy loyalty. Oh, there's a thought; satisfy my curiosity Shove: do you, as Chief of Police, get a vote to elect the government? I know I don't.'

'No, I don't either. I'm not even sure that the local branch of Anglia Ruskin University gets that many votes. I think it's just the Urban and Rural Councils, and the Senates of The Universities of East Anglia and Cambridge, who get those votes.'

'It sometimes has the feel of an Academic dictatorship, doesn't it? It isn't very democratic really.'

'Well, I don't know about you, but I think I would rather have the government we have than the half-witted idiots who let Britain secede from Europe. Did you know that the Prime Minister who led Britain out was someone who wanted to remain in?'

'But why would he go against his own wishes? I don't follow.'

'She,' Shove replied with ironic emphasis. 'I guess her urge to be Prime Minister was more important to her than her integrity. Power is a very seductive thing, you know.'

'No wonder she made such a pig's ear of it, if her heart wasn't in it.'

'Probably not, but she ploughed on regardless nonetheless, and then the economy collapsed and there wasn't enough money to repair the flood defences, and one country has now become five and counting.'

'But we've got a competent leader, even if he wants you to go half-way across the province just to discuss how not to upset the figure-head? Doesn't he realise you might have something more productive to do with your time?'

'Oh, I don't know it has anything to do with the King, in fact it probably hasn't. The Cambridge and Colchester chiefs have both been invited too, and I can't see why they would be invited if it involved a royal trip or anything. Satisfy my curiosity, Steff, your private eye licence is all up to date and everything, isn't it?'

I tapped my wristy and Shove glanced at hers, and in a moment she said, 'Yes, it's fine at the moment, it'll need revalidating in three months' time.' She then tapped her wrist, and my wristy vibrated for a moment, and when I glanced down at it, there it was, all updated.

'There,' she said, 'it's now up to date for another year. I'll update Dwayne's while I think about it.' It all goes to show how very convenient it can be to have the local police chief as your housemate.

'Why the sudden urge to make sure we're all up to date?'

'Well, you know your role in my life?'

'Being your landlady and stuff, you mean.'

'Not just that. There are definite things that I cannot do, as an official officer of the law, that I might want to do during the course of an investigation, as you very well know. Well, I can always ask a registered private investigator to do those sorts of things for me and no one would be any the wiser.'

'Ah, as a freebie you mean?'

She grinned at me, 'I'm sure we could arrange a quid pro quo, depending on the value of the investigation. And I'm absolutely sure that your Dwayne still considers himself seriously in debt to me for his current freedom to walk the streets un-arrested.'

There are moments when I ask myself whether Siobhan Flynn is really my friend or whether I am just a handy tool for her to use when needed. Shoot, I've only known her for the best part of a quarter of a century so what do I know? I was still cogitating this while she spread marmalade on her toast and took a bite. She hummed with pleasure. 'Mm, Mrs. Grubbs, is this still your home-made stuff from last year?' she asked.

'Yes, we've still got a few jars left,' the grey-haired lady replied.

'My mum used to make marmalade,' I remarked to keep in the conversation, and then added, 'that was before her accident,' pause, 'obviously.' I could still remember the aroma of cooking oranges in the kitchen when I was a child.

Mrs. Grubbs grinned, showing some of the gaps where teeth had once been. 'Bet she didn't make them from oranges grown in the back garden though, did she, our Steff?' she replied.

'No, perhaps not, though we did grow quite a lot of fruit in the garden in those days, some of which I haven't seen around recently,' I added, fondly remembering the sweet red gooseberries I hadn't seen really since the day my parents had their fatal accident.

Breakfast was soon over, and I tapped a code into my wristy to summon a pod. If the weather really was as foul as 'Enery had said, then I didn't think I wanted to walk in it. It wasn't far to the Cathedral Close but I really wasn't interested in arriving at the office a cold, gritty, soggy mess. My earpiece told me the pod would arrive in ten minutes. 'When are you next going to be here?' I asked Shove. 'Oh, by the way Mrs. Grubbs, I won't be in tonight to eat. I'm going to a meeting at the library.'

'Enery lifted his head, 'A meetin', eh? What nasty habit you trying to get shot of, then?'

'Not that sort of meeting, Mr Grubbs, thank you very much. It's a crime fiction writer who's going to be there talking about her books, especially the latest one, which is only just out.'

'Oh, OK. What's 'er new book about then?'

'No idea, I haven't had a chance to read it yet. Probably diamonds and dirty doings, that seems to be what the rest of her books are about. Our Dwayne likes them, though – she's got a disgustingly sexy detective with really long legs...'

Shove chipped in, 'I'll let you know when I've got back from Norwich. I'll have some idea then what this is all about and we can play it accordingly.'

'Got it.' My wristy tingled, and I glanced at it. Its screen told me there was a pod outside the front door waiting for me. 'See you', I said cheerfully. Like Oates, I went out into the snow, where a duck egg blue pod-for-two was waiting for me expectantly with the sliding door nearest to the house open and ready to take on boarders.

Chapter 2
The Rail

We're a nice, democratic little firm, Flack and Associates, which is why, when the woman walked through the door, it was the sight of me making coffee and Sabrina hammering away at the laptop that greeted her huge eyes. I am the Flack in the title, and Sabrina is the receptionist, secretary, human calculator and all the other useful sedentary 'associate' components of the business, but if you had just walked in off the street you wouldn't know it was that way round.

The woman was as thin as a rail. Who knows, she could possibly have been around the same age as me, but she could just as easily have been at least ten years either side. When the defining features of a face are cheekbones like hatchets, and two huge dark eyes, but nary a line nor a crease to mar their fearful symmetry, these things can be pretty hard to judge. Well, it was beyond me anyway. Someone had to have spent a lot of money on that look, and my immediate thought was that it might well have been the person who had put the gaudy diamond-studded knuckleduster onto her left hand. That probably wasn't the same guy who had followed her into my reception, although at least he was of an age that made the concept tasteful. He stood, you know, far too obsequiously behind her to have been the donor of an expensive ring, unless of course it had been a payment or a bribe of some sort. Physically, she was by far the smaller person standing in the doorway, and yet she was definitely the dominant character there, not him.

The Rail looked at Sabrina behind the laptop, tapping away busily, earnest expression, brown skin and Pakistani dress code, and me with a mug in each hand walking towards her. I could understand her being confused; she wasn't the first person to have been bewildered by the Flack democratic system in action.

'Is this Flack and Associates?' she asked, with a slight East European inflection in her voice that was beginning to fade over the passage of time. She raised an eyebrow, the effect of which was slightly disconcerting, as her eyes, being already too big for her face, didn't need any further enhancement.

I put the mugs down on the desk on my side of the laptop and replied, 'It is. I'm Stephanie Flack. What can we do for you?'

She looked me up and down for a moment. I'm used to being appraised. Private eyes aren't that common anyway in the Royal Province of Anglia, and if one turns out to be a young – well, all right, if you insist on my being totally honest about this, a young-ish woman – potential clients have a habit of looking me over. I don't find this in the least bit threatening or sexist.

'And you're the private detective?' she asked.

'I am she,' I replied. 'To whom do I have the pleasure of speaking?' I noticed that Sabrina had stopped typing and had picked up her tablet and was poised to take notes. I also noticed that the silent type behind The Rail had spotted Sabrina's actions and was showing interest in her in turn. I was beginning to hope that we were all going to get introduced as, if it didn't happen soon, 'the Rail' might stick.

And then, of course, she did introduce herself, and that really didn't help at all. 'I am Adelina Paravilyenka,' she said, well something like that anyway, and I thought words to the effect of *Oh crap, I'm never going to remember that in a hurry!* 'And this,' she continued, waving an elegant and fully-armed hand vaguely behind her, 'is my assistant.' Well, that put him in his place anyway; she didn't think he was important enough to award him a name.

'Would you like to come through to my office?' I said. 'Tea or coffee? I'm having one.' I picked up my mug from the corner of Sabrina's desk.

'No, thank you,' she said, following me through the door to my office.

My office is conveniently laid out. I have a large pillar desk, probably made out of mahogany, that I had picked up some time ago in a junk shop. I find it quite useful to either hide behind or loom over. It is possible for me to loom, despite not being the tallest of people. I have the sort of face that I can make look quite fierce if I am so minded, depending on my mood, and also depending on who is on the other side of the desk. On it was a collapsed laptop and a pad of paper. There was a disused whisky glass full of various tools with which I write stuff.

14

It occasionally serves to be emptied out onto my desk and returned to its original use. I don't drink much but occasionally a client might suddenly need a stiffener. The fluids required to create a stiffener I keep locked in a drawer. I walked around the desk and sat in my chair, The Rail seated herself on one of the chairs in front of it and her 'assistant' remained standing behind her, at the half past four position. He was considerably taller than her anyway, and by the time she had sat down at my desk, it required me to go boss-eyed to get both faces in focus at the same time. 'Do sit down,' I said to him. The Rail looked up at him from where she was sitting but didn't say anything: her look was command enough, and he remained standing. I was beginning to regret that the other associate in my firm's name, Dwayne, was out on a case. This 'assistant' was presumably a bodyguard or minder and he looked the sort of person who might try to 'sort me out' just to assess how difficult that might be. It might actually have been considerably more difficult than it might first appear as I like to think that, in my case, appearances can be quite deceptive. Certainly, I keep up with my self-defence programme so, at the very least, some of the furniture would get damaged if any nonsense took place in my office. I decided that my best move was to ignore the assistant completely and focus on The Rail. This was no good, she was going to need a name I could spell to stop me calling her that.

'I need to decide whether you are the person I want to hire,' she said.

'Fair enough,' I said, 'and I suppose I need to decide whether I want you to hire me. What would you want to know to help us both make that decision?'

'Cost?'

'Two fifty a day plus expenses,' I replied, 'and I don't do stuff that might upset my professional relationship with the law if they catch me at it.'

'And if we could guarantee that you didn't get caught?' This woman was interestingly quick.

'It would probably put the expenses rate up a bit,' I replied.

She smiled at that. The smile softened her face in quite a surprising way. It didn't last very long, but it did show a different side to her. It might be interesting to get young Dwayne's take on it too.

'You do surveillance?'

'Of course, that's the bread and butter work for private eyes.' I fished a bit. 'What is your husband mixed up in?' I was pointedly looking at the knuckleduster on her left hand. Though, to be honest, it was more like her left hand was being worn by the knuckleduster.

'My husband?' she said, puzzled for a moment, and then realised what I was staring at. 'He's dead,' she replied coldly.

'And you want me to investigate that?' I asked.

'He was an old man, and death is often what happens to people of his age, why would I want to waste my money asking you to investigate the truth of life?' She started to get up as if to leave. That was not what I wanted at all.

'So what is it that you want me to look into for you?' I asked hurriedly. It wasn't often that I lost a case in the opening interview but I saw that might just be a possibility today.

She turned round again and faced me. 'How much can I count on your discretion?'

'One hundred per cent.'

'Even if I decide, in the end, not to hire you.'

'I would forget we ever had this conversation.'

'Even under torture?' she asked after a moment. She didn't look threatening at that particular moment but in my line of business you had to keep your wits about you.

'Well, that's never been tested,' I replied, and grinned. 'I tend to lose consciousness when I'm in pain, though – you can ask my dentist.'

She gazed at me for a moment and gave me another of those expressions that she obviously kept in store to maintain control of conversations.

I didn't see where she got it from, but the next moment she was emptying a black velvet bag on the desk. The contents were items that glittered.

'What do you think?' she asked.

'What do I think about what in particular?' I asked.

'What do you think they're worth?'

I looked at them for a moment. To me they were worth nothing. I don't do glittery clothes. I doubted they were even rhinestones to be honest. 'Ten Euros the lot, including the bag,' I replied.

She looked at the minder. 'I think she'll do,' she said.

'Is there a story behind this I should know?' I asked.

'That bag was put through my letterbox this morning, with this little note.' She tossed a scrunched-up bit of paper at me. I gently flattened it out and read the scrawl revealed on it, which said simply, 'I don't think so,' in dark black pencil. Well, at least someone's still got a pencil, I thought wryly.

I raised my eyes, trying to give her one of her own expressions back and failing completely. Those would have taken years to perfect.

'When I last saw that bag, it contained real diamonds,' she said.

'And when was that?' I asked.

'Yesterday morning,' she replied.

'Ah,' I said, waiting for her to carry on with her narrative.

'Diamonds can be a useful currency in these confusing times. And, moreover, they're not as heavy as gold.' I looked at the pieces of glass scattered on my desk and tried to revalue them as if they really were diamonds. Now, I'm no diamond expert, so I had no idea how to fine tune that valuation but my immediate thought was that if they had been real diamonds, and they were mine, I would never have to do another day's work in my life, and I certainly wouldn't be living in the same hemisphere as Peterborough.

'Go on,' I said.

'Well, another form of currency might be pure cocaine,' she said.

'Yeah, you either deal in it or ruin your nose with it.' I had never taken cocaine myself, but I had seen the effect it had on people, especially during my years as a junior articled clerk down in London, when Great Britain was still just the one country, and even Scotland and Northern Ireland were still only on the cusp of leaving the union. Anyway, one of the senior partners in the firm had taken a line in front of me and then offered to share it with me, as if that would impress me. After I had declined, I thought fairly politely, to partake of the powder he had poured all over my desk, he tried to force himself on me. The managing partner could tell immediately what had happened by the strange locations of the bruising on his face as the offender was shown the door. His departure didn't seem to discourage the rock apes long term. He wasn't the last of them who seemed to consider that the presence of the young clerk was specifically for their entertainment, so I started doing self-defence classes in London, a form of training I continue to this day. Don't get me wrong, I do enjoy a spot of sex from time to time, it's just that I reserve the right to choose the people I do it with. So, as I was saying, I wasn't really a fan of cocaine.

'That was the agreed rate of exchange, those diamonds for a quantity of cocaine.'

'So, may I ask what you were going to do with a sack full of high-grade cocaine? It's not a designer drug like Phantasm, so it has a rather narrow niche in the market, or so I'm told.'

The Rail rather pointedly sniffed the air. 'That smells like real coffee in your mug,' she replied drily.

'It is,' I said, 'Kenyan Peaberry, medium roast. And your point is?'

'Well it's not a Readi-Stim tablet, is it? It isn't even instant coffee. Some people are still willing to pay top dollar if they've got a taste for the real thing. It's an investment, just like claret. I don't use cocaine myself, but there are people with serious money behind them who do and, like all good investments, when you have something that somebody else wants, there will be people who are willing to buy it off you.'

'Fair enough,' I said, 'so what happened?'

'Well, that's partly what we are asking you to find out. You already understand why I've come to you rather than gone to the police. I think I ought to ask if you're interested in taking the case before I go any further.'

I thought about it for a while. This sounded like it could be fun, certainly an improvement on hiding in parked pods with a long-lens camera, hoping to catch some businessman in flagrante delicto with his secretary, or maybe the businessman's wife doing the business with a tennis pro. 'I'm interested,' I said, 'but I think the expenses will have to be higher.'

'I understand,' she said and paused. The tone of her voice turned back into narrative mode. 'I gave that bag to one of my assistants yesterday morning and sent him off to do the trade. He was due to come back in the evening with the cocaine in the back of a pod. I was becoming a little concerned when I heard nothing from him as late as this morning. I was even more concerned when I found that bag in a padded envelope stuffed through my home letterbox with my morning paper. And yes, I still read a newspaper. I find it much easier to flick through than reading the news on a screen, and the diagrams in particular are much easier to follow. The post had not yet arrived.'

'And your courier?'

'Nothing from him at all.'

'And the cocaine?'

'No sign of that either.'

'I need to know the courier's name and where he usually hangs out, and how you contact him when you need him. I also need to know from where you get your newspapers delivered. And, probably most important, I need to know who you were doing the business with, and how I would get in touch with him.' I paused. 'Her?' I queried.

'I think Sigmund, as the businessman calls himself, is a he, yes. I suppose he could be a woman masquerading as a man. For all I know, he might think I am a man pretending to be a woman. We've never met; we contact each other through a message drop.'

'How long have you been doing business with him?'

'I inherited him from my husband: he was someone my husband did business with before he died, and I just carried it on. It has seemed mutually beneficial so we never changed it. I know, I know, every form of business goes belly up sooner or later if you don't mix it up a bit. This was one of the next bits I was planning on changing. We just hadn't got there yet.'

'If I wanted to get in touch with him, how would I do it?'

'You'd ask me very nicely, and I would put out a letter-drop and you would go and meet him, or his representative, as my assistant. It might take you a little while to get accepted, I suppose.'

'So, who is your current assistant, and where would I find him?'

'I don't know where you would find him right now. He wasn't at any of the places we expect to find him when we need him, was he, Yuri?'

'No,' was the first word I heard the silent minder say. And I now had a name for him – well, a forename anyway.

As Yuri didn't say anything else, I carried on. 'Do you think it's possible that your assistant swapped the diamonds for those, ah, glass beads, and made off with the real ones?' I asked.

She looked at me for a moment. 'Well, they didn't fool you for a moment,' she said. 'He isn't stupid, so he must have realised they wouldn't fool Sigmund either.'

'Unless he told your Sigmund that you were trying to pass off the beads as diamonds.'

'I would doubt that Sigmund would believe that. We have, after all, been doing business with him for a considerable length of time, and neither of us had ever had any problem with the other.'

'It was your husband who did business with Sigmund ...' I started.

'Mrs. Flack, my husband died ten years ago. I've done plenty of business with Sigmund since then.'

'It's Ms. Flack, if you're going to be formal. I've never been married. But why not just call me Steff? Everyone else does.'

'Steff,' she rolled the word round her mouth to see if it left an unpleasant aftertaste. Obviously it didn't. 'All right, then,' she said giving me another smoke detector special expression. 'Call me Adelina.'

'Well, Adelina,' I said: yes, that worked okay, 'tell me about your courier.'

'Ruke,' she said. 'Late forties, early fifties, I suppose. He spent a lot of his life in prison, relatively recently released.'

'Why did you trust an ex-jailbird with your diamonds? Wasn't that a little brave?'

'He had worked freelance for various people when he was young, my husband being just one of them. He wasn't working for my husband when he was locked up for a long time for people trafficking and homicide. He never stole anything from us, and my husband told me to look out for him if he ever reappeared.' She tapped her left temple. 'Eidetic memory. Anyway, he was so grateful that we gave him a job when he got out that I don't think for a moment he would want to rip us off, let alone dare to try.' She looked up quizzically at Yuri, who produced his pet monosyllable for the second time: 'No.'

I took a pull at the mug on my desk but the coffee was distinctly tepid now, so I put it back down again. 'Ruke,' I said. Somewhere in the deep refuges of my mind, the name Ruke rang a bell, but I couldn't remember where from: probably in London, though if it was a Ruke in London, it wouldn't have been this one, because from what Adelina Rail was saying, all the time I was in London, this one was behind bars. 'What was his full name?' I asked. It would be as good a starting point as any to see if I could run this fellow to ground and see if he really was a Light-Fingered Larry.

20

There was a movement in front of me. Adelina was exchanging a knowing glance with the man behind her, and a woman with an eidetic memory shouldn't need reminding of the full details of a missing man's name. There was something else they weren't telling me, although whether it was important or not, I would find out in the fullness of time.

'Farrukh Ahmed's his full name, but we never heard anyone call him anything but Ruke.' That sounded very obviously the last sentence of a conversation.

'And how do I make contact with you?' I asked.

She pulled a ballpoint out of the whisky glass and scribbled a telephone number on a piece of blank paper I had conveniently left on my desk. 'That's my current contact number,' she said. 'I do change it fairly often but, if I do so, I will call your office and let you know the new number. If you feel we need to meet, call the number you have and we'll arrange a meeting. Anything else?'

'I'll get in touch tomorrow with an agreement. Personally, I'm old enough to like a contract on paper. It gives me a sense of unalterable permanence that electronic media can't quite do. That way we at least know what we expect of each other, and we'll take it from there. However, we can produce it in any format that you prefer.'

'Fine,' she nodded and then said, 'Anything else?' again.

I couldn't think of anything else off the top of my head, so I shook it. She stood up and stretched a hand across my desk and I shook that too. It was not a big hand at all, but it didn't feel weak. It was a slightly alarming handshake from such a small person. 'Until tomorrow, then,' she said and added with a pause, 'Steff.' At school our music teacher taught us that syncopation was done with a slight sniff before the word: it was exactly the same effect.

To which I replied, also with a sniff, 'Adelina.'

As they walked out I put my hand into my top left drawer. It went straight to the back, behind the bottle of scotch, to the pieces of Mars hidden there. I pulled one out, peeled it and popped it into my mouth. For a brief moment I concentrated on the sensation it gave me. There are times when a girl just needs chocolate.

Chapter 3
Ruke

Sabrina looked up at me as I followed them out of my office. She raised her eyebrows as a question mark.

'Can you knock out a contract?' I asked.

'A complex one?' she queried.

'I think the full Mark Three is appropriate, yes.' I replied. 'I'm going to nip home to get us some more coffee. I won't be very long, just buzz me if you need me.'

''Bye.'

We weren't actually that short of coffee at the office, but there were one or two things I wanted to find out for myself before I committed us to a binding agreement with The Rail. I summoned a pod, which took no more than five minutes to arrive, so it must have been parked nearby. I climbed in and sat down in the left hand seat, as is my preference. I still find it disconcerting to sit on the 'driver's side' without a wheel and pedals to hang on to. I strapped myself in and programmed in the postcode of the City Hospital mortuary before shutting the blinds. There are very few things I find difficult to cope with, but one of them is watching pods just miss each other by inches, especially if I'm sitting in one of them. I don't think I've ever got used to the fact that every pod is a far more skilled driver than I ever was. While swirling about in traffic is second nature to them, those close shaves would be fatal to most human drivers. After all, that is why I was orphaned as a twelve year old. My father had bought an Aston Martin and then, perhaps to test how strong it was, he drove it into a tree at high speed. Sadly, he proved to my mother, who was also on board, that the tree he had picked was far more resilient than his Aston Martin. To prevent that happening now, aside from not travelling as quickly as the Aston Martin, pods have 'eyes' all around them like some sort of Ordovician sea monster, and their 'brain' is programmed to be monitoring every direction at once. Moreover, at least in Anglia anyway, all road vehicles are state-owned and they won't even think about picking up a fare unless every eye, among other things, is in perfect working order. Private ownership of transportation is a thing of the past. Or, at least, that's our government's promise.

There were occasional moments when the pod slowed and accelerated but when it finally actually stopped, I knew I was at the spot I had programmed in.

The back entrance to the hospital is round the services area and is not a place you would expect to find members of the public milling around. I jumped up onto the loading dock and was through the swing doors immediately. I strode down the corridor and turned left through the door that had the word 'Mortuary' emblazoned over it. Beyond that door, again on the left, is another marked, 'Mortuary Technician'. This was the first door to which I showed any deference, and I knocked politely and waited.

'Hello?' came from the other side, complete with question mark, and I stepped inside.

The technician was a distinctly elderly man with a mass of white hair. He sort of half-wore a blue paper hat on top, which I supposed he could pull down to cover his head properly if he really wanted to.

'Shteffy!' he cried as I walked through the door, in the thick Polish accent that hadn't changed one iota in the years I had known him.

'Yertsi!' I replied, mimicking his inflection completely.

'Vot brings you to my humble abote?' he asked. Oh, to heck with the accents, you get the picture.

'Tea, coffee, a spot of information, why do I usually come to see you, Jerzy?'

'Coffee I can do, if you will put up with cheap and nasty. I think I might even have a tea bag I've only used once.' He grinned at me.

'Why don't you ever bring your own jar in?'

'The hospital provides this stuff for the wards, and occasionally a tin falls off a trolley in my direction.'

I decided that I would just as soon do without, and then started on the second reason for my visit: information. 'Tell me, Jerzy, have you had a recent customer called Farrukh Ahmed?'

'I think so,' he said, looking over at his computer terminal. 'Yes, here he is. Do you want to have a word with him?' Jerzy always pretended that his visitors were still in some way alive.

'If it's not a problem.'

'Follow me, there's nobody else but us actually breathing down here at the moment.'

We walked through into the cold room and he led me over to the row of fridges.

'Here he is,' said Jerzy, pulling out a drawer.

It was a face I had seen before, though I couldn't offhand remember where. I very much doubted that he'd had that bullet hole in the middle of his forehead when I last saw him. The bullet hole was in exactly the place where Hindus put their red kum-kum marks. That was a little disconcerting. He was in his mid-fifties and greying round the edges. The lines around his eyes showed his life in prison had not been that easy. I pointed my wristy at him and snapped a picture. It was possible it might be handy. Working magic on photographs is one of Sabrina's many gifts: for instance, being able to make bullet holes disappear if you don't want them to be there.

'Came in in the early hours of this morning.'

'Any idea when the autopsy is scheduled for?'

'Probably this afternoon—this is a police case, as you can see.'

'Any chance you can get me a copy of the report when it's done?'

'For you, Steffy, the world!'

'Thank you, Jerzy, you're a diamond,' I said, shaking his hand, and he palmed the banknotes I passed over. The banknote kiss was a technique we had both perfected over the years in case it needed to take place when someone else was in the room. That had never actually happened, but we still practiced. Very few people use banknotes any more, but they're still legal tender, probably because their cancellation has never risen high enough up anyone's agenda to happen. I haven't seen a new banknote for a long time but they became pretty much indestructible when they all became plastic, even the Euros and the US Dollars. Anyway, they're useful as bribes or a discreet backhander. I guess Jerzy and I were old pals.

I summoned a pod again; it was there so quickly, and with the blinds down, that it was probably the same pod I had just left. Who was that guy in the mortuary? Where had I seen him before? It really wasn't possible that I actually had; The Rail had said he'd been in prison until recently. Maybe I had done business with a relative somewhere in the dim and distant. It was possible Sabrina would be able to get a line on that. She had made it her business to know her way round 'the Sharon filing system' that predated her own tenure in our front office.

The other thing that my meeting with Jerzy had reminded me of was that I had promised Sabrina that I was going out to get some more coffee for the office. There was absolutely no way that I would put up with instant coffee powder, whatever the kids would let past their lips. I strapped myself in – very securely – gave the pod the postcode of my home and crossed my fingers that it got there in as few pieces as possible.

Part of the finger-crossing was that the direct route from the hospital to where I lived would take the pod straight through the Western Sub Quarter. Okay, so I had the curtains drawn in the pod, so no one could see who was on board, but I would not have wanted to stop anywhere down within the walls of the Western Sub. The walls were now as tatty as the road surface inside them, as the pod reminded me, fairly brutally, every moment it was crossing the quarter. Most of the time I was in contact with some portion of the seat, but I was well aware that was only because I was so well strapped in. I could tell immediately that I had reached the other side of the quarter when the road surface suddenly improved. Thorpe Road is the main arterial road from the town Centre to South Mercia, and points west. Someone in the council had decreed that the four main thoroughfares, one in each direction of the compass, should be properly maintained. It had struck me as pointless that the eastern road was equally well maintained, as you hadn't even got out of the city limits when you hit The Wash, and the only way to get to Kings Lynn nowadays was by following the south road as far as Huntingdon and then following the coastline round.

It was a mere hundred yards on Thorpe Road before the pod turned off it again, but there were very few bumps left before the pod pulled up and meeped at me. 'You have arrived at your destination on the left,' it announced in a vaguely metallic but nonetheless female tone. I pulled the curtain back to look out before I pressed the door release button. I would hate to step into a passing neighbour when getting out of a pod. I looked through the front screen down the hill in front of me. I didn't think the water level had changed much recently, but I had no idea what effect the new snowfall would have on it, especially as the grit that was coming down with it would be unlikely to evaporate off. I still felt uncomfortable looking at the roofs of the houses appearing out of the river in front of me. The water level had been much lower than it was now when I first moved into the house. There were moments when I wondered whether the water level would ever stop its inexorable climb up the street. Still, if it got to my front door it would also be embarrassing the Cathedral and even the steps of the Town Hall. So, hopefully, by then the Anglian Government would have invested in further flood defences, the lack of which had triggered the Anglian Independence Movement in the first place. I am not sure the English can still believe the success we Anglians have made of our ten years of independence. In the absence of any flood defences whatsoever, the sea level at my front door would be as high as it had been since Roman times, when the land that is now urban Peterborough had been an uncultivated swamp.

I walked up the front steps and tapped the pad on the front door. It thought about it for a moment, coughed, and then obligingly opened. 'It's only me, Mrs. Grubbs,' I called out cheerily as I walked in.

'Morning, Steff,' she replied from the kitchen without coming through, so I wandered in to join her. 'You're back early.'

I reached up and grabbed a pressed cube of coffee beans from the larder cupboard and remarked that we needed some at the office. Mrs. Grubbs looked up at me, smiled, and said, 'Are you still going to that thing in the library this evening?'

'As far as I know, but I'll let you know if things change,' I replied. It must have been seriously irritating for Mrs. G. not to know who was going to be in for supper in the evening but she never betrayed the slightest annoyance to either of us.

I pottered back out of the front door to the pod, which was still there, obediently waiting for its master's return. I could almost picture it wagging its rear windscreen wiper at me. I strapped myself in and asked it to take me the several hundred yards back to my office. I would hate to have been mugged for a small pack of coffee.

Hopping out of the pod in the Cathedral Square, I went back upstairs to the front office of Flack and Associates. Dwayne was back and was slouching all over Sabrina's desk, looking very pleased with himself. All of the operatives who worked at Flack's had been born in

Peterborough. It wasn't a required qualification or anything; it had just worked out that way. The other interesting thing was that none of the parents of the operatives had even been born in what was to become The Royal Province of Anglia. Admittedly, my dad had only been born over the border in Market Deeping, now part of the English Province of North Mercia, but Dwayne's parents had come over from Barbados, I gather in a band and, for one reason or another, had never gone back.

'Oh, the band broke up and they couldn't afford to stay in London, so thought they might try their luck in somewhere like Newcastle or Leeds. Problem was, the train's ticket collector found them in the baggage compartment and threw them off at the next stop, which was Peterborough.'

He was lucky that the train hadn't stopped at Ardley, wherever that is exactly. Every time I had been to London recently, the train had stopped at Ardley. There had been no one on the platform, and no one had ever got off or on there, but the train had stopped there nonetheless. Anyway, our Dwayne had a lively start in life, which kept bringing him up in front of one DCI and upwards: Flynn of the local constabulary. Now, if you regularly come face-to-face with Siobhan Flynn and you're not a junior police officer or, even less commonly, one of her personal friends, then you are bound for big and long-lasting trouble.

To cut a long story short, one morning three years ago, Shove brought Dwayne round, pretty much dragging him by the ear, parked him in my front office and suggested I might care to do something with him because, if I didn't, the next time he ended up in front of her it was likely he would go down for a long stretch, even if it was just for 'loitering with an unpleasant expression on his face'. Obviously she saw something positive in the rangy young man who was forever getting into trouble and, as our then-secretary/receptionist, Sharon, was pregnant at the time, and therefore it was inappropriate that she should come out on surveillance with me any more, as a favour to my housie I took him on.

Well, since then, Sharon decided that pregnant was how she wanted to be for the foreseeable future, and is still showing no signs of growing out of that. She changed jobs from being my general factotum to being a full-time mother, and Sabrina replaced her. However, I had kind of got used to Dwayne being around and, as he didn't steal any paper clips, he's still here and is now an associate detective, Shove having recently awarded him his licence and everything. Yes, you really do need a licence to be an official Private Eye [in capitals] in the Royal Province of Anglia. Not so in London or in North Mercia: in those provinces you only get capital letters on proper names, or at the beginning of sentences.

I pulled out my phone and flashed up the picture I had taken of Farrukh Ahmed. 'Anybody recognise him?' I asked.

Sabrina and Dwayne both looked at him carefully and shook their heads. 'He's not going to recover from that in a hurry, is he?' remarked Dwayne drily.

'He's not an ex-client or anything?' I asked.

'Not in our time,' was the tenor of both their replies. Sabrina offered to look through the filing system, and I replied that I would appreciate it if she did, then I went through to my office, Dwayne following me.

'How did it go?' I asked him.

'As we thought,' he said. 'He's not a guilty man. He really is just working late at the office. His secretary does go home shortly after five and he stays late, on his lonesome, working at the desk.'

'You managed to get pictures of him working late?'

'You want to see them? I've got hundreds of the buggers at roughly a couple of minute intervals. It was arguably the most boring stakeout I've ever done.'

'Any evidence he knew he was under surveillance and was putting on a show for your benefit?' I asked.

'It was an Oscar winning performance if that was the case. I couldn't be that boring solidly for three days on the bounce, I'll tell you that. He got up for two reasons only: to go for a slash, and to make a cup of coffee.'

'And you saw him slashing?'

'Err no, but the light went on in the room with the frosted glass next to his office for less than a minute, and then it went off again and he came back. If he's got a popsy in the bog he doesn't seem to care about her over much. The coffee machine is on screen, though.'

'Are you going to tell the wife then?'

'Well, it's what she paid us to do. Oh, I see what you mean, yes, I'm quite happy to go and tell the poor woman that her husband's every bit as boring as she feared.'

'Ask Sabrina to prepare a completed bill then, and a few selected printouts of your snapshots on heavy glossy paper, and give her a copy of the chip. Then come back, I've got another job for us.'

'A good one?'

'Well it's already got some stolen diamonds and that corpse with the bullet hole in his head, and it's only been going an hour and a half.'

'And it's got a pretty girl?' he asked. 'It's got to have a pretty girl.'

I thought about The Rail for a moment, then said, 'Well, if you like them stick thin and about as old as me but with pots of money, I would imagine you might think she's quite pretty.'

'You're not old, Boss,' he grinned at me, 'and I reckon you would buff up all right if you made an effort.'

I threw a ballpoint at him, which he caught deftly and returned with a neat underarm throw.

Chapter 4
Two Contracts

At this dramatic juncture in our narrative there came a tap on the door and Sabrina walked in. She waved a 3D printed tablet at me, asking, 'How does this look?' It was the report she had created for Dwayne's job. I tapped the screen a couple of times and saw there were a few photos as well, and in the bill, she had factored in Dwayne's time too: the whole thing looked just fine.

'Have you got a copy for us?' I asked.

'Of course,' she said with the unspoken comment, 'as if', which she left hanging.

'Well, we'll take this round to her,' I said. 'While I think about it, did you sort out that contract for the Russian lady from earlier this morning?'

'Of course,' she replied, and produced another 3D tablet from under the folds of her hijab, like a magician taking a rabbit out of a hat. 'I've set it up to be authenticated twice so, needless to say, I've printed two tablets. Incidentally, boss, she's not Russian; Paravilyenka's a Ukrainian name, but she did say she was of Slovakian origin.' She slid the tablets apart and fanned them out and I could tell that she was internally smirking, even though her face showed no signs of it.

'I'll take a couple of paper copies as well. You never know, she recognised real coffee and ballpoints, she might be even more traditional in her thinking than I am.'

'Even people of my generation are not unhappy about having a physical contract to sign, rather than just tapping in a code. It still works,' Sabrina grinned at Dwayne, 'even for us kids.'

'Within reason. For example, nobody who's still breathing listens to that strange stuff you listen to,' was Dwayne's take on the situation. 'All those people on your playlist are dead, boss.'

'Most of the people on yours are too, they're the same people,' I shot right back at him, cheeky rascal. 'Plagiarism isn't clever, you know.'

'It's not plagiarism, it's called sampling.' However, Dwayne realised that it wasn't doing his case any good to carry on with that line of discussion. 'Do you want me to take that round to the customer?'

I had already calmed down again and I told him, 'No, it's all right. I've met The Rail already, and it was I who saw the remains of her courier in the mortuary, so I think it should be me telling her all about it, as a free goodie, so to speak. Sabrina, once you've got the pad and the printouts ready, bring them in and I'll summon a pod. Oh, and while you're at it, can you create a paper copy of the picture of the courier for that pack too.'

'Wilco, Boss,' said Sabrina and walked back through the door, firing me a jaunty salute. 'I assume you want me to leave the bullet hole in place?'

'I think so,' I replied and tapped my wristy and called the number The Rail had given me.

'Yes?' came the soft Eastern European voice. So she answers her own calls. Interesting to know.

'Flack and Associates here. I have a contract here with me, where would you like to meet to go through it? Oh, and I have a little information to give you, just to prove how good I am, even if you don't want to take it any further.'

'You know Lincoln Road in Millfield?'

'Yes.'

'Well, there's a little café on Lincoln Road, among the shops on the left as you go north. It's called The Borscht, you'll find me in there in about twenty minutes.'

'I'll be there.' That was a guarantee – I could walk it from the Cathedral Square in twenty minutes if I got a wiggle on, assuming no one was digging up the road again this week. At least the pods seem to know about any roadworks by instinct.

I strode through into the outer office to see Sabrina standing over the printer while it firstly created a pad, and then, in changing to 2D mode, two printed sheets of text and a photo. She put them all into a hemp bag and passed them over to me. 'The pod's outside,' she said. 'I summoned it myself on the office comm.'

I had had a further thought about how we were going to do this, and I called back to Dwayne, 'I've had a rethink—why don't you come along too? After we've sorted the contract with Mrs. Ukraine, you can take your report round to Mrs. Very-Dull. It'll do everyone good for us all to know who we're dealing with.' And with that, he followed me out, we walked down the stairs and emerged into the square where a pod was obediently waiting. Climbing in, I tapped in the address I had been given. Once again, I closed the blinds before the pod started moving.

'You really don't like things whirling in front of your nose do you, Steff?' said Dwayne grinning.

'I really don't,' I agreed. 'How can you cope with it?'

'I think it's all rather fun,' he replied. 'I play games with myself trying to guess who the person in the other pod is, where they're going and what they're going to do when they get there. Or if a pod has its curtains drawn, I ask myself why that pod is wearing a burqa and what it is that they're doing in there that they don't want anyone else to see.'

I shuddered internally but wasn't going to let Dwayne see it. 'They're probably trying not to let the passers-by see how absolutely terrified they are. You have to remember that people of my generation actually drove cars, and I remember how dangerous they were. My parents were killed in one you know.' I tossed him a grimace and took out the pad Sabrina had made, tapping it just to make sure I knew exactly what it said in case The Rail had any questions about the contract that I didn't expect. There wasn't anything on the pad that I found particularly surprising, but you never knew.

The front door of The Borscht was a nondescript, rather old-fashioned thing, which had to be at least sixty years old. It had a window in it, which was covered on the inside with a net curtain, which rather defeated the point of there being a window in the first place. We walked through the door and Dwayne pushed it shut behind us. Adelina was sitting at a table with her associate, who was proving he could indeed talk; he was deep in discussion with her. As we approached them, I was aware that a lad who had been sitting at a table by the door nursing a cup of something brown and cold-looking had stood up, flicked the latch on the door, and had changed the sign on it to closed. He had then sat back down again and was once again minding his own business and his cup.

The minder stood up to greet us, while Adelina remained seated.

'Yuri,' he said, offering me his hand.

'And this is Dwayne,' I replied. 'He's the associate, as in Flack and Associates.'

'Tea?' said Yuri, 'something stronger?'

'Tea would be fine,' I replied, aware that Dwayne was goggling at Adelina. Funny, I thought, it hadn't actually occurred to me that she was attractive, but then my system is definitely female. Now Shove, she's what I would understand to be attractive, her features are soft and gentle. This woman was all eyes and angles, but Darren seemed to approve. He goggled a bit more this time at the kitchen door, when Yuri popped his fingers and an elfin girl, of probably little more than eighteen, appeared from the back room There are times when I worry about Dwayne.

Yuri spoke to the girl in some Eastern European tongue that I, for one, didn't immediately recognise, and she disappeared back through the door again. Meanwhile Dwayne had produced the pad and put it in front of Adelina.

'Who's this?' she asked when she got to the picture.

'We think it's your courier, Ruke,' I replied.

She looked at the picture a little more closely. 'So it is,' she said. 'I didn't recognise him with that red kum-kum mark on his forehead.

'That's not a kum-kum mark, it's a bullet hole,' I replied, watching their faces carefully.

'Oh!' Adelina's eyes enlarged, and Dwayne appeared suitably impressed. 'That puts a different complexion on the issue.'

She turned to face Dwayne directly, 'I assume it wasn't you who shot him. She's not brought you here as a gift, has she?'

'What? No!' Dwayne was a little thrown.

I rode to his rescue, in case the minder was going to do something we would all regret at our leisure later. 'No, he's my associate, you know, another detective, we work together.'

The elfin girl returned from the kitchen carrying a tray on which there were four glasses with something clear in them. Dwayne's eyes glued themselves to her again and I couldn't help wondering whether Shove ought to have had something done about Dwayne's hormones before she gave me the responsibility of keeping him out of trouble. The girl was pretty enough for the job, assuming that the job was to be a distraction and put people off their guard, but she really wasn't *that* pretty.

'It's okay,' said The Rail. 'I was just checking to see if he actually talked as well as stared. Mrs. Flack…'

'Steff.'

'Steff. You have impressed me, so I'm willing to get this contract signed immediately.' She tapped the pad and then pulled out a rather nice old pen, which still used liquid ink, and signed both paper documents. I tapped both tablets and then signed the paper copies with her pen—oh, that pen felt nice and heavy. Dwayne witnessed my signature and then I then passed it across to Yuri.

'That's not necessary,' said The Rail. 'Yuri is bound by anything I sign, aren't you, Yuri?' She picked up one of the glasses, and tossed back its contents in one gulp. She then glared at us, and we followed suit. It was fiery in my throat, and made me splutter. But as it went down I felt a nice warm glow in my chest, once I had stopped coughing.

Yuri raised a salt and pepper eyebrow at us all, and said softly, 'If you say so.' There was more than a touch of menace in his soft voice. I wouldn't want to cross him.

'Well, if that's everything sorted,' I said hurriedly, waking my wristy with a thumb and summoning a pod, 'I think we'll get on with the job.' I stood up, and Yuri nodded at the boy sitting at the table by the door.

The boy stood as we walked towards him and, unlocking the door, he pulled it open to let us out. The pod reappeared round the corner with our number flashing on its front, its doors sliding back to let us in.

Buckling myself in to the left-hand seat, I asked Dwayne, 'Well, what did you think?'

'Scary lady,' he said. 'I really don't think I would want to cross either of those two. I think it wouldn't be painful for very long, though. Still, if you sort out her business for her I think she'll be straight with us.'

'My thought too,' I replied. 'Changing the subject,' I said, 'time to run that report round to your client. Do you want me to come with you?'

'Not especially,' he replied.

'Good, then you can drop me off at the office on your way and I'll let you get on with it'. And that was what we did. I couldn't help wondering which one of them drank the fourth shot.

Chapter 5
Steffy Aloft

Ah! It was my earpiece that was making that horrible noise. 'Yes?' I tapped my wristy and spoke into it.

'Steff, is that you?'

'Yes, and that sounds like the greater-spotted Shove your end.'

'It is. Now, I'm still in Norwich and I need to see you face-to-face as soon as possible. Is that okay with you?'

'You mean you want me to drop everything and head the best part of a hundred miles to where you are right this minute?'

'Can you do that?'

'Am I going to be back in time to hear Melissa Landry's talk this evening?'

'I would imagine so, yes.'

'May I ask what this is all about?'

'If I could talk about it over the airwaves, then I wouldn't have to see you face-to-face to discuss it, would I? I will put a ticket on your wristy as soon as we disconnect. There's a container-car leaving Peterborough railway station in twenty minutes. Be on that and the rest of it will happen automatically. I'll meet you at Norwich Hardwick in an hour.'

'Do I need to bring anything with me?'

'No, just your brain.'

'I'll make sure it's plugged in. Okay, see you then, if only to witness you meet the challenge of getting me to Norwich in an hour.' I disconnected and summoned a pod. My earpiece tinged as I went down the stairs and there was a pod outside my door, obediently wagging its tail, as I walked out. I climbed in and within five minutes it was depositing me at the station. Having walked across the concourse, I pointed my wristy at the sensor, and the turnstile let me in. The sign on top of it told me I was to go to Platform Two.

I have always thought that container-cars look shabby compared with straight railway carriages, even when they're brand new. They are fundamentally a bog-standard shipping container seated on top of a flatbed truck, kitted out inside with windows and seats. What was far more important, these seats had seat belts which held you in place.

I opened the door, found a seat and parked myself. A child with a very inquisitive look on its face came and sat in front of me, staring straight into my eyes.

'Are you going flying, lady?' the child asked. I was still uncertain of its gender, as the hair was short and the clothing was colourfully non-specific.

'I expect so,' I replied.

'I am too,' the child said. 'I bet I'm going further than you. I'm going to Mumbai.'

'You sure are, then,' I replied with a grin.

An anxious-looking bearded man suddenly appeared.

'Adake,' or something like that anyway, 'what have I told you about talking to strangers?' The name gave me no further hint of the child's gender. The child dropped their gaze and wandered off, following the person I presumed to be its parent down to the far end of the carriage.

I moved across to a seat by a window. There weren't many people in the container-car. There was the Asian family up front, there was me next and, towards the back, an elderly couple obviously together, and a German businessman working on a pad. How did I know he was German? Nobody sits that upright while working on a pad without being German. I know, I know, guilty as charged of racial profiling, but I could have been right, and it wasn't as if this snap judgement was actually going to be used to convict him of anything. I looked out at the grey surroundings and the falling snow, which continued to melt as soon as it hit the ground. The platform, however, was beginning to look wet and slightly muddy, so the snow was having some effect on the environment. A voice issued from the speakers. 'This container is bound for Huntingdon airport and will be shortly loaded onto the Zipa airship bound for Norwich, Antwerp, Cologne, Stuttgart, Zürich, Florence and Rome. If you are not intending to board this flight, please alight from this container now. Once this train is moving you will be unable to get off and your account will be charged for the distance you have travelled. You will additionally be charged separately for the return journey. You will also be unable to get out of this container at Huntingdon Airport, as it will be loaded directly into the airship.'

A youngish woman in a flight uniform swung herself into the container and sashayed down between the seats, checking that everyone in the compartment was actually where they should be. I wished I could walk like that. She looked down her nose at me.

'Norwich only?' she asked in a slightly disappointed American accent.

'My boss called me fifteen minutes ago and this flight just happened to coincide with her need of me. Otherwise I would have gone by train,' I replied, accentuating the consonants. She gave me back my wrist and, smiling wanly, announced in a loud voice that carried throughout the container that we may as well fasten our seatbelts now, as we would be at Huntingdon Airport in ten minutes and would be loading immediately.

I slotted the steel tongue of my belt into its buckle and pulled it tight. A glance out of the window showed the marshland whizzing by at quite a distance below us. They had built the railway up onto a bank, as it had become blatantly obvious to the Anglian government very early on in its existence that the water level was continuing to rise, and very soon Peterborough would be cut off from the rest of the province if they didn't do something fairly sharpish. The bank was called 'The Causeway,' and the railway was accompanied along its top by two roads suitable for pods and shuttle-buses on either side of the railway tracks. The swamp below us was most certainly still greenish, as far as I could see, which admittedly wasn't very far, the air above it being opaque white. Ten minutes later the container started to slow, and it felt like it swung sharp right and then put on its brakes.

The steward remained strapped to her seat as a clanking noise announced that we were being attached to a skyhook helicopter, and almost immediately we started moving again, though this time directly upwards accompanied by the sound of beating rotors. On the far side of the container I could see half a dozen skyhooks parked up, presumably on charge for the next time they were needed. They looked strangely incomplete, with their rotor at either end and the gaping space, where a container wasn't, in between. Peering out of my own window, I watched the Zeppelin itself loom past me. I could see faces in the windows of the huge airship, but none of them were looking back at me. They were talking or drinking coffee, or something stronger, perhaps, in a glass. As I moved up past them, my mind's eye conjured an image of watching someone strangling someone else, like they had in that famous detective story. In my imagination, it would be someone sitting in the lounge of a Zeppelin watching the crime take place in a container as it floated past the window. And, of course, that mystery would be even more tricky for the detective if the container was being disembarked, as the detective would be heading on to the next destination, whatever happened. Maybe I would write that one, one day, when I was too old and decrepit to be doing active detective work any longer. I hoped people would still be reading mysteries in twenty-five years' time. If they weren't, then maybe I would have to learn how to write a holo-vid script.

The skyhook had reached as far up as it needed, as the container was now moving sideways. It looked very strange to be moving away from the snow coming down. And just as we had started to move sideways, it stopped and there was a 'clank'. The sound of the whirring rotors faded and the container started to descend, or at least that was how my brain analysed feeling lighter. Not that I was exactly heavy anyway. I looked down the carriage at the Asian kid to see if he/she had taken off, having become critically lighter in the descent, but s/he was well strapped into the seat. For a few moments longer it was dark outside the windows until the movement stopped, and then I could see through two layers of windows – firstly those belonging to the container in which I was strapped, and then through the windows into the cabin of the airship itself. The container moved forward into its berth, the doors of the container matching up with doors in the airship and, with a hiss like gas releasing, the doors opened automatically.

The stewardess stood up and announced to everyone, although she seemed to me to be looking directly my way, 'Welcome aboard the Wolfgang Niedecken. This is Deck B. Those of you wishing to get off at Norwich Hardwick,' she said looking directly at me, 'must return to Deck B in no longer than twenty minutes' time. Meanwhile, enjoy the facilities of this Zeppelin Intercontinental Passenger Airship.' And she stood aside as everyone got up and shuffled through to the door. As I was passing through it I heard her explaining to the Asian father that their luggage was automatically being moved to their cabin to the fore of the Zeppelin. He looked bewildered, so she went on to explain that it was up the front end of the airship, and that he should book his family in at the office at the entrance to the forward quarters. In the old seafaring days, when iron men crossed the Atlantic in wooden ships powered by the wind, many of those men of metal slept in those forward quarters, or foc's'le as they were called in those days. Of course, this ship had already crossed the Atlantic and was now heading across Europe, once it had deposited people like me in Norwich.

Once I was sure that no-one needed to ask her something pressing, like 'where's the lavatory?' or whatever, I asked her about the name of the airship, the Wolfgang Niedecken. 'Oh,' she replied. 'He's a German poet. All the Zeppelin airships built in Stuttgart are named after German poets. I'm told he's like the German Bob Dylan, and his poetry was invariably accompanied by music. I expect if any airships get built in England again they'll probably name them after English poets.'

'More likely pop groups,' I replied drily. 'I hope at least they name them after classical pop groups like the Beatles and the Rolling Stones, and not one of these modern copycats.'

'Do you remember the Beatles when they were actually active?' she asked me, all wide-eyed and star-struck.

'How old do you think I am?' I replied, and then softened my voice. 'Wouldn't that have been a thing, though?' I waved my wrist at her, pretending to be a DJ, 'And for the first time, here's the new Beatles' record, "Lady Madonna."' Anyway, I'll go and park for the flight to Norwich. But I must find a cup of coffee first.'

I walked over to the bar across the walkway and bought a cappuccino, then took a seat by the window, which looked downwards and out at the countryside. Mostly all I could see was falling snow. I could see that the ship itself was moving across the ground but, at the height we were travelling, I couldn't sense any feeling of movement. Back in the day, I remembered the sensation of taking off in an aeroplane, where I felt pushed into the seat where the belts were already holding me. There was none of that pressure here. All I could see was that the ground was moving gently away from us. The airship didn't really cast a shadow on the ground below, as there was no sun to cast it, but I couldn't help imagining that the big ship would have blotted out the light over Ely Cathedral, which was still visible beneath us, surrounded by the blue-green colour of the marshland all around it, despite the murk. The airship would have appeared huge to those down below and would have blotted out the light even more effectively than any cloud cover. If I had decided to walk the length of the passenger quarters I would miss the rendezvous with Deck B that I had in twenty minutes. It really was an air [hyphen] liner. Not the old, single word airliner, which was a seventy-five seat jet aeroplane from the 1950s. There was a stack of leaflets about the Zeppelin fleet on the bar where I'd got my coffee, and I'd grabbed one to have a glance at during the journey. The Wolfgang Niedecken was, apparently, bigger than most of the container ships that plied the oceans and was over a mile long, and powered by several nuclear fusion motors, whose by-products, most conveniently, were alpha particles or, by another name, helium nuclei, which were constantly replenishing the gas bags that were keeping us airborne.

The airship was probably far too big to be bothered much by weather. It wasn't a form of transport I used very often, but I could never remember having a problem when I flew in an airship.

As Ely cathedral disappeared quite quickly behind us the murk closed in completely. I was becoming concerned that we were flying blind into the clag. Quite why any fool would want to be out flying in this I had no idea and anyway, any aeroplane powered by fossil fuels was banned from flying over Anglia at any time. But then, in stuff like this, an aeroplane headed for Heathrow wouldn't have to be very off beam to drift into Anglian airspace. Quite what a mess a wide-bodied jet would make of the Wolfgang Niedecken if they tried to occupy the same bit of air, I had no idea. If the impact had been with a light aircraft I suspected that they would find to their surprise the little plane's remains nestling in between the gasbags when they came near the ground again at Antwerp, and would need to involve the local forensics experts in trying to work out where the unfortunate collision took place. Helium is not flammable, so any trauma to the airship would involve a gas leak and loss of buoyancy, and it would require a large impact to disrupt an airship of this size. I was imagining the captain up front, and I really hoped he was up front, having stepped out of one of those golden age adventure novels my dad had read to me when I was a kid. I was very young then and I couldn't help wondering, when he read them, whether he was really reading them for his own pleasure. It certainly would have sounded odd if it had been my mum who was reading those tales of derring-do. I could picture the captain, in his very smart peaked cap, peering through the murk and at least trying to look where he was going. 'I say, Number One, pretty ropy weather this clag, what?'

'Yah! Almost as bad, sir, as it was when I was doing the Murmansk run back in Twenty-Eight, froze the giblets off a brass monkey.' The fact there had been next to no standing ice in the northern hemisphere for at least the past five years didn't alter my image of a British stiff upper lip just beneath a handlebar moustache and a peaked cap. I sipped my coffee and closed my eyes.

A gong sounded to wake me from my reverie, followed by an announcement, first in English. 'All passengers disembarking in Norwich Hardwick, please return to Deck B.' It then proceeded to give a similar length statement in Dutch, German, Icelandic and Italian, before repeating the whole rigmarole. I was seated in the container-car again and was belting myself in by the time the automated voice had finished its encore performance. There was no change of speed that I was aware of but the windows of the container-car disconnected themselves from the passenger cabin of the airship and we started to ascend. Once we had stopped climbing there came the familiar clanks as a skyhook attached itself to the container-car. And we were heading off down the outside of the airship, which did not appear to have stopped moving. I watched the ground of the small airfield appear out of the murk to meet us. There was a further series of clanks as the skyhook uncoupled itself from the container, which then rolled gently up to the passenger terminal and stopped. The doors of the container opened, and the German businessman and I got out. Then I lost sight of him. I was looking for someone who might have been sent by a senior Anglian policeperson to collect me and was pleasantly surprised to see the senior Anglian policeperson herself, still in her smart dress uniform with turn-ups at the cuffs of her trouser legs. She looked at me as she walked over. 'Morning, Steff,' I looked at my wristy; yes, it was still morning, just. 'Is that it? Nobody came with you?'

'Was I expecting company?'

'Well, I had rather hoped that Inspector North would be on that carriage with you, and one or two of the city councillors.'

I looked over my shoulder and then back at the middle-aged woman in uniform in front of me. 'Nope,' I said, 'only me.'

The German businessman leapt up behind us. 'Here I am,' he said in an Estuary accent, not German at all.

'Well, I'm delighted that you two could be bothered anyway,' she said acidly. 'Shall we go?' And we walked out the other side of the passenger terminal. Shove pointed at a family-pod, which I was just about to climb into, when it screamed metallically at me, 'This pod is already taken, summon another.'

Shove tapped her wristy and climbed in, the pod not objecting to her getting in. 'Sorry about that,' she said, beckoning us in, 'Welcome aboard my mouthy pod.' The businessman opened the back door and settled in, tossing his bag on the seat beside him, so I clambered into the front seat and strapped myself in.

'Well?' I asked.

Chapter 6
In Which Siobhan Takes Steffy to a Meeting

Shove pulled the curtains inside the pod, much to my relief. 'I don't want people lip-reading me,' she explained.

'I'm not unhappy about the curtains being drawn, but if you're afraid of anyone hearing what you have to say, surely it is important to know that there isn't someone standing on the other side of that door with his ear up against it when we're stopped?' remarked Inspector North from the back seat of the pod. I can't remember the last time I travelled in the back seat of a family-sized pod. I don't often bother with them as, most of the time, when I am using a pod I am on my own or have maybe one other person with me. It seems that this is generally the case, as I reckon that there are at least ten basic two-person pods around for every one family-sized one, and the basic pod is so much cheaper to hire.

'Would you stick your ear up against the door of a pod that had just stopped for a moment on the off chance you might hear something interesting?' Shove tossed over her shoulder. 'You'd be at a considerable risk of losing that ear if the pod started off again suddenly. Tell you what, how about we stop talking every time we think the pod isn't moving. Okay?'

I nodded at her, 'Okay then, so what's this all about?'

'Do you mind waiting until we get to the Witan?' she replied. 'The Senior Lecturer has sort of briefed me, but he said he would like to brief you two himself. That way I can't get it wrong and confuse the issue.'

'It's that complicated is it?'

'Oh yes, it's that complicated,' she assented.

So I changed the subject to what I had been up to so far that day. 'We've got a new job,' I said, 'which I think Dwayne and I are going to be working on together. Can I ask you a question without either of you asking me why I want to know?'

'Of course, but at the same time, we may just remember at some time in the future that you did want to know.' We grinned at each other. 'Shoot!' she said.

'What does the name Farrukh Ahmed mean to you?' I asked.

Shove did raise her eyebrows at that one. 'I have to say I am surprised to hear that name come out of your mouth after all these years.'

I was thrown by that response. 'Why?' I asked, with a similar sort of echo from North behind me. 'Who was he?'

'Well now, here's another thing,' she replied. 'You also know to describe him in the past tense, and it hasn't been very long that that's been the case. I have to tell you that his demise is still part of an on-going investigation. Do I need to be concerned?'

'I don't know yet. Why? Who is he?'

Shove made a steeple of her hands for a moment and then said, 'I can't tell you about the current investigation, apart from the fact that there is one. But there is a sort of irony in the fact that, had Farrukh Ahmed never have existed, then you and I would probably never have met.'

Now, that threw me even more. How was the corpse I had seen earlier that day in the mortuary anything to do with me and Shove, and what we have together? I framed that into a question and asked her.

'Farrukh Ahmed was the man who put you in hospital all those years ago.' Shove was looking at me very closely by now, and I could almost feel my mouth forming a very wide 'o'.

'You mean he was the bastard who raped me?'

'He was the last surviving member of that gang, yes.' As Shove said this, a 'Whaaat?' came in harmony from the back seat.

'Why wasn't I told that he had got out of prison?'

'He was never actually arraigned for your rape,' she said. 'By the time that came up, he was already behind bars for people trafficking and child abuse. The powers that be deemed that it was kinder to you not to put you through the trauma of a court case, especially as your appearance would have been to demonstrate to the jury how damaged you were by the whole affair, in that you couldn't remember anything about it. Add on top that your uncle had just died too, and the prosecution wasn't minded to take it any further, especially he was already on trial for multiple cases of trafficking, so it wouldn't have altered the time he would serve. I suppose that if, by some fluke of nature he got away with those, then the prosecutor would still have had your case to throw at him at a later date.' Neither of us were taking any notice of the strange noises North was making from the back seat so he just shut up and, presumably, listened.

'What did you think?'

'Me? You have to remember that at that time I was a simple PC Plod, but yes, I didn't want to put you through it either. As I said, he probably wouldn't have got any more time added on to the sentence he was already serving, so what would have been the point? Life is life, however long that actually turns out to be. Anyway, I think you must have still been in London when he was released for the first time, and I wasn't involved in the second case, so I didn't know to tell you. It was only when notice of his shooting landed on my desk this morning that I remembered him, and now here you are this evening mentioning him as well. Steff, hopefully it wasn't you who potted him after all these years.'

I grinned, 'Nah, you can rest assured, until you told me just now, I didn't know who he was. Besides, it wouldn't have been me who did for the bastard. It might well have been my son, though.'

'But you haven't got a son.'

'Exactly.'

Shove looked at me for a moment and then smiled gently and said, 'Can I ask you, semi-officially, but off the record, how he fits into your case?'

'You can,' I replied. 'Quite what it means I am not sure. It appears he was involved with some missing diamonds, or at least missing paste, and it is our job to see if we can find them.'

'Were they stolen diamonds?'

'Not as far as I know, until they were stolen from my client's courier – which was Ruke's role incidentally. That is what my client is paying me to find out.'

'You said "my client" twice. Does that mean you were trying not to say "she"?'

She was sharp, was my old friend. 'Look, can we not talk about this any more? I don't know much about it, apart from the involvement with Farrukh Ahmed and that he's wearing a bullet hole in the middle of his forehead.' Shove's eyes widened when I said that too. She now knew that I knew where he had been shot. 'At the same time, you know that I and mine are involved. If you need to talk to us officially, can we do it that way? Thanks for telling me he was the man who put me in hospital. I at least won't shudder if I find out that his demise was somewhat longer and more painful than it currently appears.' I coughed to clear my throat and to change the subject. 'So, where exactly are we going?' I asked flicking at the curtain and seeing buildings rather than countryside going past the window.

'We are heading for the Norwich City Hall. It's where the Witenagemot has its meetings. The bureaucracy of government takes place elsewhere in the city, in the County Hall, a big, ugly monstrosity outside the city centre, but the City Hall was selected as its seat, as it is an elegant Art Deco building right in the middle of the town centre. And, Steffy babes, you have been selected to be our civilian sidekick in North West Anglian law enforcement.'

Almost as if the pod had a telepathic connection to Shove's mind, it stopped and the screen in front of us announced that we were at our intended destination. The door opened and I found myself staring straight into the eye of a slender but angry-looking lion waving a claw at me. It looked as if it was cast in bronze, which had tarnished somewhat over time. Nevertheless, it was still impressive, and had a hungry glint in its eye. 'Wow!' escaped from me before I had a chance to stop it.

'Smart, aren't they?' asked Shove.

'They, you mean there's more than one of them?'

Shove jerked a thumb over her shoulder at the matching lion on the other side of the steps leading into the building. 'And we have to walk between them,' she added, grinning.

I looked at them both. They were identical, down to the fact that they both had an admonishing right paw held forwards. The one under which the pod deposited us had the paw nearest me raised. The other lion had the paw nearest the building raised. 'It looks like that one is saying, "you're not taking that out of here, are you?"' I remarked, 'Do you know their history? They look like dogs with a lion's head, rather than real lions, with their long, thin bodies.' The design of the brickwork caught my eye as we got closer to it. 'It's the same with the bricks, it looks like the builders stretched them while they were building the place.'

'Uh huh. Anyway, we're not here to admire the architecture, we have a meeting to attend,' Shove announced and marched into the building, while Inspector North and I followed behind.

The room to which we were directed was a typical meeting room, with a table in the middle and seats all around it. 'You found them then. We're just waiting for Derek to get back from the station and then we'll get on with this,' said a voice from the end of the table. The owner of the voice got up and walked over to us. 'Apologies, Chief Inspector North,' he said to me with a wave of his long, rather elegant, mane. 'I always assumed you were of the male persuasion.'

'North is, I believe,' I replied. 'I'm Stephanie Flack.' He looked rather more taken aback than I expected when I said that.

'Oh, and I'm Douglas Potter, I'm the Minister for the Interior.' He turned and faced Siobhan, 'And who is Stephanie Flack, and why is she here?'

'Stephanie is my ear to the ground in Peterborough. She is a registered private investigator.' Shove came to my rescue, though I could probably have answered that one all right on my own. 'May I also introduce Inspector North,' she waved a paw at the man who had finally come into the room. Where had he been?

'An unofficial law-enforcement officer?' The man harrumphed thoughtfully, looking at me.

'Oh, I'm official, look.' I replied drily, waving my wristy at him, with its newly re-minted licence on display.

He glanced at my wristy for a moment, without apparently taking any obvious notice of it, and then announced to all the rest of the room, 'Well, we've got the contingent from Peterborough now. Is there anybody else we are waiting for?'

Douglas Potter announced, 'I don't think we need wait for Derek to get back from the station. Ladies and gentlemen, may I request you stand for the National Anthem?' He pressed something under the lip of the table and the room was filled with Gustav Holst's famous tune. To show what a good pick it had been for a National Anthem, pretty much all of us knew the words and we all joined in, 'I vow to thee my country ...' and so on.

Once everyone, slightly teary-eyed, had sat down again, Douglas Potter said, 'Right, firstly may I apologise to those few of you to whom the Senior Lecturer has already spoken. Take this as an opportunity to ask further questions now you have had time to think about it. For everyone else, you see that snow outside?'

There was a murmur of assent from round the table.

'Exactly,' the Minister continued, 'it's the result of a volcanic eruption.'

'Like it did in Iceland, way back when, and the aeroplanes couldn't fly until it stopped?' somebody approaching retirement age from down the table chipped in. 'I remember that. Do we know when it's going to stop?'

'Yes,' he replied. 'And it's not, and it's not from Iceland.'

'It's not?' I asked puzzled, 'not what?'

Well, if he wasn't going to get umpty if people asked questions as he went along, and if he was going to be deliberately opaque, I was going to make sure I was following his train of thought.

'At least, nobody knows when it's going to stop, not in the foreseeable future, anyway.' He paused, and then he dropped the next bit on us. 'And it's not from Iceland. It's come from America. Yellowstone Park's gone off bang.'

The pit of my stomach dropped through the floor.

'But isn't that supposed to be a mass extinction event?' came a wail, definitely a wail, from down the table. I don't know who she was, but again she looked older than Shove.

His 'yes' that followed that question was every bit as chilling as it reads. Then he added, 'It all depends on how long it goes on for.'

'So what happens now?' asked Chief Inspector North. Well, at least everyone from Peterborough was listening.

'To start with, it will get colder as that cloud up there shuts off the sun. The snow will start to settle. But it won't be very long before everything starts to warm up again, as the lava flows will start burning vegetation, and release a load of carbon dioxide in the process. That, and the sulphur dioxide which is coming out of the caldera of the volcano, are both greenhouse gases, so the Earth will get considerably warmer. And of course, those two gases, when mixed with water, make weak acids. So we'll get acid rain. And, what's more, if the volcano heats the sulphur dioxide up enough to react with the oxygen in the air, it will form sulphur trioxide, and we'll get a very strong acid rain, and metals like steel will start dissolving. We talk about global warming now, but that is just peanuts compared with what is going to happen.'

'So what do we do?'

'Is that a "we" as in as individual people, or "we" as in the people of Anglia, or "we" as in mankind in general?'

'Well, any of them.'

'Well, you, me and the people of Anglia have one choice: we pick the deity we most fancy, pray to it like mad and hope the bugger's a) listening and b) at least half as powerful as it claims. Mankind, on the other hand, well, there are half a dozen people on Mars at the moment, and there's another half-dozen on the Moon. I guess they're going to have to get busy fast creating a generation of new humans not born on the Earth.'

There was a silence for a moment. Whether that was a moment of deep thoughtfulness, or whether people were picturing the reaction of the scientists who had recently landed on Mars responding to the instruction to stop what they were doing right now and start copulating, I couldn't tell. 'Can't they plug the volcano?' I asked, breaking the silence.

'I believe there are some technical wizards from the University of SoCal who claim to be looking into the problem but, speaking as a linguist, I have no idea how they think they can stuff a cork in an angry volcano thirty miles wide and two thousand degrees hot. Whether there are any bright ideas coming out of our clever boys in our local think shops here in Anglia, well, you can ask the Senior Lecturer when you meet him.'

'Is that his subject, Geology?' someone asked.

'No,' replied the minister and waited without saying any more for the next question, which came from the Colchester Chief.

'So what will you be requiring us to do?' I had met her once before, when she had come up to see Shove and we had put her up at the house overnight before she went back the following day. A pleasant woman, I seemed to remember.

'I think he'll be requiring you to keep order in your respective cities, and particularly those of you whose cities include a border. As you probably are aware, England is becoming increasingly unstable and nobody, at least on this side of the fence, knows what is going to happen next. As soon as the extent of what is happening in America becomes obvious to the population as a whole, all the natives will become more restless, even our own. The Senior Lecturer will want us to make sure society in general doesn't break down. Global warming was one of those things that politicians with connections to the oil industry chose not to believe in until as little as ten years ago. I know things have calmed down since the Secession that followed the rise in sea level but all of a sudden society is going to get another big tasty kick up the b.t.m., at least in part due to a new variant of global warming we haven't met before. That's the trouble with belief systems, sooner or later they become blindingly obvious to everyone apart from the actual cult members, whether they're right or wrong. Those people who are wrong become more and more irritable that they voted for the wrong side, even if they actually won the vote. They still look stupid and become more irrationally violent as time marches on.'

'You mean, it doesn't matter which side you voted for, sooner or later right will out. And even if only 5% of the population voted for the right side ...' came from a rather disagreeable-looking detective from Bury St. Edmunds.

'It doesn't make them any less right. Yes.' Shove's steel-blue eyes glittered at him. I got it, even if he didn't. 'So where do we go from here?' she went on.

'In a nutshell,' replied the Minister, 'we need you to keep order. The Witan's general concern is that, when people realise that the survival of the human race is at risk, then there will be a general breakdown of good behaviour on the streets.' Douglas Potter seemed very calm, considering what he was discussing.

'Where do you see particular problems coming from?' asked a voice from further up the table.

He looked directly towards us. 'Peterborough may produce problems of its own,' he began, 'with its diverse ethnic mix and its large refugee population from the salt marshes. Remember, its only land-link with the rest of the Anglian peninsula is the Causeway.'

'Ah! Pottyborough,' muttered the detective from Bury St. Edmunds, but carefully didn't make eye contact with either of us. 'Why don't you just flog the whole shebang back to the English and be done with it?'

Shove responded quick as a flash that that wasn't going to happen in a hurry. The Suffolk detective replied that as 'Pottyborough' was policed by time-served 'dolly-birds', a phrase that surely predated him by a decade or two, how were we going to be able to stop whatever was going to go down? At that point my hackles started rising too, and the Interior Minister was forced to intervene. 'Children, children, may I remind you that we really have to work together on this.' He then promptly changed the subject. 'Chief Superintendent,' he looked at Shove, 'please tell me about the person who calls himself the Qardinal, with a "Q".' He wasn't keen to encourage the Bury Saint Edmunds detective any further.

'He is a non-denominational preacher, who pontificates from the equally non-denominational church in Kingsgate.' Shove still sounded quite terse. I don't think she particularly wanted to defend the Qardinal, but she absolutely did want to defend the status of Peterborough against that unpleasant man from Suffolk.

'What's a non-denominational church?' asked one of the other uniformed figures from around the table.

'Well, it was constructed during the building boom on the east side of town about thirty years ago, so that any group from any religion could use it, either for religious or secular meetings. We have a number of very different religions in Peterborough, so I suppose it was quite a nifty idea. In practice its main use has been secular.'

'Apart from the Qardinal.'

'As you say, apart from the Qardinal's activities. His performances seem to draw quite a crowd at Kingsgate.'

'Is he an entertainment or what?' asked the Bury detective from across the table in a more serious tone.

I looked at him for a moment and gave him a straight answer, 'Well, I don't personally find him so, no, but then I've only ever seen him in action just the once. He was preaching against all formal religions and all the things you must give up in order to be a member of their gang.'

'His main point is that God is God, no matter what you care to call him: Allah, Yahweh, Jehovah, or even just Tracy. However, the cults that surround these individual creations are man-made and for the most part restrictive, even destructive. Needless to say, the Muslims, the Orthodox Jews and some of the more evangelical Christians don't take kindly to his preaching. They see him as a threat.'

'And you?' asked the Suffolk detective, looking for an entry to get another pot shot off.

'Personally, I find him a bit of a bore.'

'Well, that's pretty much it isn't it,' he agreed. 'You join a Church, become a believer, and you have to give up eating pork, drinking wine, you name it. Like it? So you have to give it up, just to prove you can, to fit in.'

'That's the Qardinal in a nutshell,' I replied, successfully suppressing a giggle about the large man across the table chuntering on about pork and booze, 'so you can see why I didn't bother going to a repeat performance.'

'And he gets an audience?' asked the Interior Minister.

'So I'm told,' said Shove. 'Sometimes quite a big one.'

'Well, rumour has it that he has already heard of the gist of what we've been talking about today, and that he is going to preach about it later this evening. Something of the ilk of fire and brimstone from the heavens, with an angry God descending from Valhalla with his cohorts tum tiddley all burnished with gold.'

'Well, he's certainly got the ice and brimstone bit,' I remarked drily.

'Quite,' said the minister. 'Now you two have to get back to Peterborough to shut him up PDQ. That sort of oratory we can do without at this moment in time. Can we hang on to Inspector North here for a moment, there are issues still developing and we may want to brief him later today prior to his returning to you tomorrow?'

'What would be the quickest way for the two of us to get us back from here straight away?' Shove asked.

'Well, we can get you a fast train to Kings Lynn, and from there we can set you on a hovercraft to cross the saltmarshes directly to Peterborough. Shouldn't take you more than an hour and a half if you leave straight away.' He looked down at his wristy and tapped it. 'There will be a pod waiting for you at the main entrance in five minutes. Go!'

And so we went. As we rushed down the steps between the lions a pod drew up and threw its doors open. Once again, Shove leapt into the right side and I jumped into the left. We had hardly finished buckling our belts when the pod set off. I did check the time on my wristy and it was six and a half minutes flat when the pod stopped again and the doors flew open. We were parked right in front of a 'train' consisting of a single carriage that appeared to be itching to set off. There was no one on the platform to ask whether this carriage went to Kings Lynn, but as there wasn't any other train in the station at all we looked at each other, shrugged and climbed aboard. We had hardly sat down, when the carriage set off at breakneck speed. 'I have to say, I'm quite impressed,' she said.

'Someone takes us seriously,' I replied. 'That is, unless the train's next port of call turns out to be Lowestoft.' Glancing around the carriage at the few people travelling with us, we realised that every single one of them was looking at us. Well, maybe it was Shove's braided uniform that caught their eye but, 'Do you think the train was kept waiting for us?' I asked her quietly.

'That's a possibility. I hope we didn't keep them waiting too long.' She raised her voice a little and asked, 'This train is going to Kings Lynn isn't it?' She looked relieved when she received a general murmur of assent.

Looking out of the carriage and the rate at which the windmills sped past us in the snow and fog, if the train had been waiting for us, it sure was making up for it now. I felt very sorry for the people working in the fields in the snow but it might even be quite pleasant in a strange sort of way. The snow would certainly cool down the August mugginess. I wondered how long that would last. We were travelling so fast that it was difficult to make out the details of the land passing beside us. First we were going past a field of what might be cabbages or lettuces, being green blobs against the background. Next there was a field of solar panels all facing southwest. Then there was more vegetation, with more people working in the fields, and everywhere there were wind turbines rotating slowly but inexorably. There may not be an inordinate amount of light to drive the solar panels or nurture the plants, but there was wind enough to drive the turbines. It didn't look like the Royal Province of Anglia was going to be in financial difficulties this week.

We travelled through the small town of Swaffham at a frankly disrespectful speed, too fast to read the signs on the platform, but one of the voices behind me remarked that 'this is Swarff'm, not long now,' in a broad Norfolk accent. Now I suppose that was no absolute proof that was where we were, but there really wasn't any other built up area of any size at all on a direct line between Norwich and Kings Lynn, so it was a reasonable bet that the speaker was right.

As we drew into the southern edge of Kings Lynn, there was water all around us. We were travelling slowly enough by then to be able to read the signs identifying the place. The carriage pulled up at a platform and the doors opened automatically.

We had hardly got out of the carriage, when a young man in a turban bounced up to Shove and announced, 'Superintendent Flynn? I'm Iqbal, I'm to be your chauffeur from here, follow me.' And he turned on his heel and bounced off, not offering to carry anything. I looked Shove, and we both said, 'The uniform' in sync to each other, and followed our guide for the next part of our journey into the salt marsh out behind the station, though perhaps not mimicking the antics of a rubber ball quite in the way that he was. I couldn't help wondering why a young man carrying a Muslim handle like Iqbal might be wearing a turban.

Chapter 7
Across the Saltmarshes

Iqbal bounced out of the station, across the road, and through a gap in the fence. Intrigued, we followed. On the other side of that gap was row after row of masts. We were in some sort of harbour, rather reminiscent of times past.

'Stay on the planking,' he said over his shoulder. 'If you slip off there's nothing but water and mud down there, and I'm afraid the mud may well behave like quicksand and drag you under before we can get you out. We never found the last person who fell off the dock. Of course, it's always possible he was running away from Anglia for some reason and swam all the way across The Wash to Boston, who knows?' He hardly took a breath as he spoke. Shove and I moved into a line astern formation, rather than walking side by side, to increase our distance from the edge. At the end of the jetty, instead of a sailing yacht there was a small, umm, well, I didn't know quite what to call it at first. It reminded me a little of the flat-bottomed boats that featured in those old movies set in the Louisiana Bayou, except that it was considerably bigger. It was low and flat, with what looked like a funnel coming vertically up out of the middle of it to a height of roughly six feet. It wouldn't actually be a funnel, would it? If it was a funnel, that suggested there was some sort of internal combustion engine and, as far as Anglia was concerned, that would be illegal, wouldn't it? Behind the thing that looked like a funnel was a casing that abutted against it, and behind that was a large four-bladed fan, fixed vertically and enclosed in a large wire safety cage. It suggested that, when it rotated, the fan seriously moved and would make mincemeat of anything that collided with it, be it sea bird or human being. In front of the thing that looked like a funnel was a sort of cockpit facing forwards, and in front of that, and below, was a cabin, with glass windows round the sides that went more or less to the front of the device. On the top of the cabin, slowly rotating, was what I took to be a radar scanner.

Behind the screen in front of the cockpit sat a white peaked cap with goggles in front.

Iqbal turned round to us, beaming, waiting for me to catch up. 'Here it is, one of the three active Anglian Navy electric hovercraft. This is Anny-Aitch-Two. And this,' he said waving at a young man in a yellow waterproof coat, a leather flying helmet and goggles, who was fiddling with a large halogen lamp on a pole on the other side of the cockpit, 'is my cousin, Able Seaman Vipal. He is going to be our lookout for the crossing from here to Dogsthorpe Docks.' He jumped across to the deck beside the cockpit and pulled open a door down to the cabin. He then leaned back over to the dock, waving a hand at us. Shove took it first and he helped her aboard. Then it was my turn, and I was eased past a lamp on a tall pole, through the door, and down into the cabin. Iqbal followed us in.

I could stand up straight, just, in the cabin but I noticed that Iqbal had to stoop somewhat. 'Make yourselves comfortable down here,' he said. 'We'll keep the outside door shut, as once we're underway the spray gets everywhere, and spray from the salt marsh can be quite unpleasant and may not do much good to your nice shiny uniform.' He smiled at Shove. 'Now, you will realise quite quickly that we will not be going anywhere near as fast as Anny-Aitch-Two's top speed. The mist and snow will reduce the visibility quite considerably and I have been instructed to look after you two, on pain of something that wasn't actually specified, so I estimate that the crossing should take about an hour. My cousin will be on the lamps and will try to keep you informed of anything worth looking at. If you see something solid coming up in front of us, come up and tell me as soon as you see it. The hovercraft doesn't have brakes and can't just stop like a pod. Hopefully I will be able to swerve round any object you might spot. In a conflict between a hovercraft on the move and a building standing still I know which will win, and it won't be us, even if most of the building has been underwater since the flood.' He grinned cheerfully, handing us an A4 card each. 'These are the safety instructions, do read them.'

Shove asked him, 'Just out of interest, what is that thing that looks like a funnel that stands behind the cockpit? It isn't an exhaust is it?'

'Oh, goodness no,' he replied, 'that would be quite illegal. It's an intake. The air is sucked in through there and squirted out underneath the hovercraft to lift us off the water.' He paused for a moment. 'Shall we go?'

Shove nodded and we went and sat down in the row of three seats up at the sharp end of the cabin. They were comfortable enough, albeit plastic. The floor was of a sort of non-slip, slightly glittery material in one piece that curved up the sidewall. There were no ashtrays or sweet papers anywhere, but there was a cup holder in the armrest of each chair, although we hadn't been offered a cup of anything to put in it. The smell was vaguely reminiscent of disinfectant. Somebody had given the cabin a good scrubbing recently. The one thing the smell didn't remind me of was that of marine diesel, which I remembered from the last time I was on board a ship. You have to remember that I was in a car at the time and was crossing the channel from Dover to Calais on holiday. Yes, it was that long ago. I was still a lawyer in my twenties and I have to admit that I don't remember who was doing the driving, but it certainly wasn't me.

'Ever been in one of these things before?' I asked my companion.

'No, this is my first time too.'

I looked forward into the driving snow and murk and could see very little. The noise level suddenly increased and we felt like we were being lifted up in our seats. The snow started flying into the screen and windscreen wipers started at a slow beat, keeping time perhaps with the radar scanner on our roof, sweeping spray as well as the snow from the screen in front of us. We were off. The hovercraft wasn't a particularly smooth ride – it bucked and dipped, and every time it plunged downwards the spume flew up onto the windows in front of us, putting far more water on them than the wipers could clear away with a single swipe. I began to understand why someone had had to clean the cabin recently with disinfectant. While I didn't suffer from motion sickness personally, I could certainly appreciate how someone who did would find the whole experience quite unpleasant.

For a while we said nothing, as the lights of Kings Lynn slowly faded behind us and all we could see was what the big spotlights displayed to either side of the cabin. I had no idea what speed we were actually doing, as there was absolutely nothing apart from the grey green water ahead of us to give us a hint. I had an uncomfortable thought. 'You know,' I said, 'we're absolutely at their mercy, if they want to do unpleasant things to us.' Where the hell did that come from? I wondered. It wasn't as if I had any problems with Asians, well, not that I could remember, at least not since I was fifteen, and I have no actual memory of that episode. But only a couple of hours ago Shove and I had been talking about Ruke Ahmed raping me to within an inch of my life. And yet here I stood – well, technically sat – guilty as charged of racial profiling. Or was it racist profiling? I was going to have something interesting to discuss with Melissa Landry, forensic psychologist and mystery novelist, this evening, always assuming I got there in time. That whole thought took the same amount of time as it took Shove to rummage in one of the pockets of her uniform. 'You speak for yourself,' she said, producing a pistol. Where had she been hiding that? I wondered. 'I'm a very good shot with this, so I feel safe enough. Are you carrying?'

'Er, no. I don't think I would have been allowed anywhere near the airship if I had been armed.'

'Oh, I'd forgotten for the moment that you came to Norwich by airship, yes, I agree. They'd have taken you to the trap door they don't advertise in the Airship Tourist Guide and dropped you through it if they'd found you carrying a gun. The security on those airships is very effective. Just as a matter of interest, can you shoot?'

'You know, Ben's given me a few lessons on his range, but I haven't got a gun or anything myself.'

'Ah, Ben, I knew he was useful for something, apart from painting that intermittent very silly smile all over your face. I must meet him some time. Anyway, if we're going to need to be keeping control then perhaps we ought to get you something out of the armoury.'

'And Dwayne?'

She thought for a moment, 'Perhaps not. He has got a police record, after all.'

'Let me think about that,' I said. 'I'm not at all sure I want to be armed. After all, Peterborough isn't the mean streets of San Francisco in the thirties.'

'Not yet it isn't but,' she shrugged, 'who knows how this'll all turn out?'

A blast of cold air behind us told us that we had company from above deck. It turned out to be Able Seaman Vipal, his goggles hanging round his neck. '

Just to let you know, we're absolutely bang on target. What you can see on your right is Wisbech.' It was obviously Iqbal who was playing the light on the right side of the cabin over the tops of the buildings emerging from the water. The scene was very spooky. There was no light apart from what was reflected back from the spotlight on our hovercraft. It looked desolate.

'Is there anyone there anymore?' I asked.

'I'm sure there is,' Vipal replied, 'living in the third floor of those buildings, which of course is now sea level. I understand there is quite a thriving fishing community. They have boats and trade with Boston and Skegness, where of course you can still buy petrol for an outboard motor. It's only Anglia where petrol is banned.'

'How many people are we talking about?' asked Shove.

'Twenty, maybe thirty tops.'

I shuddered: that was all that was left of a once thriving market town with well over thirty thousand inhabitants, and then the floods came. In Wisbech's case the sea came in really rather quickly, as one of the dykes around The Wash gave way, ultimately triggering the Anglian Secession. Much of the debris washed up on what has now become the rather trendy beach round the Isle of Ely to the south. Well, it became trendy after the bits of Wisbech had been cleared off it. The survivors from Wisbech and the places round it mostly ended up in Peterborough or on Spalding Eyot. Two of the Wisbech survivors are now resident in what became my house, being 'Enery and Alice Grubb. I had never heard 'Enery ever talking to or about his wife in any way apart from as 'Mrs. Grubb'. I wondered if, even in moments of extreme tenderness, he still addressed her that way. 'Ooh! Mrs. Grubb, I don't 'arf fancy you.' I shuddered and smiled simultaneously, remembering the way my Mercian major addressed me.

Vipal made for the door. 'The tops of the next lot of buildings we will see should be the village of Guyhirn, which will be passing on our left. There isn't a lot of Guyhirn left,' he added laconically. As he pulled the door to behind him, the wind level dropped. I looked at the clock on my phone: it read five o'clock and, in the middle of August, the sun should still be high in the sky; certainly we should not be surrounded by this strange grey twilight. Vipal was so right, the lights on the left played over the surface and we could just about make out the tips of buildings breaking through. Guyhirn, of course, had been built below sea level anyway and was surrounded by dykes. Whether they had been breached in any way, I had no idea. I think the water level had simply risen above them, and there Guyhirn wasn't any more. The next spot on our right would be Thorney Island, which still stood proud above sea level. We would pass between the island and another island, now known as Whittle-in-the-Sea, on our left on our way into the Dogsthorpe Docks in its lagoon by Parnwell, and its Kingsgate Church.

Iqbal slowed down when we passed Whittle, and he opened the cabin doors as we crept into the lagoon. 'I have no idea quite how shallow it is here. I would hate to pull the bottom off the hovercraft just because some fool tipped a shopping trolley into the water.' After we had drawn up to the edge, and Vipal had jumped ashore with a rope to tie us to the dock, Iqbal turned the engine off and the craft settled in the water. Once the fan stopped spinning, Iqbal also went ashore and, holding a hand back to us, he helped us onto the planking.

'Captain Iqbal,' said Shove, and was about to continue when he interrupted her.

'Oh, I'm not a captain, Superintendent, nothing so grand.'

'Well, at the very least you must be a commander, because you commanded the hovercraft during the crossing.' Iqbal looked embarrassed, and I thought she was obviously after something, being such an inveterate creep. She continued, 'Where would we find you if we needed you and this craft in a hurry?'

'Well, until Four is launched in a couple of weeks' time, this craft is based in Kings Lynn, but after that, I don't know.'

'If I were to want to request if it could be based here instead of Kings Lynn, who would I have to ask?'

'Hang on, I'll ask the chief,' he said. He tapped his left wrist a couple of times and then spoke into it. 'Hello Chief, Iqbal here from the Anny-Aitch-Two. I've just delivered our customers to the Dogsthorpe Docks and the Superintendent's just come back at me with a request that she would like me to stay.' There was a pause. 'I don't know, I'll ask her.' Iqbal looked at Shove. 'The boss wants to know how long you would like us to be available.'

'Indefinitely,' she replied assertively.

Iqbal repeated the word into his wristy. There was a pause and then he said, 'The able seaman and I have family in the Western Sub, so that wouldn't be a problem for us. Very good, sir, I'll tell them.' He tapped the phone and put it back into his pocket. 'The chief says that's all arranged. Anny-Aitch-Two's new base is here in the Dogsthorpe Docks from this moment. Apparently the Minister of the Interior had already floated that idea past him earlier this afternoon. Thank you for bringing it up now; that saved us a double journey to Kings Lynn and back again.'

'Can we make Vipal a Petty Officer?' I asked cheekily, just to remind them I was there. 'It sounds much more important.'

'Ssh! Don't say things like that, he might hear you. And if he hears you he might get ideas and believe me, we don't want Vipal getting ideas.' Iqbal looked horrified. 'Vipal's mother is my mother's elder sister and my poor mother will be nagged incessantly until it happens if he actually hears you.'

'How do I get in touch with you in a hurry?' Shove asked Iqbal while glowering at me. She and the seaman went into a little huddle involving them and their wristies, both of which were alight.

Meanwhile I tapped my own wristy and summoned a pod. I had a date with a forensic psychologist, which I could just about keep if I got a wiggle on.

Chapter 8
A Cancelled Talk

The pod pulled up on Park Road in front of the library, maybe a quarter of a mile north of my office in Cathedral Square. The door to the library was still open but there wasn't the hubbub of people milling around that you might expect before an event. Maybe they had already been ushered into the room. I picked up my feet and went swiftly in. Up the steps I noticed that the concessions stand, which was usually open when there was something on, was shut and boarded up like when there wasn't.

There was a young man with a slightly lost expression on his pale, rather unremarkable face standing near a sign which had a poster featuring Melissa Landry, with a sticker taped diagonally over the front of it which simply said 'CANCELLED' in big handwritten letters. 'What happened to Melissa Landry's talk?' I asked him.

'Oh,' he said, 'haven't you heard? She couldn't get here.'

'But I've come all the way from Norwich for this!' I exclaimed, omitting the fact that it had been the return journey home.

He looked at me sadly, 'I'm so sorry for your wasted journey,' he replied. 'Melissa died in her sleep last night.'

That grabbed my attention. 'What? What happened?'

'They found her this morning, when the hotel housekeeping went up to do her room.' He paused for a moment, recaptured his breath, and then continued, 'and they said she had been dead for some time. The poor girl, it must have been quite a shock.' His eyes glistened. He was obviously very upset.

I tried to picture the fifty-plus-year old Melissa Landry from the photo on the poster in front of me as a 'poor girl' and failed utterly. 'Girl?' I said quizzically.

'The girl who went in to do the room. They said she was very upset.'

'Oh, I can imagine that, yes, poor girl.' I then changed the angle of the conversation very slightly. 'You and Melissa, were you very close?' I asked.

'No, I'd never met her. Today was going to be my first time. I've read all her books, of course, and they're brilliant, and I was selected by the library committee to host this event, as I like to think that I'm her biggest fan in Peterborough. Isn't Sue Laking a brilliant character?' I could have sworn he stifled a sob at that moment.

I have to say that I've only read a couple of her books, and it isn't the protagonist who's impressed me so much as the thought processes that went behind the structure of the novel as a whole. There was a cold logic to the crimes Landry created, and especially in the one I had recently finished, which is why I wanted to meet her in the first place. The reasons why her killer did what he did made him or her far more sympathetic, to me anyway, than her detective, who simply annoyed me. I got the feeling from the book she was beginning to annoy the author too. One of the questions that I was minded to ask was if she was going to kill off DS Laking soon, just so that she would be able to write about someone else for a change. It is one of the crosses that mystery writers must have to bear, having to write about the same protagonist over and over again, though a lot of them seem to enjoy watching their characters change and grow. Killing Laking was not a topic I would have wanted to put to the young man in front of me, who obviously liked the lanky detective that had lived, perhaps unloved, in her late author's mind.

Well, there wasn't a lot of point in my hanging around in the library if there wasn't going to be any talk. I touched him on the shoulder and just stopped myself from saying that I was so sorry for his loss. In some way that was exactly what I was thinking as I wandered out of the library. As I wasn't expected home for supper, I wandered up the road just a little bit into a takeaway. A doner kebab with salad and pickled chillies rather appealed to me at that moment, especially when the hunk of processed meat rotating on the spit right in front of me as I walked in filled my mouth with saliva from the smell of cooking meat and spices. Okay, so there was absolutely no provenance on that meat, and it could have come from absolutely anything, possibly not even originally a member of the animal kingdom, but I wasn't that bothered. It appealed to me and I went for it. The young man behind the counter used a very long knife to carve thin slices off the roast onto a sort of metal tray with a handle that he held in his other hand.

He added the sliced meat to some salad in a pitta bread, finally topping the whole thing off with a couple of pickled chillies from a jar on one side. He then deftly wrapped the whole caboodle in plain paper and presented me with a very neat parcel. I tapped my wristy and then held it up against his reader, and the 'kerching' that came from both of them drew satisfied smiles from all concerned as our business was completed. While he was parcelling the kebab up, I had already tapped my wristy and ordered a pod to pick me up outside the shop. The pod's timing was exquisite. I had just pulled the takeaway's door shut when the pod pulled up in front of me, its sliding door nearest me opening for me to jump in. I thought I would need to check with Sabrina in the morning that we were not paying over the odds for this admittedly superb VIP service.

I programmed the pod to take me home, while I munched contentedly on the kebab. I had got halfway through it when the passenger door flew open and there I was, as close to the front step as I could be without actually being thrown through the door and into the hall. I wrapped what was left of the kebab in its paper and took it in with me.

'Aren't you supposed to be at a meeting?' asked Mrs. Grubbs, as I walked through the kitchen door.

'No, yes, but it got cancelled,' I said, adding 'at the last minute,' so she wouldn't think I had taken an opportunity not to enjoy her cooking. She was eyeing my kebab wrapped in paper a little like something I had brought in on my shoe.

'Can I have a plate?' I asked. I was going to finish this kebab and enjoy it too.

She smiled at me like an over-indulgent aunt and I knew I had won that round. 'Of course, Steff,' and then she added. 'Is it nice?' just to ensure I didn't get too cocky.

'S'okay,' I replied, and changed the subject. 'Is Shove about?' I asked mid-munch.

'Oh, didn't you know? She had to go off to Norwich at short notice.'

'Yes, and I've just come back with her,' I replied.

Mrs. Grubbs looked at me quizzically, 'You mean you went too?'

'Oh, I've had a fun day travelling all over the Province in vehicles I would never have imagined this morning. We've just come back from Kings Lynn in a hovercraft.'

'Ooh, my word!' she exclaimed, 'whatever next? What was it all about then?'

At that point I thought it was up to Shove to discuss the purpose for the Norwich trip with whosoever she wanted. 'Well, I'm not sure what it was all about, to be honest, I certainly didn't follow it all,' I fibbed. 'That's why I was hoping that Shove would be back from the Dogsthorpe Docks, so I could go through it with her.'

'I'll let her know that you're looking for her as soon as she gets in.' It was Mrs. Grubbs' turn to change the subject. 'Bloody weather,' she muttered. It was probably the strongest language I had ever heard her use. 'Is it snowing like this in Norwich?' she asked.

'From what I hear, it's snowing like this all over the Island.'

'Very peculiar isn't it,' she said, 'middle of August and all? I wonder what it's all about?'

'I'm sure that is one thing we will get an answer to,' I replied, pushing the last piece of kebab into my mouth. I chewed happily and swallowed. 'I am sure that everybody will be looking into this. The only thing we mustn't do is believe the first story that comes out. There will be a lot of lunatic theories.'

'Witches and goblins,' she muttered. 'Anyway,' she said picking up the plate with the empty paper on it, 'I can't just stand here gossiping, I've got things to do.'

I wandered through into the sitting room. I'd just been wondering what to do with myself when Shove walked in.

'Hi there,' I said, 'I was just about to put some music on. Interested?'

'Not right at this moment, but I do think we need to talk about what happened today.'

'Okay,' I agreed.

Shove subsided into a chair. 'Sorry about that,' she said, 'I just think we ought to talk.'

'Two things:' I said, 'the first thing is Mrs. Grubbs, who wanted to know what Norwich was all about. I pretended I hadn't really followed what was going on so that she ought to ask you. That way you can let her know how much, or how little, you want her to know; the second thing is the talk I was supposed to be going to was cancelled because the speaker was found dead in her hotel bed this morning. Is there anything about Melissa Landry's death I might like to know about?'

'Why, has someone offered you a fee to investigate it?

'At this stage, the only person who might do that is me. She was a forensic psychologist who also wrote mysteries. There is any amount of potential in that back story.'

'Local girl, was she?'

'Not at all, and hardly a girl. Older than either of us and she came in from over the border somewhere – Manchester, I think – she was on a public relations tour as she's just published a new book.'

'Well, I think you know where to start then, don't you? Download that book and get reading.'

Chapter 9
A Pluperfect Murder

And this is what met my eyes:

Detective Constable Aaron Gold sat on the sofa, reading his copy of the briefing. The text was clear enough on the tablet, he supposed, but he was having great difficulty concentrating. He was distracted. Any one of four things might have relieved that distraction but none of them took place. Detective Sergeant Susan Laking could have shut the bedroom door. But she hadn't. Then again, she could have kept her trousers on. But she hadn't. Or she could have drawn the curtains so that the sunlight didn't shine directly onto her long, slender legs in a way that Aaron couldn't help noticing. But she hadn't. There again, Gold could have simply rotated himself through ninety degrees so that he wasn't looking directly at DS Laking's legs. But he didn't.

Laking had gone into the bedroom to change for their walk down Pelikaan Straat. Her slacks had already been removed in preparation for replacing them with an elegant mid-length skirt, when she was distracted by something on the bed. She picked it up and then she sat down on the end of the bed to look at it. It was probably a flyer that had been left there by one of the hotel staff. They did that sort of thing when a couple that they took to be the Earl and Countess of Flint occupied one of their VIP suites.

Nobody spoke Flemish in the Duchy of Lancashire – well, certainly not in the police force anyway – so the next best thing for a mission to the Diamond Quarter of Antwerp was to find someone who spoke Yiddish, which has been one of the business languages of the Quarter for centuries. That was where Aaron Gold came in. Aside from being quite a presentable young man, who would pass as a credible consort for a countess, he also had a smattering of the language of his forefathers. Why Aaron had signed up to be a policeman was perhaps his own secret and one that, at least for the time being, he was keeping to himself. There was certainly nothing about his manner that suggested that he was cut out for a life directing traffic or strong-arming drunks into the tank on a Mancunian Saturday night after the local team lost. Being involved in a piece of undercover work abroad in a place like Antwerp, however, seemed much more up his street. Maybe it was because he looked a bit like James Bond. His role was, of course, subservient to that of his boss on the case, Detective Sergeant Laking, though, provided she wasn't wearing heels, he was very slightly taller. Their mission was to masquerade as the Earl and Countess of Flint, while in fact they were investigating a haul of diamonds that had cropped up inside a corpse near the Pier Head in Liverpool earlier that week. Quite who the corpse was, or where he had come from, was as yet unknown to the Manchester police or, if they did know, they hadn't shared that information with Detective Sergeant Laking or DC Gold.

Aha, or words to that effect, I thought. As she did with the previous two books I had read, she starts her novels in the middle and then goes back to the setup later. Once again, she opens with the beauty that is Laking and introduces it from the point of view of somebody new, in this case Gold. He may, of course, have cropped up before, just not in any of the books that I had already read. There are disadvantages in dipping into a series at random as I was doing.

Aaron pulled the little bag out of his pocket again. He let the shiny stones run through his fingers, looking closely at them as they tumbled from one hand to the other, glittering as they fell. They looked crystal clear to him, and rivetingly beautiful. 'So, run this blood diamond stuff past me again,' he said, looking across at the leggy detective. Perhaps she would move if he spoke to her. 'They don't appear to have the slightest trace of red in them.'

She looked horrified at him, the way he was playing with them. 'They're not called blood diamonds because of the colour, you halfwit, they're called blood diamonds because of their history.'

'That doesn't make the name any clearer.'

She walked over and stood over him. 'Give me those,' she snapped. He poured the diamonds back into the little velvet pouch and put them in her waiting hand. 'Here,' he said, riveted by the sight of her long, bare legs.

'And incidentally, my face is up here.'

'Yes, but my face is down here, just on a level with your knees. You wouldn't want me to get a crick in my neck gazing into your eyes when I could just as well sit here and talk to your knees? Explain to me blood diamonds.'

She came very close to clipping him round the ear. How had he got this far in this operation without understanding the basic tenet? 'Blood diamonds are those mined secretively in places, usually somewhere in West Africa, by slave labour and are used to fund civil wars anywhere on the planet, often not far from where they are mined, though that is by no means the rule. Because they are illicitly mined by slave labour, without any provenance, they are much cheaper than the real McCoy from, say, Kimberley. They are usually used as currency to pay mercenaries in a conflict.'

'So they're not real diamonds then?'

'How do you mean?'

'Like the Koh-I-Noor?'

'Oh, they're real diamonds, all right, just without any certification or anything. That's why we're here. Antwerp is the diamond market of the world and we're going to find out whether anyone knows anything about these little beauties, and therefore their value.'

'And I'm playing the part of their owner?'

'I think I'm going to pass you a cigar in a moment.'

'I don't smoke.' If Aaron had been looking upwards, instead of at the knees in front of him, he would have seen her eyes roll.

'And I'm playing the part of your beloved wife, for whom you intend to buy some diamonds of similar provenance to those we are showing them.' She was aware he was getting closer to her knees. She was happily unaware that what he really wanted to do was lick them.

Oh my God! Eww! I thought: Melissa would never have got away with that sort of writing if she'd been a man.

'And, as you were told in the briefing before we even left Manchester, I am only playing the part of your wife on the other side of that door. In here you just behave yourself, got that?'

'Yes, Boss,' he replied.

'And moreover, your job is to support me in making absolutely damned sure those diamonds remain safe. They belong to the English *government and it expects to get them back in exactly the same quantity and quality that they left London.'*

'Well, technically they belong to the person who owns them,' Gold replied drily. 'It's just that we don't know who he is yet.'

'Hmm,' Sue thought for a moment, 'and you could buy a pretty large part of Manchester nowadays with that bagful. Fancy owning Old Trafford, Constable?'

'Not particularly, Boss,' he replied.

Detective Sergeant Laking still wasn't sure about DC Gold. She was certainly sure that the silly young man was on her side, and he wasn't bright enough to be a double agent or anything like that, but she was far from convinced that he would be able to stand up to hostile action. She wasn't sure that he would even be able to tell a hostile if they came up and talked to him if they weren't waving a weapon and making threats. Could he even tell whether someone was a Welshman for example? Caerdydd wouldn't employ anyone as a spy if they only spoke Welsh. And as for Anglians and Wessexmen, well all right, they had accents too – well some of them anyway – but it was only straight English they spoke. So if he was expecting to protect them from Russians or Arabs he would be somewhat disappointed; the enemy was far closer to hand.

I looked at the text. Hmm, that's why I hadn't seen Aaron Gold in earlier books; he was a 'redshirt'. He was to be a fairly early casualty in the narrative to put Detective Sergeant Laking, the heroine, in jeopardy and she would have to play the grieving widow. I decided to have a sweepstake with myself: I bet myself that Gold would die, probably painfully, at around the 14% mark in the book. What this particular piece of text was showing me was how much of Laking's grief would be an act and giving her a perfectly good excuse not to grieve too much.

I was beginning to feel sleepy; it had been a long day. It looked as if there was going to be a long, useful discourse on diamonds in general and blood diamonds in particular, to say nothing about the writer's views on the British Provinces that had achieved independence. Various locations in Antwerp where such gems would be found and frowned upon would also be part of the narrative. Bearing in mind that The Rail's diamonds might well have little or no provenance either, the book could be a very good place to start looking. Melissa Landry might well have already done a lot of my research for me.

I would formally buy the book in the morning but, as always, I had put my wristy in its charger overnight and its charger was securely located on the dressing table on the other side of the room to avoid my marmalising it if I thumped it when the alarm went off. Ordering the book could wait till tomorrow. It was seriously tedious trying to do it through the reading tablet as I had never put my bank account details into it in case I left it somewhere by mistake. I turned over and my eyes shut themselves automatically.

Chapter 10
Gone Book

One eye opened. I looked around, vaguely hoping that the greyness and snow from yesterday had all been a bad dream; that I hadn't been to Norwich by airship or come back by hovercraft; that Yellowstone hadn't exploded; and that the world wasn't about to go through another mass extinction event, either slowly and inexorably as a result of the volcano or rapidly at mankind's own hand. The other eye joined its pal and opened as well. If it wasn't still snowing, it was either very early or awfully grey out there. One leg crept out of bed and its partner obediently followed. I parted the curtains and looked out. It was still snowing. So I had been to Norwich yesterday and Yellowstone's explosion had caused the biggest snowstorm since sixty million B.C.

Once again, I was second down for breakfast. This time I really felt like a couple of poached eggs. 'Do you have any crumpets to put them on?' I asked.

'I think I can rustle you up a couple of crumpets, our Steff,' smiled Mrs. Grubbs. 'Would you like them buttered?'

Paradise indeed. I tried to work out how Mrs. Grubbs kept everything in stock 'just in case' without them going out of date and her having to throw the lion's share away. And I knew that didn't happen as I knew how much the housekeeping cost. The house was part of my business after all.

The other thing Mrs. Grubbs knew was how to poach an egg properly. This is not a skill that a great many people have, including a number of chefs in hotels where I have stayed. Mind you, I didn't usually stay in the sort of hotel described in the novel I had dipped into the previous evening. That reminded me – as soon as I had finished these delicious poached eggs, which came from the chicken house at the bottom of the garden, and probably had a second cup of coffee, I needed to formally buy a copy of the whole of Melissa Landry's new book.

'Morning, Steff,' came Shove's Irish brogue from the door. She was in mufti today, though neat as she always was and certainly as neat and tidy as would be expected from the guv'nor. I wondered carelessly where she might hide her sidearm in this get-up.

Coffee, toast and marmalade were what she fancied. The very large chunks of peel in the dark jam had me thinking that I would like a piece of toast and marmalade too. I had been hungry after all. Last night's kebab had only been a rather short fix against hunger pangs.

I tidied my things into the kitchen where I was waved away by Mrs. Grubbs. She was feeding her husband his breakfast at the kitchen table – bacon, eggs, black pudding and the largest mug of tea I had ever seen – and she didn't want me getting in the way. I have no idea why the Grubbs ate in the back room and not with the rest of us. I had suggested regularly that we should all eat together, but there was always a reason why that wouldn't be a good idea at that particular moment. Perhaps they really liked being 'the servants' and keeping themselves away from the rest of us. I wonder whether it had anything to do with the fate of their previous home, and its current location underwater in The Wash.

I wandered through into the sitting room and tapped my wristy, opened the 'Nene Books' app and looked for Melissa Landry's *A Pluperfect Murder*. It should still have been there right in front of me. The previous night I had found it easily enough and had tapped the 'would you like to try it' button, and it had appeared, ready to read, on my tablet in a matter of seconds. So where was it now?

I went back to the search engine and typed in Melissa Landry. There were all the books that that sad young man from yesterday evening would remember, and there *A Pluperfect Murder* wasn't. It wasn't even on the screen. So I typed in A PLUPERFECT MURDER and the search engine thought for a moment and replied 'The requested item could not be found'. Well, that was ridiculous. I bolted back upstairs. At least my tablet was where I had left it, on charge on my bedside table. I picked it up and turned it on. It didn't default to what I had last been reading as it usually did. It went to its top menu, effectively asking me what I would like to read next. I ran my finger up and down that menu. No *A Pluperfect Murder*. Where the hell had it gone?

I turned my tablet back off, leaving it charging, and went downstairs.

Shove was finishing the last morsel of toast and marmalade. I asked her, 'Has it ever happened to you that your tablet has lost a book you were reading the night before?'

'No. Why? What's happened?'

'Well, you know last night you suggested that I should read Melissa Landry's latest book?'

'Yes.'

'Well, I downloaded a taster last night and read part of the first chapter. I decided this morning I would like to buy the whole book and read it at my leisure. It has completely vanished, no taster on my tablet and the book no longer appears to be available to buy.'

'Oh, you enjoyed it then?' she asked, missing the point completely, not understanding what was rattling my cage.

'Not especially, but it had some interesting things to say about diamonds and I thought Adelina's expenses would cover the cost of a copy if it got me closer to finding her missing horde.'

'Well, in answer to your question, the answer is no, it has never happened to me that my tablet has ever lost a book I was reading. It does, however, unload books I have merely borrowed or rented but if I actually buy them then they remain on my reader even when they're no longer available, like in the old days when you bought a physical book.'

'I must get hold of the man at Nene Books and see what's going on,' I said, tapping my wristy and finding the Nene Books voicemail app. It said that there was high demand right now and that I should call again later. Of course, there was probably no one there at this time in the morning. I did, however, browse through some of the big international market places where people bought stuff. I tended to avoid those completely, probably out of loyalty to support struggling Anglian individuals. I always assumed that Anglians were struggling but actually they were less likely to be starving than people on the other side of the fence. To my surprise none of the 'international plutocrat' suppliers appeared to know anything about Melissa Landry's latest novel either. Certainly none of them had it on sale.

I summoned a pod and went and waited by the front door. The snow wasn't settling or anything but the gravel on the drive was beginning to take on a grey tinge. The volcanic grit in the snow was beginning to establish itself even if the water wasn't staying solid. The pod arrived quickly and I tapped in Cathedral Square and off we went.

Five minutes later I was in the office offering Sabrina and Dwayne a cuppa. Both of them waved full mugs at me to show they were way ahead of me and Dwayne made work for himself by offering to make me a cup. Needless to say, I accepted, and he was left with the job of keeping his boss happy.

I went through into my office, installed myself behind the desk and checked my wristy. In five minutes it would be nine o'clock and I would call Nene Books again. I tapped in Jerzy's number in the meantime. 'It's me, Steffy,' I said, 'I have another enquiry about one of your guests.'

'Who is it this time? I haven't any more information about your Mr. Ahmed yet.'

'Did they bring in a Melissa Landry yesterday?'

'Woman from the hotel in the town centre?'

'That's the one. What's happening about her?'

'Well, as far as I know there's going to be a post-mortem. She's not an Anglian citizen and she has no medical records in the Province. What usually happens in situations like this is that the locals require some sort of documentation before they release the body over the border for disposal. If someone from, say, Manchester, lays claim to the body for disposal there, and can justify why the person had died here, and can provide adequate paperwork, we just box it up and ship it back to them lickety split. Any post mortem they require will be up to them. If there are no requests for the body then we do the usual post-mortem to make sure there was nothing untoward about the whole thing and then dispose of it ourselves.'

'Which means?'

'The remains are composted, although if any family members really object we do what they require, unless it's against the law. You know, we even launched a Norwegian out into The Wash in a burning boat not so long ago. Nobody could find anything in the Anglian by-laws formally prohibiting traditional Viking funerals, so we did it. Got quite a crowd it did. A by-law probably did get written the following day. We're not totally against pumping carbon dioxide into the atmosphere, especially if the wind's blowing from the south.' He chuckled down the phone.

'So, if no one claims her, and there's nothing on the autopsy, we'll compost her ourselves. Do we keep the compost for our own agriculture?' I asked

'That's the bottom line. We've done all the work.'

'How thorough will the autopsy be?'

'I'm already concerned, Steff, that your asking these questions suggests that you think the post mortem ought to be a very thorough one.'

'I don't know. I'm just concerned that her latest book has been removed from circulation overnight, within twenty-four hours of her demise, and I had just started reading it.'

'Has your copy been withdrawn?'

'Oh yes.'

'I think you ought to be notifying the police about that if you're worried about it.'

'I've already done so.' I thought for a moment and decided telling Shove while she was munching on toast and marmalade was probably not what you would consider to be a formal notification. 'Probably not officially, though. How long have I got, to make it an official report?'

'They wouldn't even schedule a post mortem at this stage for at least a week, unless the police give us a giddy-up. They did that with your Mr. Ahmed, even though it was obvious to anybody how he was killed. The police, you know, when they want to know something, they want to know it yesterday. It'll take the various bureaucracies at least until the end of the week to come to an agreement as to what the next step is, unless they have decided she was murdered.'

'Thank you for that, Jerzy, I'll get on with it straight away.'

I disconnected. Well, that was a starting point. I peered at my wristy: five past nine. I thought I would give Nene Books a call.

There was no response for a few moments and then a slightly sleepy but fairly cross voice replied, 'Yeah, Nene Books, how can I help you?'

'Hello, this is Stephanie Flack, Flack and Associates, I'm a private investigator,' I waited a beat in case he came back with a 'wha-a-at', as some people do when you tell them they're talking to an eye, and then continued, 'I ordered a taster from you last night and liked it so much

I tried to buy the whole book this morning, but it's disappeared off the face of the earth and I wondered if you could revive it for me.'

I could have sworn he yawned before he replied, 'Which book was this?'

'Melissa Landry's *A Pluperfect Murder.*'

'Oh God, not another.'

'What do you mean?'

'My wristy has not stopped buzzing about Melissa Landry's fucking *Pluperfect Murder* since stupid o'fucking clock this fucking morning.' He sounded furious. I couldn't imagine anyone swearing at a customer like that on a regular basis and hanging on to his business very long. He must be feeling very frayed round the edges.

'Since you got up,' he couldn't see me grinning, but I was.

Not expecting his reply though. 'I'm still in fucking bed, haven't had the opportunity to do anything yet this morning. I just wish the fucking bugger would just shut the fuck up so I can get washed and dressed.'

'Would you like me to come round and deal with the calls while you get on with your ablutions? I am currently in the centre of Peterborough. Where are you?' I asked, flying by the seat of my pants. I knew this man knew something and I wanted to know it too. He might be a bit potty-mouthed this morning but really, he's a bookseller, how dangerous could he be?

His reply was surprisingly welcoming, 'Would you? That would really help. I live at fourteen Guyhirn Mews, in North Bretton. Do you know where that is?'

'Personally no, but I'm sure a pod will be able to find it. Do you have a postcode?'

He gave me the code and I scribbled it down before jumping up from the desk and brushing past Dwayne coming through the door with a mug of coffee in his hand. 'Sorry D, I've got to go out,' I said.

'Do you need me too?' he asked. 'I'm not doing anything. I can look after you if things go wrong.'

'No, you stay here and look after Sabrina. I'm not going to be very long, I'm off to North Bretton, just to help a bookseller get up.'

'Huh?'

'And once he has done, and I've got the info I need, I'll be back and we'll have a formal morning meeting, and I'll tell you all about yesterday. If I'm not back by lunchtime, call me. If I don't answer, here's where I've gone.' I gave them the post-it note I had just scribbled.

'Yeah, I was going to ask you where you got to yesterday, 'cos you vanished off the face of the earth.'

'You could always have called me,' I pointed out, waving my wrist at him.

'I did, and you didn't answer.' We both glowered at my wristy, which flashed silently into life and told me there was a pod waiting outside. 'Gotta go. See you shortly,' I said, tapping at the silent mode button which I had obviously activated before the meeting in Norwich yesterday and then forgotten I had done so. Oops, sorry Dwayne, my bad. I was off down the stairs as fast as possible and out the front door before the pod gave up waiting in disgust.

Guyhirn Mews was one of those synthetic, modern, terraced estates that had been thrown up in the previous few years to fill the hole in the housing stock that the floods had more than decimated. This particular estate was full of streets named after villages that had disappeared into The Wash, like Gedney Square, and Gote Street. I couldn't help thinking that the architects who had got that contract had a slightly sick sense of humour. As I got out of the pod, which had opened up right outside number fourteen, I noted number twelve on its left and fifteen on its right. So, actually, it was number thirteen, wasn't it? A train thundered past, well within earshot. Yes, that would figure, the marshalling yards would be just on the other side of that fence at the end of the cul-de-sac and would effectively be the border with North Mercia, which was still a part of England. Half the road freight from the North would be entrained in those marshalling yards to go to the Anglian ports of Lowestoft, Felixstowe and Harwich, to name but three. So this house wouldn't be the quietest place on the planet, even before the incessant buzzing and trilling of frantic devices from within. The people living in twelve and fifteen must be thrilled to bits with the noise next door. I walked up to the door and pushed the button under the number.

'It's open,' came a voice from within, which sounded frantic and sore.

I walked through the door into the front room, which was full of tobacco smoke and howling terminals. Speaking into the headset was a dishevelled young man in pyjamas, his hair askew, and his voice beginning to sound rather more than frayed round the edges. 'You're Steff Flack, right?'

'That's me,' I assented.

'You're a godsend,' he said, too tired to smile.

'What do I say?' I asked, picking up a spare headset.

'That the publisher's recalled it and that you don't know why.'

'Is that the truth?'

'Near as dammit. I'll tell you what they actually told me when we cop a break. Meanwhile, can I go upstairs and get washed and dressed?'

'Go! Go!' The man really needed a wash, that much I could tell from across the room.

'I'll fix you a coffee when I get back down. Ten, fifteen minutes?'

'Fine,' I said and, plugging in the headset, proceeded to field the calls. It wasn't difficult. There were a fair number of really pissed off people. It appeared that there were people who had actually paid for the book and theirs had vanished too. I took their names sympathetically, in case we needed to send them a refund, if it hadn't happened automatically. It was probably the longest fifteen minutes that I had spent recently.

Chapter 11
A Bookseller's Story

I looked around the room as I half-listened to the vitriol going into my earpiece. It was obviously designed to be the house's living area. Through the open door at the back of it and to the left I could see through into the corner of a kitchen. There was a kettle and a heap of hopefully empty takeaway containers on a built-in surface in my line of sight. At the other end of that back wall there was another door, through which the young man had disappeared, and behind that door was presumably the staircase, as he had clumped upwards fairly loudly once he had gone though the door. Between those doors, on the nicotine-stained back wall, was a fairly large old-fashioned plasma screen. Standing on an upturned beer crate underneath it were a program box and a couple of games consoles. Quite what they were I didn't know, but that was my ignorance. I don't do electronic games. There was one rather elderly but well-loved armchair in the middle of the room facing the screen. Otherwise there were two dining chairs, one of which was under me. On the other, standing beside the right arm of the armchair, were a couple of pizza boxes, one of which was open, showing a couple of cold slices still in it. Rotating myself through a hundred and eighty degrees, I came face-to-face with four full-sized screens, each with their own keyboard in front of them, three of which were the standard QWERTY type, the fourth being a piano style keyboard. I wondered whether he was musical or whether this was something else altogether. Each of the keyboards had a freestanding black box beside them, even the piano keyboard. Each black box had a column of lights on the front and on each box it was the second one down that was flashing red. I tapped a flashing light and it stopped flashing as a voice yelled into my ear, demanding to know where the [very rude word] was the book they had bought three days ago as they were really [a different rude word] getting into it. I apologised, just like the bookseller had told me, and said we would be back to her as soon as we knew something. I tapped the red light and it went out as the line disconnected, leaving me free to connect with another flashing light. After a couple of those I thought I might amuse myself and, while the customer still talking, said, 'Hang on, this might be the wholesaler on the other line,' and pressed another flashing light. It went still and the previous one reverted to flashing. Of course it wasn't the supplier, it was just another whingeing customer whom I sorted with another platitude, and then spoke to the previous punter again. Very nifty piece of kit, I thought. I must ask the bookseller where he had got his VoIP from. We could use a system like that at our office.

It was astonishing how many people thought that it must be a conspiracy set up by Nene Books that their book had disappeared. They blamed me, well him, for everything. The more abuse I took, the more puzzled I became as to why he had given me his address. I wouldn't have told any of these animals in which province I was hiding, let alone giving them details of exactly where to find me. Had I really been the only friendly voice he had heard all morning, and one that had allowed him to vent his own frustration?

I was surprised that the chair he used was the dining chair I was sitting on. If his IT system was his main raison d'être then surely he would have a comfortable chair to sit on. Obviously not. There was no dining table to go with the dining chairs, unless that was it under the right-hand bank of screens, with rings where hot mugs had once stood and a pad of paper and a ballpoint on it.

There were odd cuttings stuck to the wall, set only fairly straight. They were mostly publicity shots about books. Maybe they were free posters that he had been sent by publishers, to be displayed in a walk-in bookshop where customers had actually gone to buy a book. They didn't exist any more, well, they might in places like Norwich and Cambridge where residents still value the past but certainly there wasn't such a thing in Peterborough. The posters must have taken his fancy and he had stuck them up on the wall. Certainly the only thing they had in common was that they were eye-catching, in a very masculine way. Yes, that was definitely the thing that was missing – there wasn't a trace of a feminine touch anywhere in that room. Even the curtains that effectively blocked all the light coming in from the street behind the bank of computers were simply impenetrably black.

The room was lit by a single powerful, unshaded bulb hanging in the middle of the ceiling.

Meanwhile I was fielding calls. Whatever else, the young man appeared to be doing pretty good business, if the cancellation of one book was anything to go by. It had annoyed a good many people very quickly indeed. The terminal on the right, the one with the piano keyboard, had also been fairly active, though quite what the scrolling codes actually meant I had no idea. Perhaps they were registering sales and downloading books into people's tablets. During a ninety-second gap between bursts of abuse I had noticed a name and address come up on the screen, followed by a load of code. So he was doing business as far away as Chelmsford. The screen didn't tell me what it was that the person in Chelmsford had downloaded, perhaps that was buried in the stream of code that followed the identifier. Then there was an irate buzz and I was back again listening to someone complaining about the absence of Melissa Landry's book. At least this one hadn't had one and then lost it. She had been expecting to buy it today, and she was a regular customer, and what were we playing at? Nene Books always gets the best books first, don't we? Now there was a facer; this tatty little enterprise in the downstairs of someone's house was apparently one of the best e-bookshops around, and able to compete with the big boys. I really had to know who this young man was. I hadn't even got a name or anything.

The shower had stopped upstairs and he was stamping about in the room above me, presumably throwing on clothes. Please be putting on clothes. Then came what sounded almost like a tumble down the stairs, but he swung through the door the right way up, and fully clothed, so he had apparently simply been moving fast. 'Right,' he said. 'Coffee?'

'Yes, please.'

'Milk and sugar?'

'Just milk.'

'Help yourself to some cold pizza if you want,' he said, waving at the box on the chair.

'No thanks, I've had breakfast,' I explained, without having to tell him that nothing short of having my nails pulled out slowly would induce me to put that detritus anywhere near my mouth. He disappeared into the kitchen. The kettle in my eyeline was switched on and there was a sound of running water. A couple of moments later he was out holding two chipped mugs, also bearing publicity slogans. 'Yours is the Maurice Clark, no sugar.' He plonked the mug down on the table, beside the pad of paper. Well, that explained the rings on the table. I had no idea who Maurice Clark was, but his mug had seen good use in this house.

As an opener to conversation, I asked him who Maurice Clark was.

'No clue, it came with a package from a publisher. Just because I sell all this stuff doesn't mean I read any of it.'

'You mean you don't read any books?'

'Oh, a bit of sci-fi, a bit of fantasy, you know.'

'Sorry, I've been sitting in your house all this time and I don't even know your name.'

'And I know all about you,' he said. 'I'm so sorry. I'm Allo Wood.'

'Allo?'

'My mum thought it would be fun to give me a really posh name, so she called me Allowishus but she had no idea how to spell it and anyway, she got fed up with all of them syllables, so she shortened it to plain Allo. It wasn't till I was eleven, when I got to see my birth certificate, that I found out I'd got more letters in my name.'

'What did your dad have to say about all this?'

'Dad? I never had a dad.' He paused for a moment and then continued, 'Well, obviously I had a biological dad, I just never knew who he was. Still don't.'

I couldn't help being nosy. It's my job after all. 'So whose name was on the birth certificate?'

'It blamed me on Hickory Wood.'

'The guitarist?'

'That's the one.'

I looked at him and then said, 'But you're rather too old to be Hickory Wood's kid. He really only got famous in the last twenty years.'

'That's what I said to Mum but her reply was that he had to be playing before he got famous, otherwise he would never have got famous in the first place.'

'But Hickory Wood's not his real name, everyone knows he's called Cameron Cragg.'

'All things of which I'm well aware. Bottom line is, I have no idea from whose gene pool I came and nor did my mum. I think I'm the result of a one night stand when Mum got loaded, smashed and knocked up without waking up in the process. Not a problem, here I am and here is Nene Books.' He waved a proprietorial hand at the stack of servers and flashing screens.

I looked round the room.

'I have to ask how you got a place like this on your own. Don't worry, I'm not going to drop you in it, I'm just interested.'

'I didn't get it on my own; Mum was alive then. We were in a similar sort of place in Cardea, you remember the township down south of the city on the way to Whittle? Well, of course, that flooded, and we were moved into this new development, single mum and child, two bedrooms, perfect. They moved a lot of people from Cardea into this estate. It's a bit noisier here, with all the trains and stuff, but I don't mind, not with them next door in number twelve.'

It was beginning to fall into place. He had moved here during the floods. He must have been in his mid-teens, I supposed, at that point. We answered a couple of rather more polite enquiries about Melissa Landry's book and one about a book by Hans Hellmut Kirst, of which I had never heard. Allo had, however, and he explained that the firm was still in the process of getting that one typeset and uploaded. He would contact them as soon as it was available.

'That was slick,' I said, thinking I had just heard a bit of elegant 'BS'.

'Fuck no, all genuine stuff. There's all sorts of companies I deal with who digitalise old books which predate the invention of the reading tablet. Some of those books from the fifties through to the noughties are dead good, especially the sci-fi and war stuff, so naturally I stock all those at Nene Books.' I was beginning to understand why he was such a successful business.

'Mum?' I cocked an eyebrow.

'She died about five years ago. Poor love, she'd been ill a long time. So now it's just me here. Me and my bookshop.'

'Do the council know about you running a business from your home?'

'I've not formally told anyone but I've not kept it a secret. I pay all my bills in advance or on time. So I guess they're happy, it's the one place on this estate they don't have to worry about. The junkies next door can't possibly be on time with their rent and the deaf old couple in fifteen, well, they must be on a pension so their rent gets paid automatically, doesn't it?'

He had an answer for everything, except for his solitude. He was talking nineteen to the dozen to me, telling me all his secrets, and we had first met half an hour ago. Didn't he get to talk to anyone else, apart from disgruntled customers? A customer wouldn't call him unless there was an absence of gruntle. I mean, why would you contact a bookshop just to have a chat? 'Don't you get lonely?' I asked. Oh, that hit a spot, his eyes got two sizes wider.

'At times,' he nodded, 'but it's good to have an income and I do get to talk to publishers and the people next door, when they're in orbit round the same planet as I am, so I'm not completely alone.'

'But you're obviously highly qualified, running this business.'

'Skilled, possibly, but not qualified. I didn't get any box tops. When my mum got ill I stayed here to look after her while I set the business up and then, when she was gone, it was already here, up and running.'

'When did you last really get out properly?' I asked gently.

'When mum was really ill I took her to see Hickory Wood in Huntingdon. Nobody any good ever comes to Peterborough.'

'Twas ever thus,' I muttered.

'"And there," Mum said, "that's your dad." Well, you had only to look at him once and you knew that wasn't possible. The man's as black as the ace of spades for fuck's sake, er, no racial slur intended, but it's true, innit, there's no way someone as pale as me could have been spawned from those loins. Now, he plays a sweet guitar and all, but when he opens his mouth to talk he's as thick as shit. Those pretty lyrics he sings must have been written by someone else. Now, though I say it myself, I'm quite bright, especially in maths and programming and stuff. So no, whoever my dad was or is, he wasn't Hickory Wood, but I got the guitarist's stage name. So now I work my own bookshop and take the occasional spot of medication from next door,' he chuckled. 'Only a spot of Phantasm, none of the hard stuff.'

'You've actually taken Phantasm?' I asked.

'Yeah, I take it from time to time, it's not addictive, certainly not to me, anyway, but it makes me feel good.'

'What's it like?' I had heard of the new designer drug on the streets but I had never got up close and personal to anyone who had experience of it.

'Well, 'im next door described it like, "Remember when there was this girl, and you had never seen anything like her, and you adored the water she walked on?" and I said, "Yeah," and he went on and said, "Remember when you first got her into bed and how that felt?" and I said "Yeah", and he said, "Well, multiply that feeling by twenty-five and that's what Phantasm is like."'

'And was it?' I asked.

'I don't know, I never got that girl into bed.' He paused for a moment. I could see immediately this was a story he had wanted to tell someone for a very long time, so I waited and finally he continued, 'When we came here from Cardea, I got enrolled in the local comp. I was fourteen at the time and there was this girl, we all called her Angel, though I guess her real name was probably Angela. Angel was the most beautiful girl I ever knew and she liked me, honest. We had this really shit maths teacher we called The Slug, who was just rubbish. It didn't matter much to me 'cos I didn't need him to explain stuff to me, I knew how he got there without him trying.

'Well, when I arrived at the comp they put me in the row behind Angel and I could sit there and sniff her hair without her realising. She had fair hair – like yours, only longer and wavy – anyway, one day, after a particularly bad maths lesson, she turned round and shone her eyes straight through me, well, that's how it felt. I'll never forget, these were the first words she ever said to me, she said, "You understand this crap don't you?" and I said "Yeah," and she said "Will you teach me so it makes sense to me too?" Well, what could I say? I said "Yeah."

'All that summer term, we met after classes were over and we went through what The Slug had tried and failed to teach us. Now, I didn't do her homework for her, she didn't want that, what she wanted was for me to explain to her so she could do it herself. Once she had got the idea locked in, Angel could do it herself and all those straight 'As' she got from maths were her own work, promise. She was bright, that Angel. Towards the end of that term she said to me, "You know, you should teach everybody maths, you're so much better at it than that Slug. Can I ask my friends to join us? You can have a whole class all of your own. They'll make it worth your while, promise." Well, I thought about it for about ten seconds flat. I didn't want those other dozy pillocks diluting the time I got to spend with my Angel. And I really did consider her my Angel, you know. So I said no and she asked why not and I said that I didn't want to teach anybody but her. And she looked at me with those really big eyes she had and said, with a little giggle that often gave me an instant stiffy, "Don't tell me you're in love with me or any of that stuff, 'cos Collin would get really pissed." Now, Collin was this biker bloke from Market Deeping with tattoos all over. Everybody knew Collin and most of us were shit scared of him. I knew she knew him too but I didn't know he really mattered to her until a few days later she said, "I've got a tattoo, do you want to see it?" Did I? I mean, all I ever got to see of her usually was her face and her hands and sometimes her legs if she was wearing a skirt. She lifted up her shirt at the back and on her back was this huge dragon, with a tail which went round her side to fuck knows where.'

I couldn't resist it. 'What did you feel?' I asked.

'I was fucking heartbroken. This beautiful girl with this wonderful skin had had that done to it. Why had she done it? Course, I knew the beginning of the next term when she came back with a metal stud in her nose. And six months after that she dropped out of school completely. I heard she was up the duff. But I never forgot my Angel and there has never been anyone else like her since.'

'Do you ever hear from her?'

'Them at number twelve know of her. She's got four kids with a fifth on the way. She's still with that Collin bloke. He races motorbikes at Silverstone and places but, of course, motor racing isn't allowed in Anglia so I guess they don't come here. I don't know why they know of her at number twelve. I thought they only knew drug people, so I don't ask. I don't want to know.'

It was the saddest story I had ever heard. This poor Allo Wood had got to me. But I wasn't there to sympathise with him. I had put myself through those twenty minutes of hell, listening to a barrage of four letter words, for a reason. I needed information. 'So,' I asked, 'tell me how a book might disappear from someone's tablet out of the blue.'

'Well, it happens like this. If you're a library then you are licenced to lend books or rent books on a short term loan. Libraries are owned by the council and you pay a subscription to be a member of one. Are you a library member?'

'No, I've never got round to it. I get my books from you,' I added to keep him on side. It worked.

'In which case, I won't try terribly hard to try to persuade you that libraries are good things to be a member of. You can taste and try before you buy from me. Anyway, while you are a member, you can borrow as many books from your library as you previously agreed when you took out your membership. And when you have borrowed the maximum number of books then you can't borrow any more until you have returned one. Now, in the old days, when books were physical lumps, you literally had to take one back before you got to take another one out. Nowadays you can either return one yourself by 'returning it', which means, in reality, you deleting it and letting them know that you've done it; or they can claim it back when the time is up and it just deletes itself. I'm not allowed to be a library but I can, like a library, rent books. You pay me a fee, or you pay the library a fee, to loan a book from either of us. Sometimes I'm cheaper than a library, sometimes they're cheaper than me. Those books that people rent are often research books. Sometimes they may be plays that a drama group is rehearsing and will then take through to production. Quite cool, sometimes, to suddenly find that a whole wodge of your favourite play is being rented in, say, Huntingdon. Then you know that there's going to be a performance of that play and it's fun to find out exactly where it's going to be put on. Sometimes I even go and see it. I can remember taking Mum to see *The Accidental Death of an Anarchist* in Wisbech before it got flooded and she thought it was seriously funny. Anyway, they'll want the book for a fair length of time but probably won't want it, apart from for sentimental reasons, after the last night. Now, the library isn't allowed to sell books but I am. Once you buy a book it should remain in your reader's memory, either in the device itself or in the cloud, for as long as you want it, even if the book has gone out of print and is no longer available to buy.'

'So, if you've bought a copy of a book, it ought to remain in your reader no matter what happens to the outside world. Okay,' I continued, 'so what happened here? I know for a fact that a number of people had actually bought that book, not borrowed it or rented it, and their copies vanished too.'

'I know, and I don't understand that either. While I was upstairs putting my socks on I had a word with the wholesaler on my wristy and he said he had had a number of booksellers from all over the island on his case. It's just that we booksellers are, for the most part, more polite than our customers.'

'Where is your wholesaler based?' I asked.

'Exeter,' he replied. 'In darkest Wessex.'

'Nice,' I replied. 'Does he supply all the independent provinces?'

'I think he supplies a lot of England itself too, and a fair amount of the E.U. as well. He specialises in English-language editions.'

'So I couldn't get an original Jules Verne in French from you, then?'

'Oh, I have other contacts all over the reading world. You would have to ask me personally but I could get you a Verne in French. Which one would you like?'

'No, no, that's all right, I was just trying to find out how the system works.'

'Up until this morning, my reply would have been "very well".' He looked mournfully at me. 'It only takes one glitch and everything falls apart.'

'It isn't as bad as all that,' I replied, 'and it certainly isn't your fault.' I thought for a moment. 'Tell you what, I wanted to read this book as I thought it might help with a case I'm working on at the moment.'

'Oh, what's that about?'

'That I can't tell you, client confidentiality and all that sort of thing.'

'You mean that, if it got out, your client might tip you into The Wash wearing concrete wellies?'

'That might be truer than you think. However, if, as a spin-off of that case, I find out what happened to that book, and I can fix it so that it doesn't involve my client, I'll let you know.'

'And if you can find a copy of that book I'd be fascinated to read it. There must be the odd paper copy about that hasn't been burnt or pulped.'

'Do they still make paper copies?' I asked.

'A few. They're only made for successful authors. You know, once you've got half a dozen best sellers under your belt they'll make a few paper copies which the authors will sign and rich collectors will put on their shelves. Mind you, I doubt many of them actually get read. Even those collectors will probably read the book on a reader. No, that's not fair, I have customers who tell me that they still prefer reading physical books. I can sometimes get hold of the odd one for individual punters. That's what we're here for. I may not have a shop to walk into but I'm still all about books.'

'Well, I must go,' I said. 'I promised my crew I would see them shortly and they'll be starting to worry.'

'Thank you for all your help and I'll keep my fingers crossed you can find something.'

'I'll keep my fingers crossed too,' I replied, pulling out a card which I left on the table beside the screens. 'That's me – stay in touch. I'm sure it will be worth our while to meet again.'

It was difficult to know whether I should be hugging him or shaking his hand as an au revoir. I'd only known him for, top whack, thirty minutes but during that time I had found out all about his life. In the end I did neither; I just tapped my wristy and summoned the pod, which appeared to have remained parked outside the house all the time. I waved farewell and walked out into the snow.

Chapter 12
Steff has an Adventure with a Box of Bullets

I had just eased myself into the pod and it was making its way back to Bretton Way, at which point I would probably close the windows, when my wrist tingled. 'Hello,' I said into my wristy.

'Is that my favourite poppet?' came back to me.

'That sounds like a Ben in my ear,' I replied. 'Is that a Ben I might like a bit?'

'I hope it is,' came back at me with a chuckle. 'Listen, I have just got the indoor range all to myself, do you want to come round and share a box of bullets with me?'

'Hang on. I'll just check with Dwayne and Sabrina that they won't need me in the immediate, and if they don't, I could use a little shooting practice. Listen, if you don't hear from me, I'll be at the gate in the fence in about ten minutes.'

I called the office and delayed the staff meeting till just before lunch, then redirected the pod round to the border post. Oh Ben! Ben is what I would call my boyfriend, though that is probably not an appropriate way for people of our age to describe each other. He is, after all, older than me – not a lot, perhaps, but if you add our ages together, the sum you would get wouldn't get much change from ninety. It's just that if you put the word 'manfriend' and 'womanfriend' into a spell checker, it gets agitated, whereas put in 'boyfriend' and 'girlfriend', it doesn't. Ben is the local police chief over the border in Market Deeping, and we have developed a 'friends with benefits' relationship, with added small arms training for me. So, every now and then, he gets access to a range and over I pop to fire off a pistol or two. It was interesting that yesterday Shove had asked me if I was armed and, less than twenty-four hours later, my secret beau comes back at me offering some shooting practice.

The information screen in front of me became excited, asking me, *You are aware that the address you have requested to travel to is over the border in England? Y/N.* I tapped the 'Y'. *Are you willing to accept full responsibility for the reimbursement of the Royal Province of Anglia for the full value of this pod if it fails to return? Y/N.* Again, I tapped the 'Y'. The screen went quiet again and at the same time my wristy made a definite 'kerching'. The Anglian exchequer had taken its deposit.

I reached the Bretton Way junction and, instead of turning south towards the town centre, the pod turned north towards the border. Past Walton and what was left of Werrington there wasn't a lot of traffic on the road. There was only one further village before the border fence anyway, and that was Glinton. But you don't go through Glinton to get to the border, you follow the road round it, down the fenced channel. The fence is about four metres tall, topped with razor wire. Ben and I often muse who the wire is supposed to keep out. He is convinced it is to keep the Anglians out of North Mercia. Me, I'm not so sure. The main road by-passed Glinton, as I said, and headed up to the main border crossing, surrounded on both sides by the security fences. On the right, behind the fence and then a tall privet hedge almost as tall as the fence itself, was Glinton, the border trying to be gently discreet for the residents. On the left, behind two layers of fence with perhaps a couple of metres between them, was the Marshalling Yard. This was as far as you would be allowed to drive a lorry into Anglia. From here on in, all freight crossing the Province to the European ports of Lowestoft and Felixstowe went by rail. Here, the drivers must remain in their lorries, while the containers were lifted off their trailers by crane and put onto flatbed railway trucks. The driver would then move his lorry to where he was directed, an incoming container from the ports would be placed on his trailer and, once it was secured, he would be signalled to leave the marshalling yard back into North Mercia forthwith. The only people on the ground wandering around the marshalling yard all wore uniforms and, at least from the south side, the only way they got into that odd no man's land were by rail or on foot. The railway workforce wore tatty brown overalls. In dark blue, looking smart, were the Anglian customs and border police, and in bottle green and, I thought, less smart, were the English border police. If you weren't wearing brown, it appeared that you were required to be armed. I couldn't help thinking that there was a real battle just waiting to happen if one of the border guards tripped over and his pop-gun went off accidentally.

My pod slowly and respectfully moved towards the border crossing, which was the little bridge over the Maxey Cut, the narrow canal
that took much of the water from the River Welland down below
Market Deeping. The fencing over The Cut itself reminded me of the
topiary we had at the house in Sutton when I was a child. It divided
the recreational garden from the vegetable garden, and it too had a
tall privet hedge. Ours, however, had an archway cut into it just wide
enough to push a wheelbarrow through. The poor gardener was forever moaning about having to keep its insides trimmed. This 'topiary',
however, was not green but made up of the same wire fencing with its
razor wire round the edges. There was a small gap in the fence that a
man could walk upright through, and a pod, shuttlebus or a van could
pass underneath, but you certainly couldn't get anything larger, like
a container lorry, through there without pulling all that razor wire
down round your ears. Before the bridge over The Cut was a barrier,
and on either side of that barrier, which was down, stood uniformed
men rather pointedly not speaking to each other. I secretly hoped that
they would all get together and chat after I had gone, and this cold
hostility was just for the tourists' entertainment.

The Anglian Customs officer, in blue, waved me down, and the pod
automatically opened its window. 'Papers?' he said, pushing round a
device that looked a bit like a pair of binoculars on top of a rather
shabby wooden post at me. I looked into the binoculars-device and it
flashed. An electronic beep sounded somewhere nearby.

That border post must have been set up immediately after the sep-
aration, and at that time everyone needed a real paper passport to
pass through it, so they still asked for 'papers.' He passed me a wristy
reader, and I stuck my wrist out of the window and rubbed it. The
guard looked at his screen for a moment, checking the reading from
the retinal scan that I had just undergone agreed with my 'papers.'
Smiling gently, he asked, 'Police business?'

'Yes,' I nodded.

'Be careful,' he said. 'It's a little brittle over there.' He pressed a big
red button in front of him and the barrier went up, allowing the pod to
creep politely forward over the bridge until it came to the next barrier.

This time a corporal in bottle green asked for my papers. I waved
my wrist at him and added, 'Chief Inspector Watson's expecting me.'

He took one glance at me. 'Ah, Mrs. Flack, you're right, he is expecting you. Open the door, and I'll ride with you.' I wasn't aware I had touched anything, but the sliding door on the other side of the pod opened up and he climbed in. His submachine gun lay on his lap with its muzzle pointing vaguely in my direction. Did he have any idea how jumpy that made me feel, especially with the sorry state of the roads north of the border? The barrier went up and the pod set off. I looked over my shoulder to see another soldier moving out of the shed to take the corporal's place at the barrier. I chuckled quietly to myself, wondering if they were clones.

The pod moved fairly slowly, as if it knew that the road surface was going to be as bad as it obviously was. We passed one pod parked at the customs office, but I didn't see another one until we pulled in to the range, which was to the west of the small town of Market Deeping. The corporal waved at the soldier standing at the gate behind the fence surrounding the building in front of me. There was a large sign with the paint beginning to chip, announcing that it was the property of MOD Market Deeping, with 'NO ADMITTANCE' emblazoned below it in fierce-looking capitals. The soldier was standing with his submachine gun hanging from his shoulder, all of them getting covered with gritty snow. He drew himself up into a rather sloppy salute to the corporal. 'The major here yet?' he was asked.

'Yes, Corporal,' the soldier replied.

'Good, I've got his toy with me.' I decided not to feel insulted and get cross, certainly not with that submachine gun still pointing in my general direction.

'He'll be happy, then.' The soldier pulled the gate back and the pod, which appeared to have been following the conversation, eased through the gate and crept slowly to the front door of the long, narrow, brick building ahead of us. The front door opened and a tall, beautifully built man stepped out and waved at me. 'Can you run me back to the office after we've finished?' he asked.

'I expect so,' I replied.

'Then you can take my pod to go wherever you want,' he said to the corporal. 'Dismissed!'

The corporal saluted him and then turned to me and politely nodded before climbing out of the pod and walking over to the other one in the car park. Meanwhile, I pressed the pause button on the control panel of mine and headed through into the brick building. I was well aware that it would cost me a fair bit to hang on to a pod but then at least I knew it would get me home again later, and that sense of security was worth paying for.

We just stopped and looked at each other for a moment. 'Steffy, poppet!' he said. 'Come here'. What could I do? I jumped at him. This was certainly a man who excited me just the right amount. When I was with him I wanted to eat him up. When I wasn't, I kind of forgot all about him.

After a few minutes of enthusiastic kissing, he pulled away and said, 'Are we going to spend all our time necking, or are we going to shoot something?'

'Well, I came here with the intention of doing a spot of shooting,' I said breathlessly, not at all sure that that was actually true.

'Here's your first one,' he said, tossing a pistol at me.

Absolutely terrified, I caught it. 'What the ... ?' I spluttered.

'Don't worry, it isn't loaded,' he replied gaily.

'How do you know?'

'I've just checked it.'

I looked down at it. Well, at least its safety catch was on. I flipped the catch off and shouted, 'Range live,' pointed the pistol down the range at the target at the far end, then, like he had taught me, I squeezed the trigger. There was a loud bang, and smoke came out of the barrel.

'Oh, oops!' he said with a giggle.

'Pillock,' I said. 'You could have killed me, or I could have killed you. You've taught me never to mess around with guns. And then you do something like that.'

'And now you know why. And I tell you something, you will remember that lesson far better than my ever just telling you not to play with guns. Empty the weapon.'

I did so, and the brass casing bounced on the mattress in front of me. He passed me the binoculars. 'How did you do?'

I scanned the targets at the far end. I couldn't see a hole in any of the targets. Shit, I hadn't hit anything. I wasn't that bad a shot, even though I had been a little agitated when I took it. 'Missed,' I said ruefully.

'Now look at the shell casing, it should be cool enough.'

I switched on the safety catch on the pistol and put it down on the table. 'Range clear,' I shouted. I picked up the case. It was still very warm. Then I realised I was holding a blank, as the open end was still crumpled. It had never held a bullet.

I wasn't sure whether to be really cross or laugh. I have no idea what my glower told him, but I gave it to him anyway.

'Come here, you,' he said, pulling me to him and kissing me, this time on the forehead. 'Okay, let's get down to business.' He passed me a Lee Enfield .303 rifle, which I put on the table beside the Browning pistol while Ben picked up a small cardboard box and pulled the tape off a box of bullets, with 'Major B Watson, mixed', and the date written across it in thick black ink. He rifled through the box and pulled out half a dozen long slender rounds, all of which had a bullet in the business end, then passed me ear defenders. That was something he really should have done before he started horsing about with the pistol, but there you go. My ears were still ringing. I put on the defenders, which were like lightweight headphones. My experience of headphones dated back to Volffy's collection too, and those at home were far more comfortable than the things you stuck in your ears. Volffy said the sound was mellower than the 'new digital things', and Shove and I both agreed with that. It was like being cuddled by the music.

Next, Ben pulled a metal clip out of the box, slotted five rounds into it, and passed the thing to me. I picked the Lee-Enfield off the table and pulled the bolt up and then across, opening the chamber. I looked into the magazine to check that it appeared clean, then fitted the clip into it. I pushed the rounds down into the magazine, then pulled what was left of the clip out and put it on the table. Finally, I pushed the bolt back away from me and locked it shut before I lay down on the mattress with the barrel of the rifle pointing towards the far end of the range.

At this point Ben and I settled down to some serious shooting, using the rifle and the Browning pistol as well. I was back to my 'reasonable shot' status. I could remember the first time he had taken me shooting, he had remarked that I had needed a group of very tall men with another group standing on their shoulders, and with that arrangement I might hit one of them. I now put every shot on the target and most of them were kill shots with both weapons.

After about half an hour he turned the box over and nothing fell out. He looked at me and I looked at him, and we mouthed something at each other. Whether he actually made a noise I don't know but I certainly didn't. I opened the weapon I was holding and did shout, 'Ceasefire'. Once I had deposited my last weapon on the table, I turned over and lay on the mattress face up, looking up at him.

To which he replied, 'Range Clear'. He put his weapon on his table and crawled across with something that looked suspiciously like a rather soppy smile, joining me on my mattress. Or should I have written joining with me on my mattress? The opening kiss was just the start, and both of us found fastenings on each other's clothing that we felt it was important to undo.

Chapter 13
Aftermath

I felt both tingly and rather scruffy once I had got dressed. He had insisted I put my trousers on last, so he could have one final look at my legs. I had no idea why he was so fascinated; I must be at least six inches shorter than the fictitious 'Sue Laking with the lovely legs' in Melissa Landry's books. Didn't your legs have to be really long to fascinate men?

I was slightly disappointed that there wasn't any sort of mirror at the shooting range, but then it was hardly likely that squaddies would want to do their hair after a morning's shooting on those mattresses. They were, after all, provided simply for lying on and practicing killing an enemy with your gun, not for playing about on. Heigh ho. We left the building, and Ben locked up while I reactivated the pod outside. It opened both doors as instructed, and I got in as quickly as possible. Ben soon followed. 'Foul weather,' he muttered. 'I wonder what's causing it.'

That threw me. 'You mean they haven't told you?' I asked, surprised.

'No, have you been briefed?' he replied, raising both eyebrows.

'Well, yes.' I answered. 'After all, I am sort of civilian CID – well, something like that.'

'And who briefed you?'

'The Minister of the Interior.'

'Himself?'

'Yes, why not?'

'Wow! My precious poppet moves in really high circles. Is that what happens if you've got a five-star pair of pins on the other side of the fence?' He grabbed the knee nearest him but it was a gentle and affectionate touch. 'Only kidding,' he said. 'So, what is it with the snow?'

I gave him a shortened version of our briefing and watching his expressions change, ending up in one of complete disbelief told me that no one had made the slightest attempt to share information, at least in Market Deeping.

'So what's going to happen next?' he asked.

'That I don't know,' I replied, 'but I will be told when it's decided.' We were bouncing along the road which used to run from Stamford to Market Deeping. It had been a real road once, but it was now barely more than a track. It took us into the little town, which had a very 'opsed' air about it. Do you remember back in the day, when there were petrol stations? Well, some of them had big, round Castrol signs on the roadside, which read 'open' on one side and, if you flipped the board over, they read 'closed'. Now, if the board fell off it would read 'opsed' and, somehow, that state of being neither open nor closed but somewhere in between rather described that sad little town. There were one or two grubby children playing in the slush on the edge of the pavement in front of shops that were no longer open. A dress shop, which I had occasionally been taken to by my mum back in the day, stood on the north side of the square, but now all it appeared to have on sale were the mannequins themselves. None of them were wearing any clothes, and if you looked carefully at the stained window in the door, the word 'Closed' hung aimlessly on a piece of string behind it. Even the bank two doors back seemed to have been closed for some time. There were no footprints going up to the door, and no one had appeared to clear a path through to it.

Just past the square we came to an altogether busier part of town, the police station. 'Anywhere here will do,' he said, and pressed the button to release his door. He leapt out and then leaned back in to give me a peck on the nose. 'Thank you for bringing me back, Poppet, can we meet again soon?'

'Do you really want to?' I asked semi-playfully.

'You have no idea,' he said and, having given my knee a final farewell pat, pressed the button to close the pod's sliding door. It slid to, and he bounced up the steps and through the front door of the police station. I programmed the pod to take me back to the Cathedral Square via the fence. The pod was obviously aware of the quality of the road surface. There were no signs posted saying 'uneven road surface' or even simply 'ramp'. In France I remembered signs saying '*Chaussée Déformée*': deformed road, and in Germany they said, '*Strassenschade*' meaning 'surface we're a little bit ashamed of really.' Here in England you just took it as read, and the pod understood it anyway, as it meandered its careful way to the border post at the Maxey Cut.

As I approached the English side the corporal waved me down with a grin, but didn't ask for papers or anything. 'Thank you for taking the major back to HQ, he much appreciated it.' Winking, he pressed the button, up went the barrier, and the pod crept underneath. That man knew everything about what his boss had got up to that morning.

'Papers, please' said the man in blue on our side of the border. 'Oh, it's you, Detective. You seem to have made a few friends over on that side. Shall we have to start keeping an eye on you?' I think it was said in a friendly enough manner but I wouldn't have bet my life on it. He still took another retinal scan and a read from my wristy, but, as I explained to myself, he had counted me out, so he had to count me back in again. The barrier went up and the pod eased forward. My wristy went 'kerching' again, showing my deposit had been returned, and the pod accelerated on the road back into Peterborough, apparently much relieved to be rolling on an acceptable road surface again.

Dwayne was sitting on the corner of Sabrina's desk, drinking a cup of what was probably coffee, when I walked through the door. 'Good grief, Boss, what has happened to you? You look like you've been pulled through a hedge backwards. Who did that to you? Tell me and I'll go and hurt him. Well, perhaps I'll go and borrow Yuri from that Adelina first and get him to do a spot of hurting, he looks right handy …' He paused for a minute and his expression changed from its look of concern into what would pass for a leer. 'Oh, wait a minute, I know what you've been up to. At this time in the morning, really, Boss!'

'No, you hang on a minute,' I started, but Dwayne was already responding to Sabrina's 'What?'

'Indoor sledging,' he grinned at Sabrina and, rather worryingly I thought, Sabrina grinned back.

I raised my voice sharply and filled the room with it. 'Now hang on a minute. My office, the pair of you, now.' And I stormed through to my room – well, as much as it was possible for me to storm, considering the quantity of mellow dopamine that was still coursing in my veins. Ben has always had the ability to ring a full peal on my bells, and that day he had given me the complete Nine Tailors. I was already parked in my chair facing the door by the time they had made it through the door. 'Leave the door open, just in case someone comes in.' Dwayne took hold of the chair in front of the desk. 'I didn't say you could sit,' I snapped. I was enjoying this.

Sabrina looked worried. I had never shouted at her before. 'What have I done?' she asked.

I let a smile break through my scowl, 'Oh, sit down you idiots, I'm only teasing you. I have a fairly complex briefing for you both, much of which is seriously confidential.

'Right, in case you didn't know it, among other things, Adelina's a drug dealer. She's not the dealer that your average junkie on the street gets his supply from; she's the person his dealer gets his stock from. She's a wholesaler of both legal drugs like cannabis and Phantasm, as well as illegal substances like nicotine and heroin.'

'So why are we doing business with the likes of her?' Sabrina asked crossly. 'I thought we were supposed to be the good guys.' She looked at Dwayne, obviously hoping for him to back her up.

Dwayne wasn't going to get involved. He was keeping quiet and looking at his feet. Hmm, I knew he'd been arrested for the possession of cannabis when the stuff was still illegal, and I had little doubt he had taken Phantasm too, so I decided not to push him. There was no reason why I should know what he got up to in his own time, and if I did, then I wondered if it would be beholden on me to grass him up to Shove. No, I really didn't want to lose him, he was damn good at his job.

'Oh, really!' Sabrina grinned and, with that, the air was cleared.

'Right, here's what has been going on since I left for Norwich yesterday,' I said and filled them in on the whole story: Yellowstone, Melissa Landry, Allo and, even trivialising it a bit, Ben. Partly because I wasn't at all sure what I felt about Ben. It was so much easier when we were just friends with benefits, but that wasn't what I took from what he had said today, or what the corporal said when I hit the fence. At the end of my monologue, Dwayne asked, 'So, are we getting paid for any of that?' Straight to the point is our Dwayne.

'I am pretty sure we'll be paid either a retainer or a fee per case by the City. That is one question Shove and I haven't clarified, because she isn't sure yet.' And partly because I hadn't asked her, was what I didn't explain. As two friends, we'd been having so much fun together messing about in the hovercraft, we didn't address the elephant in the room – money. 'The other stuff, I don't know yet. I got into the Melissa Landry stuff because her new book was, like Adelina's case, about diamonds, and I was originally trying to read it as a textbook. Then she disappeared and then the book disappeared, which is what took me up to Guyhirn Mews. So, are they all linked, and will Adelina stump up for all that as expenses? I don't know. If all those pieces of glass that she showed me were in fact diamonds, their value would have been astronomical. She's not poor, and her share of the case is unquestionably valuable.'

'So we're looking for diamonds?' Sabrina asked.

'Fundamentally, yes.'

'And there appear to have been two casualties already?' Dwayne added. 'I think we ought to be looking over our shoulders, Boss, and I should definitely be making sure our Sabrina's safe.'

'Well, thank you, Dwayne, it's nice to know someone's looking out for me.' Sabrina gave him another of those smiles I wasn't aware that I'd seen before. I'm not sure that Dwayne had either, but he certainly responded in kind. His beaming smile would have given Saturn's A-Ring a run for its money.

'Is there something going on in here that I should know about?' I raised an eyebrow at them. I could tell that Sabrina was blushing, and even Dwayne seemed to have gone a shade darker. 'I have no difficulty with you two being in a relationship, as long as I know, so I can predict how things might go down in a moment of stress.'

It was Dwayne who changed the subject out of the blue, 'Did you ever see the bloke who arrested me? More studs in his face than a football boot, and a tattoo on his shaven dome. Now there was a detective who didn't want to be taken for one.'

I laughed, 'He was also a detective who didn't want to be put back in uniform, ever. He's got to behave as far as CID is concerned, or he'll be out on his ear, probably working security at one of the Marshalling Yards.'

'He might end up in the drug squad,' Dwayne laughed.

'Can I just mention something?' asked Sabrina quietly, joining in the new conversation, knowing that the previous one was simply on hold for the time being. 'The chief superintendent called you shortly before you got back and asked if you would call back after our meeting.'

'What a silly billy,' I replied, 'She could just have called me.' I waved my wrist at her.

'I know, but I did tell her you were out on the case, so she said she wouldn't disturb you.'

'Well, thank you for that,' I said, relieved that Siobhan had not disturbed us when we were in the shooting range. It was a good thing we had a Sabrina to hand but, before I talked to Shove, I just needed to check up that Allo's day had calmed down a bit. I nodded at her and tapped a number into my wristy, I could tell that Sabrina and Dwayne were listening avidly. 'Allo? It's me, Steff from this morning.'... 'Yes, I know that it's quick, how's it been going since I left re Melissa Landry's Pluperfect Murder?'

'It's quietened down now,' he replied.

'That's good. Well look, I'll be keeping my eyes open for the next few days and I'll see where it gets us. Are you going to be out of town at any time?'

'Highly unlikely, and if for any reason I am, I'll be wearing my wristy so you can find me.'

'Me too, though I may take a moment to answer, and I may end up calling you back.'

'Got it.' A click told me the conversation was over.

I shooed Romeo and Juliet out of my office before sitting down to talk to Shove.

Chapter 14
Girl on a Phone

Siobhan's personal ringtone sounded in my ear. The worst she could do would be to tell me to call back later. 'Steff! Are you still busy?' She had spotted who was calling her before I had time to announce myself.

'No, no, not at all. I'm back in the office now and Sabrina briefed me you were on the lookout for me.'

'Good. Now, have you got any further with that missing book?'

'Not really, except that there are a lot of pissed off people out there who want to know where their copy has gone.'

'A lot of them?'

'Yes, that's where I was, at an e-bookseller's place. He was fending off a serious number of irate customers who wanted to know where their books had gone and he recruited me to help. And they weren't all just people like me, who had got a free taster that had vanished. There was a whole slew of people who had paid hard cash for the complete book, and that had disappeared from their tablets too during the night. Neither of us spoke to anyone who complained that the book vanished before their eyes while they were in mid-read, but a number of people were complaining that they had started reading it last night, and there it wasn't the following morning.'

'Was their money returned to them when their book vanished?'

'I don't know. That wasn't a question I asked them.'

'All sounds very fishy, doesn't it? I've been thinking that, before we release the body back to Manchester, we ought to do a proper post mortem here in Peterborough. I've been in touch with a pathologist, and she may well contact you. Meanwhile, I'll ask one of the team to try to find out whether books have vanished from tablets across Great Britain as a whole, as well as in Anglia. Stay in touch.'

'Will do. Hey, just one other thing before you go,' I added.

'Go on,' she said.

'What is Dwayne's status as far as going across international borders is concerned? I never thought to ask you before.'

'Well, obviously he doesn't have any problems going into England,' she replied. 'He'll have been to places like Stamford and Market Deeping loads of times while working for you. I don't think there will be problems with the newly independent provinces like Wales and Wessex.' She paused.

'What?' I asked, realising there might be a hitch.

'I will have to look into his status with the European Union member states like Scotland and Ireland. Why? Where were you planning on sending him?'

'Flanders,' I said, with a shrug in my voice.

'Whereabouts in Flanders? Brussels?'

'Antwerp,' I replied. 'Do you remember my telling you about that fragment of Melissa Landry's novel I read before it vanished?'

'Go on.'

'Well, that sequence was set in the diamond district of Antwerp, which I understand is still above sea level and, as I am being paid to look for some missing diamonds, I thought that that might be an instructive place to start. However, the first thing I don't want to do is to go around upsetting the locals by importing someone they may consider an undesirable.'

'Allow me to get someone to look into it. Don't send him before you've cleared it with me. I do think it's possible that you may have to do that bit of sleuthing yourself.'

'Oh, I was planning on going anyway, I was looking for a bit of company on the trip, and maybe taking someone along like Sue Laking did in the book.'

'You crafty old thing, taking a date.'

'Dwayne? Hardly! He's young enough to be our kid.'

'You and I know that,' she replied. 'Your average Belgian may deem it appropriate. Stay in touch, though, I don't want you losing our ward in chancery on a Flemish fishing trip. The Senior Lecturer might not be amused. Contact me again before you go,' she said cheerily and disconnected.

I pondered what I was going to do next. I was still thinking about that when my wristy fizzed again. It was a local number, but not one on my contacts. 'Hello?' I answered it carefully, in case it was someone spamming me. Nothing irritated me more than being told that I had had an accident and they wanted to help me or, even more, that I was in debt and they were offering to set up a loan.

'Is that Stephanie Flack?' a pleasant enough voice asked, though it was still one I didn't know.

'Who is this?' I asked. 'How can I help?' I supposed it was always possible that it was another potential client in need of a private eye.

'Oh sorry, my wristy didn't identify me. I'm Dr. Clark from the forensics laboratory, I was calling you to get some information about an autopsy I've been asked to perform. Superintendent Flynn told you would be able to answer any questions I might have.'

'And this post mortem is on who?'

'Someone called Melissa Landry from Manchester.'

'I was just checking – I didn't recognise your voice and my device didn't recognise your device. When we speak again, we'll all know who we are. Anyway, what can I do for you?'

'Well, this woman, what do you know about her?'

'Not an inordinate amount, I've never met her or anything, though I was planning to yesterday. She was going to give a talk in the local library about her new book, a detective story. It's what she does; writes detective stories. Or rather, it's what she did.'

'And you were a fan?'

'Not especially, but the plot of her new book was rather similar to a job I'm working on at the moment, and what I wanted to do was ask her about the research she did for the book. I was rather hoping her reply might save me some leg work.'

'And what was this new book called?'

'*A Pluperfect Murder*, but it appears to have vanished off the face of the earth, and that's why I suggested to Shove that she got a post mortem done here before the body goes back to her nearest and dearest in Manchester.'

'Shove?'

'Short for Siobhan. Chief Superintendent Flynn and I are very close friends, and we have worked in conjunction for many years.'

'So it's you who's making all this extra work for me?' I couldn't make out whether Dr. Clark was peeved or amused. It was a shame that the screen wasn't transmitting a picture at the same time as the audio. 'Anyway, you knew she did extensive research on her books.'

'I didn't even know that but, had we been face-to-face, I would have known by the end of the conversation. I like to think that most writers do research their stories thoroughly. It would be a very lazy author who didn't do that, don't you think? I mean, can you imagine a book with a plotline set somewhere you know, and the framework is simply wrong?'

'How do you mean?'

'Well, if the story told you that they were going to a three-storey house at seventy-three Waterloo Avenue, and you know for a fact that seventy-three Waterloo Avenue is in fact a GP's surgery, you would find it difficult to respect the rest of the book. I know I would.'

'So this book was set in Peterborough then?'

'No, not at all. I've no idea where its substantive setting was, I didn't get that far. Her heroine was in Antwerp in the bit I read, and I was hoping to be able to avoid having to go to Antwerp myself.'

'Waterloo Avenue?' the pathologist sounded confused. 'Just out of interest, where exactly is that?'

'Nowhere in particular, it was a typical address I pulled out of thin air. There must be a Waterloo Avenue somewhere. Whether there is a GP's surgery at that location anywhere in the English-speaking world, well, your guess is as good as mine.' A thought arrived in my skull unbidden, as sometimes those things do, and for a moment I tried suppressing it but it insisted. 'You said your name was Clark, are you any relation to Tom Clark? He must be getting on a bit by now, but once upon a time, he was a doctor in this city.'

'A GP, back in the day?'

'Yes, I just wondered if you were related.'

'Yes, he's my dad.'

'And he's still alive?'

'Oh yes, a little tottery maybe, but he's still firing on all cylinders upstairs.'

'Well, I doubt he'll remember me but give him my best wishes, he was my doctor when I was a teenager.'

'I will pass that on, it'll make him happy to be remembered positively. Um, you are remembering him positively, aren't you?'

'Oh yes, he was a good doctor and he did look after me, especially after my problems.'

'That sounds as if it is something that is best kept discreetly shared between the pair of you, but I'll tell him you asked after him. If he would like to see you, can I put that on the table?'

'Certainly, I'd be delighted to show him how well I'm doing and what I'm getting up to nowadays. I think I owe him quite a lot for where I am today.'

'Anyway, may I come back to you with any further questions about this autopsy, if I have any?'

'Certainly, and I would actually be grateful if you would, even if you didn't have any further questions. I might have some for you, and I would like to know what you found.'

'I'll have to clear that with the chief superintendent first, but if she's okay about that, not a problem.'

'Thank you,' and with the usual polite platitudes we disconnected.

I had one more call to make, and then I was done.

'Hello, I assume this is Flack and Associates?' came the immediate reply.

'Is Adelina in?' I asked, remembering not to call her 'The Rail'.

'Passing her over,' came the voice.

The soft voice with the Eastern European burr came on line, 'Hello, do you have any news for me? If you've been that quick, I am impressed.'

'No, nothing positive yet. I wondered whether you could help me though.'

'Go on.'

'Do you have any more of the diamonds like the ones that got stolen?'

'And you want to know – why?'

'I want to take one of them to a dealer in Antwerp to see if he has had any of its cousins brought in recently.'

'So you want to take one of my diamonds out of the country to see whether any others like it have been taken abroad?'

'That's the top and bottom of it, yes. After all, if you had stolen your diamonds, so to speak, you would try to move them on fast, and where better than a diamond market?'

'Why not London?'

'Antwerp's better. And besides, a trove of diamonds in London will find their way to Antwerp. Where they go from there is anybody's guess. Just as an aside, you may have to be prepared to temporarily lose that diamond.'

'Exactly what do you mean by that?'

'I may have to leave the diamond in Antwerp so that if its cousins start rolling up later, then the dealer will be able to compare them.'

'I think I shall have to send someone with you to make sure the diamond is secure.'

'I have no problem with that. When shall we meet?'

'Half an hour's time. Here.'

'Your café in Millfield? I'll be there. We may not be setting off today but we'll set everything up now. See you shortly.' We hung up and I put my hand into my top left drawer. I pulled out a piece of chocolate and popped it into my mouth, savouring it for a moment. As it slipped down my throat, I got up and walked into the other room. Dwayne was still perching on Sabrina's desk burbling at her. 'Don't distract her, she has things to do,' I said.

'We going out, Boss?' he asked.

'I am, but I don't need you for this one. You stay here and look after Sabrina or something, I'll be back shortly.' I walked out, tapping my wristy to summon a pod.

Chapter 15
The Borscht Revisited

The pod told me I had arrived, and opened its door. I got out cautiously. I was well aware that it had stopped in the middle of the road, and I had to get past a van that was being unloaded before I even got to the pavement. I moved fairly rapidly, hoping that the van didn't decide to move off while I was still in front of it. It didn't, of course; they don't do that sort of thing do they? I turned to look back at my pod and was horrified to see it lurch off right in front of another pod hurtling up behind it, with another one steaming down the road in the opposite direction. The snow was beginning to settle, momentarily only maybe, but I remembered one fact from back in my childhood, snow is slippery. Pods probably hadn't got that long a memory. There was only going to be one result, an almighty smash. I jumped backwards onto the pavement and found myself clenching my eyes shut. Why my eyes decided to close, I had no idea – perhaps it was to protect themselves from the inevitable flying debris, and gravelly slush. It was instinctive anyway.

When the inevitable crash hadn't happened a second later, my eyes crept open again. Everything was normal. There was no debris and there were no dead bodies strewn all about the place. How the hell had they avoided each other? That was surely a physical impossibility. Had pods learned how to fly while I was asleep last night? Was this still the twenty-first century? I was still shaking internally when I pushed open the door of Adelina's little shop and walked in.

'Hello, madam,' said the young waitress whose name I still didn't know, 'you look a little shaken up. Would you like to take a seat? Can I bring you a drink? I know the boss is expecting you, I'll tell her you're here,' a barrage of words, mostly questions from someone I couldn't remember ever hearing speak before. When I last saw her, Yuri had spoken to her in an Eastern European language of some persuasion, and it surprised me that the girl didn't appear to have a trace of any accent in her voice, not even a local one. She stood absolutely still as

I sat down, and when I looked up at her she had a tablet out and was preparing to tap my order into it.

'Er, whatever your boss is having. No, wait a minute, I'll have a drop of brandy first if you've got one, and then I'll have a cup of whatever the boss is having.'

'Certainly,' said the girl and walked off towards the counter and the door behind it. I noticed she was moving without any sway of her hips. Good, I thought, hopefully they aren't trading her. I would have found it extremely difficult to work on a case with someone who was involved in people trafficking, however tangentially.

The waitress brought me a brandy in a little balloon glass, and said, 'You don't want ice and lemon with that, do you?' I shook my head, and she continued, 'I'll tell the boss that you're here. The tea will be along in a moment.' She sauntered off through the door beside the counter into the back. The door had hardly closed, when it opened again and Adelina walked through it, with the inevitable Yuri towering behind her right shoulder. She took a glance at the brandy glass I was holding in both hands and said with a knowing smile, 'It is getting chilly out there isn't it?' before sitting down. Yuri remained standing. Had they any idea how annoying that was? It was absolutely impossible to look at them both at once. I must have looked like a nodding pigeon as I flicked up and down between them. Once again, I decided to ignore Yuri and took a sip of the brandy. Oh wow, that was rough! It was probably not a glass I would finish, even if they were going to insist I paid for it. That was something of a surprise. Somehow I couldn't imagine this place having duff anything. They might not stock a particular spirit on the shelf, but I thought that if they actually had an item, I would have expected it to be of an acceptable quality.

'Anyway, tell me again why you want this diamond,' she said.

'Pelikanstraat in Antwerp is the main diamond market in Europe,' I explained, and went through the Antwerp plan again.

'I would have thought if I wanted to buy jewellery, I would buy it in London.'

'Yes, but if you were a craftsman and you wanted to make that jewellery, you would buy the gemstones in Antwerp.'

She nodded. She certainly didn't need to be told twice about anything. She tossed a little velvet bag at me. It almost held up in the air, it seemed so light. I caught it, and I could feel it had one stone in it. Pulling open the drawstring, I looked inside and then tipped the stone onto the table. Now that was a diamond. Its lustre was immediately apparent, and my eyes, having been drawn in, wanted to keep gaping at it.

'I think you can put it away now,' Adelina remarked drily, 'we don't want to excite the staff unnecessarily.' She popped the stone back into the bag and pulled the drawstring before she tossed it back at me. Her timing was excellent; the waitress appeared at the door with a tray with cups, a small jug and a teapot on it. There was also a saucer with slices of lemon.

Also at that moment, the outer door opened and in walked a tall man, considerably younger than Yuri, in fact younger than everyone in the room apart from the waitress. 'Dietrich,' said Adelina, 'come on in. May I introduce you to Steff? Steff, this is Dietrich, you are both working for me at this moment in time.'

That was an interesting opening gambit. I stood up, offered the young man my right hand, which he took with his firm grip, shook, and then let go. He walked over to a chair by another table, grabbed it by the scruff of its neck, swirled it round beside the table where Adelina and I were sitting, and sat on it.

'Tea?' said Adelina, looking almost exactly between where Dietrich and I were sitting. He looked across at me, nodded, and said in a soft Germanic accent, 'Yes, please.'

'Lemon or milk?'

'Milk for me,' I said simultaneously to Dietrich's 'Lemon.'

Adelina looked up at the waitress who poured a little milk into a cup, added tea from the pot on top, and gave that cup to me. She then poured just tea into the other two cups, putting a slice of lemon onto each of them. She passed those cups to her employer and the new arrival. I noticed that Yuri wasn't included in that little ceremony. I cocked an eye at him.

'I'm the Russian who doesn't like tea,' he said in explanation without moving a muscle below his neck.

Adelina ignored him, and said to Dietrich, 'Steff's a local PI who is doing a job for me finding where my diamonds went. Once you've found the diamonds, Steff, your job will be to explain to Dietrich here who was responsible for their disappearance. He'll then sort the thieves out, while you pop the diamonds in your pocket and hurry back here with them as fast as your legs can carry you.' Ah, I thought, that's who he is, a hit-man. I'm going to be travelling with a hired killer, oh joy. Still, if he was good at his job, then maybe I couldn't be in safer company.

'Tell me about these diamonds,' said Dietrich.

She looked at him carefully, 'Well,' she said, 'One of them is a big one similar to the one I've just given you. That was due to be a payment to Sigmund as part of our business arrangement. The other five were smaller and were part of a consignment of diamonds that was part of the trade we were doing together. So their absence will be a problem for the Sigmund and Adelina Partnership. The big one will have to reappear before the partnership goes any further. Do you follow?'

'Perfectly,' he replied.

'Supposing they haven't shown up in Antwerp yet when we get there?' I interjected. 'I'm sure they will eventually but when, I have no idea. You won't be wanting to pay us to hang around cooling our heels in Belgium indefinitely. It will be a waste of everyone's time and money.'

'Well, you're the private eye – recruit someone when you get there. When you've done so, arrange with Dietrich where to meet when the stones do turn up and take it from there. Do I have to think of everything for you?' Adelina's tone was taking on a fairly acid tone. I also saw that Dietrich was saying nothing, just listening to the two women squabbling, with one of them – me – thinking up and throwing out objections. I wasn't playing this very well.

'I think, Dietrich, I'd feel safer if the diamond travelled in your possession,' Adelina continued. 'Do you carry?' She was looking at me when she asked that.

'What? You mean a gun? No,' I replied.

'In which case, it's probably wiser if you still don't. People who don't carry guns routinely make mistakes when they break the habit of a lifetime and start doing so. You would need intensive training to be weapons savvy, and as you're off tomorrow morning, we simply haven't got time to start now.' I decided not to tell her that I actually had had a fairly serious amount of weapons training, especially recently. I didn't want to have to bother telling her how that had come about. I hadn't even told Shove yet.

'I do,' said Dietrich.

'I know,' replied Adelina, 'which is why I didn't bother to ask you.'

I was aware, and not a little concerned, that this conversation was being carried on in front of Yuri and the nameless waitress. Yuri I had taken to be Adelina's bodyguard, but the waitress, who was little more than a child, was also taking in the discussion about guns and retribution, without any change in her expression whatever. I was concerned that she wasn't as innocent as she appeared.

'Right,' Adelina continued, with a change of tone, as if we had finished the topic about weaponry and were moving on to something else. 'I will sort out the travel arrangements here. That seems only reasonable, as I will be footing the bill.' She slipped a tablet from under the table somewhere and tapped it. 'I assume that neither of you has any objections to travelling tomorrow?'

'And if we had?' I asked.

'We would still be travelling tomorrow,' Dietrich remarked drily, 'but Adelina would be aware you had objected.'

'Incidentally, I'm perfectly happy with travelling tomorrow, I was just interested to know about the what if.'

Adelina looked up from her tablet, seemingly oblivious to the last fragment of conversation. 'Okay, there's a Zeppelin on the route from Helsinki to Lisbon that's passing through Huntingdon Alconbury tomorrow. You'll catch it there and disembark at Zaventem outside Brussels.' She tapped the screen, and continued. 'You'll get a connection into the main station in Brussels, where you'll catch the high speed train to Antwerp. You say you want to go to Pelikanstraat in Antwerp?'

'That's the idea.' That was me replying.

'Fine, and just off the Pelikanstraat there's an Autohotel, so I'll book you both in there. I'm afraid they don't run to expensive things like two-room suites but I will stand you a room each. Do you have access to the European Transit System, Dietrich?'

'Of course,' he replied.

'In which case, Steff, don't lose him, you'll need him to get access to pods to get you about.' I didn't bother to explain to her that I also had full rights of access to the European Transit System. I had been to Paris and Cologne on business several times fairly recently and could summon and book anything from a pod to a Zeppelin of my own if I wanted. However, as she was picking up the tab, it was fine by me to keep quiet and see what happened.

'I'll come round in a pod to your place about nine-thirty tomorrow,' said Dietrich, 'We'll go by road to Alconbury. I've been told that the view from the Causeway is quite spectacular, and that I haven't lived 'til I've seen it.'

'My place at nine-thirty it is then,' I replied, aware that that would mean travelling with the pod's curtains open. On the Causeway itself I wouldn't have that much of a problem with that, but until we got to it, well. I was also becoming aware that my wrist was tingling. I let it finish its business and then, after a few moments, it wriggled a bit more to let me know I'd received a text.

'Have either of you anything further to say?' asked The Rail, after finishing her tea.

'Not that I can think of,' I replied, finishing mine. 'You?' I added, looking at Dietrich.

'I will see you tomorrow,' he replied with a grin. 'Sleep well, you may need it.'

'Do my best. Right,' I stood up, 'I must go and sort out the office and let them know they're going to have to do without me for the next few days.' I tapped my wristy to summon a pod and noted a message on the screen. It read, 'Can we talk?' and was signed by 'Ben.'

I walked out of the teashop and waited for a pod to pull into the space that had been previously occupied by the van.

Chapter 16
Ben Again

I climbed into the pod and pulled the curtains to. I was in Millfield, for heavens' sake. The road was fairly narrow and covered with personal transportation pods whirling everywhere. I tapped my wristy.

'Poppet,' a voice purred into my ear. 'Thank you for calling me back. Was my calling you just then a bit awkward?'

'Well, I'm really glad we don't have those things that ring out loud any more. I was in a meeting where it might have been difficult to explain you away if they'd known anything about who you are.'

'Are you ashamed of me, Babes?'

'Anything but, but I do have a job and, while I'm doing that job, it is not always going to be easy to explain that I've got one relationship with the chief of police in Peterborough and a very different relationship with the chief of police in Market Deeping, yet here I am doing business with someone who might be a gangster, and that's probably a hitman sitting across the table. My private life is just that, private. So you can guess in that particular meeting I was in, probably either relationship might have been a little, shall we say, tricky if they rose to the surface. Anyway, what can I do for you so soon after our last... chat?'

'I wanted to ask one or two further questions about what we just talked about. You know, the volcano and stuff.'

'Okay, I'm on my own in a pod at the moment, so ask away.'

'Well, firstly, how long have we got? I mean, I really enjoyed what we did this morning, you know, and I definitely don't want that to have been the last time.'

I sort of grinned to myself – so it had been good for him too. 'I doubt that the eruption will shorten our life expectancy very much,' I replied, 'so if you're up for a repeat performance in the not-too-distant future, count me in. I promise I will become good enough to get all my marksman's badges before the world comes to an end.'

'No, that wasn't what I meant...' he started but I interrupted him.

'I know what you meant, silly, but it has also been mentioned that it might be handy for me to be fully weapons trained in case things get difficult in Anglia too. I know our government is becoming concerned that the population may become restless. We have all sorts of different ethnic groups over here in Peterborough, and not all of them get on particularly well together. They may make it an excuse to cause a bit of excitement, you know.'

'Have you got loads of guns over there?' he asked.

'I have no idea,' I replied. 'I do know that Shove's got a pistol, I've seen it.'

'I must meet this Shove of yours sometime,' he said. 'She sounds fun.'

'In the fullness of time, I'm sure that'll come about. I guess the importance of that will depend on what happens when you get promoted. Will you get posted away to somewhere like Manchester when they make you a colonel?'

'I haven't the faintest idea,' he replied, 'the whole system hasn't been round long enough to find out. I hope not. If I was, would you move to North Wales?'

'Wales is a separate country, as independent of Anglia as it is of England. What makes you think they'd accept me as a resident?' I thought for a moment, 'You know, I've never been to North Wales in my life. What's it like?'

'No idea, but it might have me nearby.'

The pod had stopped, presumably in Cathedral Square, but I just wanted to see where this conversation was going.

'Funny how this global catastrophe might be what really brings us together,' he said, 'and that it wasn't some half-baked idiot who kicked it all off.'

'No, mankind is totally innocent of this one. Ironic, isn't it?' I replied. 'Global warming was all our fault, and ever since Hiroshima, nearly a hundred years ago, people have been twitching that someone with a low IQ, but enough inherited money to buy himself a position of power, might launch another nuclear weapon just for a giggle to see what would happen. "Goo! I wonder what happens when I push dis." And in the end, Nature herself got fed up with all the tension, and said, "Well, here's something for you idiots to think about," and pressed the button all by herself.'

'You know what I really want to happen right now? I want you to come here right this minute, so I can screw you silly all over again.'

I grinned to myself—*hoo yah*, I thought. However, what I said was, 'Well, fun as that sounds, I'm off to Antwerp for a few days first thing tomorrow morning, and right now I've got to tidy stuff up this end before I go,' I said, as far as I knew not letting on what I was feeling.

'A few days?' he asked.

'Yes, just a few days,' I replied.

'Well, tell you what, when you get back, call me, and we'll go to one of those posh Peterborough restaurants which I hear are so good and have dinner as a sort of pre-entry entrée. I wouldn't mind looking around a bit.'

'You mean you've never been to Peterborough?'

'Not in full tourist mode, being shown around by a woman I really care about, no. I'll even book myself into a hotel with a really big bed. How does that sound?'

There it was again. He was declaring more than I was feeling. Or was I? It was so long since I had really felt excited by any man but to be honest, this was the only man I had done stuff with, and then come back and done more stuff with, since before our two countries went their separate ways. 'I'll call you when I get back,' I replied.

'Thanks so much. See you then, love you.'

I automatically murmured, 'Love you too,' back as I disconnected, wondering if that was true. I stepped out of the pod and went through the door and up the stairs to my office.

Sabrina and Dwayne were both interested in knowing what I had arranged. He was certainly disappointed that Shove thought it was unwise for him to come with me. 'Don't worry,' I said. 'Once Anglia is formally a member of the EU again, she assures me there won't be a problem if you can do all our work in Antwerp. She'd be happy enough for you to come with me now but she's uncertain whether they would be so happy on the Flemish side of the border with your police record. I don't think either of us want the government, which is trying to finalise our negotiations to re-join the EU, to be distracted into spending weeks in complex negotiations just to get you back again.'

'Yeah, fair enough' he said sadly, 'I get it.' He turned to the secretary, 'Tell you what, Sabrina, once I've been there a couple of times, can I take you over and show you round?'

'I'd like that,' she said quietly. 'Provided my family doesn't object. You know what they're like.'

'Not really,' he replied. 'Am I going to meet them some time?'

Sabrina shrugged. Any doubts I had about them disappeared at that point. I didn't need to say anything further right away, but this would become a problem I would have to address in the not too distant future. Meanwhile, I briefed Sabrina about tomorrow's travelling companion and asked her just to check whether the network had any information on Dietrich that I should be aware of. She hunted around in a few databases for a little while and couldn't find any reference to him at all. 'But I'll do a more thorough search over the coming days, and if anything does appear out of the woodwork while you're away, I'll get in touch.'

'Thanks for that,' I replied. 'Anything else either of you want to throw at me before I go home?' I paused and grinned, at least internally. 'Or do you just want me to leave you two to it?'

I am fairly sure neither of them got it, but they both said, more or less in two-part harmony, 'No, you go off and get packed and if anything crops up I'll be in touch.'

So that's what I did. Returning home, I arrived in time for an evening meal with Shove, which we ate while destroying a bottle of a more than half-decent wine. We discussed what I was off to do on the morrow and finally, when we were all talked out, we both went up to our separate rooms, first to pack and then to sleep and perchance, to dream.

Chapter 17
In Which Steffy Flies South

'Steff dear, there's a pod outside the door and a man standing beside it asking for you.' Mrs. Grubbs sounded concerned.

'Is he tall and rugged?' I asked.

'Don't know about rugged,' she said, 'but he's certainly not short.'

'That'll be my ride,' I said, grabbing the handle of my bag and pulling it behind me. 'I'll see you all in a couple of days.' I walked out of the front door and there was Dietrich, under an umbrella, standing in front of a pod, which had both doors open. He pulled my bag to the pod and stowed it behind the seat, pulled the seat back up and, slightly mockingly, said what sounded like, 'Gnaydigger Darmer,' and bowed at the waist. So he could even be courtly in his own language, calling me his 'honoured lady'. Yes, I spoke a bit of German, so I replied, '*Gnädiger Herr*'.

I seated myself in the left-hand side of the pod while he walked round to the right. He tapped various buttons on the console, the doors shut and the pod set off. I was aware that it was 'his' pod, as he had specifically suggested we travelled by pod to go over the Causeway so he could experience the famous view from the top for the first time. I thought about asking him if he might consider closing the curtains until we got to the Causeway but actually, the traffic wasn't that alarming that morning, so I decided to lump it. I could shut my eyes if it got really bad. We headed out west from the city and crossed the western bridge over the Nene. It always amazed me that there were still only three bridges over the river in Peterborough, and that two of those were on the ring road. All three had been reconstructed in the past thirty years to cope with the rise in the water level, so perhaps they couldn't afford to build more bridges if they were going to have to improve the ones they had already got. Whatever!

The pod took us past the Hamptons and into Yaxley, though only people who had lived in Peterborough as long as I had knew where the one ended and the other began. The pod navigated itself out of

Yaxley and onto the Causeway itself. It had never been called any particular sort of Causeway, apart from its being awarded a capital letter up its front end, nor had it been named after anyone, or anything, for that matter. Perhaps they were waiting until the Senior Lecturer shuffled off this mortal coil and then they would name it after him; after all, I assumed it had been his idea to build the thing in the first place. As far as I knew, the English hadn't contributed anything to its construction, even though it was their village of Sawtry, on the west side of the border, that had benefitted most.

The Causeway was a two-lane road with the lanes separated by the railway tracks that ran between them, situated along the top of what was effectively a dam keeping the swamp water out of the low-lying land on its west side. Being generally about twenty yards inside the official Anglian border, it also protected the border itself. The only traffic permitted on the top of the Causeway comprised bicycles, pods, shuttlebuses and small vans, but really that was all that was permitted on any road in the Province of Anglia. Personally, I wasn't sure I would want to be anywhere near a bicycle on the Causeway – pods get very close to other traffic at the best of times and those carriageways weren't particularly wide. Looking through the murk from the right side of the Causeway, you could just about make out the Great North Road, which had been there probably since Roman times, a track then, of course, which, over the centuries, had morphed into the eight-lane dual carriageway which, in its final iteration, was the border between Anglia and that part of England which was called South Mercia. There were large numbers of container lorries going up and down the Great North Road, very similar to those I had passed yesterday at the Deeping Marshalling Yard. Some of those trucks would be heading to London to be distributed around England's capital, and some to Alconbury to load their containers onto an airship to take it wherever in Europe, or perhaps even further afield, in the hope of keeping England as financially afloat as possible.

Dietrich leaned over me to look at the greenish swamp water on my left, less than three metres below the level of the dam. We then both looked back down at the A1 and worked out that the road must be well over five metres below the level of the dam, as was the village of Sawtry that we were going past below. The water level would have been getting on for the height of a container if the Causeway suddenly chose not to be there.

'Can you imagine living in a place like that?' Dietrich asked me. 'Supposing the dam broke?'

'If the dam broke, you wouldn't be left contemplating it very long.' I said grimly. 'Mind you, it was built by Anglian engineers so, with a bit of luck and a following wind, it is very likely to be structurally sound.'

'Was it built with this sort of weather in mind?'

'Obviously not, but perhaps the weather won't last for long,' I threw the last bit out knowing that that wasn't likely to be true, but then Dietrich wasn't in on what was actually going on, was he? 'It must be rather disappointing for you to have waited for so long to see our famous Causeway,' I continued, 'and it's all so murky, so you really can't see a damn thing. On a fine day the views from up here are really quite spectacular.'

'Ah well, I suspect I'll be back before long, and be able to see it at its best. Maybe it will turn out to have been a very special time to have crossed your Causeway. I'm told that the best time to have been in Berlin over the past hundred years was when the Wall was coming down.'

'I wasn't even born then,' I replied.

'Nor was I,' he said. 'Things seem to have changed very fast. At the end of the twentieth century, everybody was coming together and getting very friendly, and here we are in the middle of the twenty-first, it's all breaking apart again. I wonder what our grandchildren will have to look forward by the end of the century.'

'Mud,' I replied and looked at him quietly, somewhat surprised that this gun for hire could be so thoughtful about the future. Only I knew, I thought drily, that we hadn't got one.

We both sat quietly in the pod, waiting for it to take us into the airport building. It pulled up right outside the main doors, and Dietrich hauled out both my bag and his knapsack. As a gag, he then patted the pod gently on its backside, just as it obediently pottered off.

Once we were through the doors we found ourselves facing a fairly empty concourse. I supposed that was only to be expected. Most people got into their containers at the nearest railway station, as I had done a couple of days before. We walked up to the ticket counter and waved our wrists at the balding, middle-aged man who sat looking bored behind his desk. He looked at the screen on his desk. 'Brussels?' he asked.

'Yes,' Dietrich and I replied simultaneously.

'You're Anglian?' he asked me.

'Yes,' I replied.

'And you're German?'

'Yes,' was Dietrich's response.

'And you're travelling together?'

'Is that such a surprise?' Dietrich asked him acidly.

If you could have seen the man's feet, they would probably have shuffled awkwardly at that moment. Then he said to me, 'You will have to go through the Anglian citizens' gate over there on the left to go through airport control, and you,' he added to Dietrich, 'will have to go through the European citizens' gate there on the right.' There was a gate marked 'English Citizens' between them, through which neither of us would be welcome.

Dietrich gave him an expression that was almost as bored as the man's own, and said, 'We know. However, we also know we will be able to get together again before we get into the container.'

'I expect you're right,' said the man, and pointed me to a desk up to the left, with a sign over the top that read 'Anglians'.

'See you on the other side,' he grinned at me, and we walked our separate ways, with me now pulling my case.

My next port of call was the departure gate. There didn't appear to be any sort of queue, so I walked up to the desk and again I held out my wristy.

'Stephanie Flack?' asked the border guard, as I looked into the security machine that checked that the face on my neck was the same as the face on the photo, and that my retinal scan was the same one that my wristy said it should be. I wondered idly whether he was going to be the same guard I had met yesterday, but he wasn't. When I answered affirmatively, he asked whether it was business or pleasure. He then added, glancing out of the window, 'Business, I assume, nobody would be going anywhere for pleasure in that stuff.'

I assured him it was, and he didn't seem to need to ask any more questions so, apart from looking at my face one last time and exhorting me to make some money for Anglia, he stood back and let me pass into the departure lounge. There were only two groups of people waiting for containers that were due to be loaded any time soon. One was the transatlantic route via Reykjavik, the other, further down the lounge, was the one that I was looking for, City of London, Brussels, Paris and all the way to Lisbon, before its long Atlantic crossing to South America. I pulled my bag behind me and parked in a seat that looked at those coming through the Aliens' gate. I was beginning to think about looking for a cup of coffee, when I heard behind me an announcement that embarkation for the container for my Zeppelin Intercontinental Passenger Airship to Brussels, among other places, was about to commence, and would passengers travelling on this route prepare to take their seats in the container. There was still no sign of Dietrich. I walked over to the woman by the embarkation desk and explained my problem, that I was travelling with someone who had been called to his container but had yet to appear from passport control.

She looked at her desk and tapped it a couple of times and muttered into a microphone. I didn't catch what she said but, as if by magic, a couple of minutes later, the doors flew open and a whole slew of people came storming through from the Aliens' departures desk. 'Is he one of those?' she asked.

I looked through them and yes, I could see Dietrich coming my way. I told her that now all was well. She grinned at me and said that it was more than a border guard's worth to hold up a Zipa's departure.

'You mean it wouldn't have left without him?' I asked.

'Not if he arrived on time, so if the system clogs up like it just has, we arrange for it to be unclogged.'

'Isn't that a bit unsafe? Supposing there was someone intending to blow the airship up in that queue and you've now just let him through?'

'Oh, everybody's been checked. We just get the border guards up off their behinds in the tea room and get them to come and do a job of work for a change.' She was grinning happily, and I felt I had met a kindred spirit.

'Steff,' said Dietrich, slightly out of breath. 'Good of you to wait, shall we get aboard?' and we hustled through the open double doors into the container. I pushed my case into the space under the seat and sat down. He did likewise with his knapsack and sat down opposite me, then we fastened our belts and waited. I sat back in the seat and closed my eyes. Any moment now, we were going to be hoiked vertically upwards under a skyhook and then jerked sideways to be deposited on the top of an airship. Whereupon we would plummet down again into the bowels of said airship until it stopped suddenly and then jerked sideways again until we came face-to-face with a glass wall through which we could see the passenger compartment of the airship itself. I was well aware that I had very recently had breakfast, but actually I had never really enjoyed the sensation of dangling underneath a skyhook and being shunted around at the best of times.

I wondered if I would have enjoyed the whole experience more if I had been travelling with Ben on this journey. Certainly, looking into those eyes would have been more soothing, and my stomach would have been really keen on not throwing up all over him. He would have been just as effective as Dietrich at protecting me should I need it, but then Ben also knew a lot of stuff about me that I wasn't letting on. I'm not a fragile little flower who needs looking after, as Ben has learned during our long, intermittent and rather complicated trans-border relationship.

'Are you all right?' Dietrich interrupted my thoughts, 'I was talking to you.'

My eyes jerked open or, more accurately, were jerked open by the sideways motion of the container in the belly of the airship as it slid into place. 'Sorry,' I said. 'Miles away, avoiding the slightly unpleasant sensation of being thrown about.'

'We are about to depart,' came over the loudspeaker system. 'Please take advantage of the facilities available on this Zeppelin Intercontinental Passenger Airship flight. If you have booked, or wish to book, a cabin, please make your way to the Purser's office. If you wish to disembark at London City, you may leave any belongings you have in this container, and return to it in twenty minutes, in time for disembarkation. If you are travelling further on this flight, please take all your belongings with you. We at Zipa and the crew of the Rainer Maria Rilke all wish you have a pleasant flight.'

I looked at Dietrich, and when the disembodied voice started speaking in tongues, brackets other, I said, 'Sorry, you were saying?'

But he was standing up, pulling his knapsack out from under the seat. He pointed at the bag under my seat. 'You'll be needing that. Come on.' And he was heading towards the doors that were sliding apart, giving us access to the sitting area in the airship. I pulled my bag out and followed him. Clever boy, he had found a seat by a window. He threw his knapsack on one seat, like any good German who owns a towel, while he took my bag off me and thrust it upwards into the locker above the window, then nodded at the seat in a manner which was as imperative as anything he had done so far. I smartly sat down in it as he swung his knapsack up from the seat where he had placed it to put it in the locker next to my bag and, having shut the locker, settled in to the seat he had claimed.

We both looked down through the window at the airfield below. We were certainly close enough to the ground to make out all the airport features, even with the grey clag that was all around. I couldn't help wondering what you would see if you looked down from the top of the airship. My mind followed that thought, duh! Airship, of course, these things are huge.

'As soon as we're moving again, do you want a coffee or maybe a stiffener?' he asked, pulling the folding table out between us from the wall below the window.

'At this time in the morning?' I asked. 'Coffee maybe, certainly nothing stronger.'

'Espresso? Latte? Do you like it with honey or sugar?'

'Just milk, nothing else,' I replied.

He popped his finger and an orderly came rushing over, very adeptly dodging people stowing cases and children. He had his tablet out and Dietrich said something to him in German, which I didn't catch, and he bounced off again. Dietrich grinned at me, 'So nice to be talking German again to someone who understands it,' he said.

'How did you know he spoke German?' I asked quizzically.

'You may claim to be something different, being Anglian, but you're quite as bad as the rest of the British. You expect everybody to speak your language, and you're surprised when they have a language of their own.'

'That wasn't what I was getting at,' I replied, getting his point but choosing not to let it rile me. 'What I was asking was how you knew he was German.'

'This is a Zeppelin Airship, it's called the Rainer Maria Rilke, who was a German Poet, the Zeppelin Service is a German service based in Stuttgart, which is in Germany. Its employees will probably be German, and will certainly speak German, because they will be given their instructions in German.' I hoped Dietrich wasn't going to get any crosser. I could see the blood vessel pulsing at his left temple, which I understood was a sign of elevated blood pressure. I had no idea what would happen if he actually lost his temper and I didn't really want to find out. I didn't think he was armed yet but then again, now was hardly the time to ask, surrounded by tourists.

I peered out of the window and I could see Huntingdon beginning to move beneath us. They were probably still loading freight containers from the airport. As long as people didn't fall over and hurt themselves during embarkation, the airline wasn't likely to get sued. There wasn't a great deal of sunlight, but the huge airship still cast an enormous shadow over the town below. It must have been fairly alarming for the people to have this nearly silent behemoth passing close over their heads. I had never been that close to the underside of an airship. I wondered if the temperature actually dropped as an airship flew overhead, as if it were a total eclipse of the sun. Mind you, with all the murk up here, there really wasn't a lot of sun to eclipse.

Dietrich had obviously been thinking along the same lines as he asked, 'So what is Anglia going to do for energy, as this snow and stuff will probably make the solar panels useless?'

'We also have tidal farms around the coast and wind farms all over the Province, so there should still be enough power for Anglia,' I said. 'But there won't be so much to sell on inland. And the other solar farming we do, being vegetation and food plants, will be okay this year but, if this carries on, we may run into trouble next year. Maybe we'll have to develop a fishing economy.' I grinned at him. 'Do you like crabmeat? There are tons of crabs up on the north Norfolk coast,'

He looked at me and shrugged, 'Is it anything like pork?' he asked. 'That's my staple.'

'Nothing like pork,' I replied, still grinning. Truth be told, I wasn't really into crabmeat either, which was quite strange as I really liked lobster. We had passed the town boundary of Huntingdon now and the airship was beginning to climb, though not so as you would notice if you weren't looking out of the window. The corridor remained horizontal, and I didn't feel any heavier, but the ground was slowly getting further away from us and features were becoming less clear.

The orderly returned with a cup and a glass on a tray and while he and Dietrich exchanged some words in German, I tried to work out what they said this time. *Milchkafee* was easy enough but what *Obstwasser* was I had no idea. Dietrich tapped his wristy, the waiter looked at his tablet and thanked him for the tip, then he put the tray down on the table and wandered off.

'*Obstwasser*?' I asked.

'Technically it means vegetable water,' he said. 'It's a kind of schnapps.'

'May I?' I asked.

'Be my guest,' he replied.

I picked the glass up and sipped at it. I could tell it was very alcoholic when it got even close to my nose. It filled my mouth with fire, and the little that passed the back of my throat burned all the way down. I could feel my eyes watering. 'Whoa,' I said. 'That's strong.'

'Yes, but did you like it?' he asked.

To be honest, I wasn't sure. Dietrich took the glass from me, muttered 'Prosit!' and emptied the glass down his throat in one gulp. After a moment of recovery, he said, 'That is how you are supposed to drink schnapps. The other thing that schnapps does is make the ground disappear, look.' He was right, you couldn't see the ground at all from the window now.

For the next half hour or so, we sat back and exchanged pleasantries, though avoided discussing the job. I have no idea whether the diamond in his pocket was having any effect on him, but I couldn't get it out of my mind.

'Ladies and gentlemen, those of you wishing to alight at London City, please make your way to Container Nine and prepare to be disembarked.' That then followed over the loudspeaker system in various languages, some of which I recognised, some of which I didn't. One of the lines which I half heard was something to the order of 'If you only have tickets as far as London and don't get off here, you will be charged more to land at the next stop and will not be allowed to disembark until you have paid.' I imagined some poor fool asleep somewhere, missing his London stop and carrying on in the airship until it finally ground to a halt in darkest Patagonia, then returning to London about a fortnight later to get off at the right place.

The airship had descended again within visible range of the ground and I could see the dome of St Paul's through the murk. Up alongside the airship I could see a skyhook flying up beside us with a container under its belly. I could see faces looking out from the side of the container looking back at me. Well, that answered one question I hadn't thought to ask before: yes, they could continue to load before they unloaded anything.

'This is a final call for passengers wishing to alight at London City airport. Go to Container Nine now.' Now that was a command. I couldn't see a sudden rush to go back to the container, so either the people who wanted to go to London were aboard the container or they were resigned to, or perhaps planning on, a cheap trip to Southern Argentina. Who knows, perhaps Argentina would be a safer place to be right now than Northern Europe.

The airship did jolt slightly as it swapped containers with the City of London down below and the airship, as far as I could tell from my view of the ground, had actually stopped moving. I sipped from my cup and was amused to see that, as the container reappeared at the door into the passenger cabin, there was a flash. Presumably a paparazzo was taking pictures of someone who had just come aboard. The person was being led forward and a path cleared for them though the milling crowd, to the area where the cabins were.

'Well,' said Dietrich, 'that's either a politician or a pop star, I wonder if we'll find out which. If he disembarks with us in Brussels then he'll probably be a politician.'

I looked down at the huge city below me. The vehicles pottered about like insects under bark on a rotting tree. They weren't only pods either, that much I could tell, there were many other shapes as well. I wondered whether they had driveable cars in the city. I knew they were illegal in Anglia but I didn't think they were in England. They merely required signal courage to travel in them. Certainly, that vehicle down there with the flashing blue light on top, presumably an ambulance, would have had somebody on board actually controlling it.

I wondered what the native Londoners down there thought about the huge dirigible floating overhead, with its extraordinary power unit that worked on the same principle as the sun. The airship's engine was an H-bomb in miniature, fusing hydrogen atoms into helium, capable of powering the ship from one end of the planet to the other, and certainly capable of obliterating the city beneath us if it lost its temper. The airship was motionless over the city while it was being loaded and unloaded, and I wondered what was going up and down in those containers. There were no more people appearing, so they had all been boarded for a while.

And then I could just see the airship's shadow start to shift over the buildings. It didn't feel like movement yet from where I sat but you could see we were drifting forwards. Dietrich, who had been looking out of the window too, remarked rather pointlessly that ours would be the next stop. Equally pointlessly, I agreed with him. I had no idea how long it would take us to get there. An hour or so, I supposed, what with getting up to speed again and then, having got up to around two hundred miles an hour, needing to start slowing down again almost immediately. A thing the size of the airship would take some stopping, and I supposed that we would need to fully stop at Brussels too. There would be a good deal of disembarkation to do, and no doubt some bureaucrats would come aboard to go to Paris and the Iberian Peninsula.

'I wonder how many people apart from the crew actually travel the whole distance that this ship will travel,' Dietrich remarked.

'Huh?' I wasn't really listening to what he said.

'Well, it started its journey beyond the Arctic Circle and it will finish it near the Antarctic. I was just wondering how many would make the whole journey.'

'Not very many,' I replied. 'Perhaps a few scientists doing research into global warming in both places, perhaps a tourist or two trying to get out of this snow. Whether it's snowing in Argentina, I have no idea. Perhaps it will be on someone's bucket list to go from the Arctic Circle to the Antarctic in a single flight. Who knows?'

I was watching through the window as the city slowly faded out of sight as we climbed, and my eyes closed.

Chapter 18
Pelican Street

Once on the move, the airship turned sharp left, quite surprising me, as we didn't actually feel the movement that was obvious through the window. The fluid in my cup didn't spill out sideways as the giant of the air turned to follow the river east. Out of our window we could see north Kent below us, although of course we were actually over the Thames Estuary. It was almost as if the pilot was being polite to the people of the Home Counties province and was avoiding blocking out what was left of their light.

We followed the north Kent coast, flying over the Isle of Sheppey. We could just about see the levees round Margate before the land was lost from view in the murk. Yes, at least the English Government had rescued some land from the rising tides before the sea invaded. It was just to the annoyance of my people that it wasn't Anglian land they had decided to rescue, and it was probably the fundamental reason why we were now an independent country.

I closed my eyes and nodded off while we crossed the southernmost reaches of the North Sea. It must have been the better part of an hour later when Dietrich muttering about the view beneath us woke me. We were coming in over marshy land, which was part water and part town. 'Where are we?' I asked.

'That's Ghent down there,' he replied. 'Not long till Brussels now. I had no idea how much of Northern Belgium was flooded. We flew over a whole archipelago of islands during the last half hour, which was the old Belgian coastline. Did you know Ostend is now an island? Pretty useless sort of port, isn't it? We finally crossed the coast properly at Bruges. You could tell it was Bruges by the buildings. We've been back down near the ground since then. Don't know why they bother to climb up to any altitude. All it does is make the ground impossible to see.'

'Maybe it's easier to fly up there,' I replied, not really thinking about it. What did I know about flying anyway? I had never been behind the

139

controls of a flying machine, even before the coastline got flooded, so how was I to know anything about it now? I couldn't help thinking that it would be easier to navigate using ground features when you could actually see them. 'I wonder how long this service will continue to run,' I remarked.

'You think it might all grind to a halt in the snow?' he asked.

'I'm quite impressed that the pumice isn't getting into the control surfaces,' I replied. 'You can see them sort of rusting up, can't you?'

He grinned at me. 'You forget that these Zeppelins are made by German engineers. Of course they'll continue to work properly; they were properly made.'

'Oh, you patriot, you,' I smiled back, looking out of the window as the marshland to the east of Ghent disappeared behind us. There was a click on the loudspeaker and the disembodied voice told passengers wishing to disembark or change at 'Zaventem for Brussels' to head to Container Nine, and to remember to take our belongings with us. 'That's us,' I said.

He stood up and pulled his knapsack out of the overhead locker and, having pulled my wheelie-bag upright, extended the handle. 'Thanks,' I said. We headed across the walkway to the container, whose doors were opening as we arrived. There weren't that many people getting off at this stop, apart from the VIP who had got on in London. I didn't recognise him. He was too young to be a politician and surely too old to be a pop star or a footballer. He was, however, surrounded by an entourage of people taller than himself, carrying bags and whatever. Maybe they were armed, who could tell? 'Are *you* armed?' I asked Dietrich. The question just popped into my head out of the blue – well, to be totally accurate, grey.

'Not yet,' was his laconic reply, but that did explain why he had been allowed on the Zipa in the first place.

A woman in a uniform was already walking up the container, advising us to fasten our safety belts and waving a probe at our wrists. Presumably she was checking that we shouldn't have already got off at London City and had cheated ourselves across the North Sea into Europe free of charge. 'Welcome to Europe,' she said as she walked along to the family on the seats in front of us. 'When you get down on the ground, you will need to leave the container and present yourselves at immigration,' she told them.

The man stood up and faced her almost nose-to-nose. 'Why us and not them?' he asked angrily in a South London accent, jerking a thumb in our direction.

'They are European citizens,' she replied, and added, 'not that it is any of your business. If you stay on the container without having your passes checked, you may run the risk of being arrested.' That was interesting. Dietrich, yes, I could understand that, but apparently they were already considering us Anglians to be European citizens. As far as I understood, that was still in abeyance. Maybe agreements had been reached since my trip to Norwich a couple of days before.

The Londoner was even less impressed, and I was watching Dietrich closely, wondering if he was going to ride to the rescue of the woman like some sort of Knight Errant. I needn't have worried. A second uniformed figure, rather more obviously armed, had disentangled himself from the 'celebrity's' entourage and reappeared at the Londoner's shoulder. 'Y a-t-il une problème?' he asked the woman in French. If there wasn't a problem, the implication was, then he was quite happy to create one. The Londoner sat down hurriedly and glared across the top of the chair at us. Moral of the exercise, if you are going to show off to your children, pick a battle you can win. Mind you, was the Frenchman actually going to fire that thing in the airship? The helium in the gasbags wasn't inflammable or anything, but it would still leak, and this airship still had several thousand miles to go on this journey, a great many of which were over the Atlantic Ocean, a long way from any land. I wouldn't want to come to grief half way to anywhere because of a trigger-happy security guard near Brussels.

The container doors slid shut, there was a jolt, and I began to feel heavier as it moved upwards. I was interested to see that the armed guard/policeman didn't appear to notice the movement and remained standing at the Londoner's shoulder. He had done this before. We reached the top of the airship, where there was obviously a skyhook waiting for us, as there was a clank as we stopped, and then almost immediately we were whisked off, passing the side of the airship on our way down. I could see the letters 'ILK' go past the left window as we went down, presumably from its name, 'The Rainer Maria Rilke'.

Once we stopped moving, a further voice came over the loud-speaker as the container doors opened. 'If you have been asked to attend Immigration, will you please disembark immediately and make your way to Immigration services to the left. Free transportation will be provided for you to continue your journey once you have been processed by Customs.' The Londoner looked up into the eye of the man who had been watching him all the time.

'You,' said the policeman, which is what I took him for. He looked at the rest of the Londoner's family. 'Disembark now,' he added in a voice that broached no discussion. They stood sullenly, and the guard followed them out of the container. The Londoner threw one final angry look at us as he walked out.

Once everyone who was supposed to have left the container, including the celebrity and the rest of his entourage interestingly enough, the doors shut again, and the loudspeaker clicked on. 'This container will take you into the Brussels Central Station.' It continued, presumably saying the same thing in as many languages as it could in the ten minutes it took to travel from Zaventem into the city's central station. Eventually, the doors opened and the loudspeaker shut up.

'That was annoying,' said Dietrich, as we got up and got out of the container.

'What was?' I asked

'That man they pulled out of the container, he was my supplier. He had my gun.'

'Hunh?' I was a little confused.

'He was carrying a piece for me in the child's things.'

'Could that be awkward?'

'For everyone,' he replied. He walked up to a kiosk that advertised '*Koffie*' and told me to wait for him there. He suggested I had a coffee while I was waiting. It would keep me awake. The coffee was actually very good, probably the best cuppa I had ever had at a railway station coffee kiosk. I parked myself on a bench nearby and waited for Dietrich to return.

His little journey took him about ten minutes, and he came back to the coffee shop wearing a grin and looked pointedly at my cup. I took the hint and swallowed the rest. I tossed the beaker in a bin conveniently standing at the end of the bench. 'Come,' he said. 'We have a train to catch.'

Considering the size of the central station in Brussels, I was concerned that we might have quite a long walk to find our connection but, fortunately, this was not the case, and two platforms over was a train marked 'Anvers/Antwerpen'. He grinned at me and said, 'C'mon.'

We climbed aboard to find there was a fair amount of seating still available. He flung his knapsack into the rack above a pair of seats before taking my case from me, which he put on the rack next to the knapsack. He then pointed to the seats, bowed slightly, and sat down. I took the seat facing him and we both waved our left wrists at the scanners beside the seats. They appeared to think for a moment and then a green light flashed at us from the top of our respective boxes and Dietrich leaned back in the seat that had scanned his wrist, so I followed suit. 'You know, in the old days they actually had a human being checking the tickets,' he remarked.

'Yes, and he wouldn't let you on the train if you hadn't got a ticket. You couldn't get anywhere near a train in Peterborough unless you had a valid ticket. Nowadays, if you've only got a ticket as far as Ardley, the difference may well be taken off you in blood and sinew when you finally get off. So, what happens now?'

'Perhaps we'll see,' he replied. 'We haven't left yet.'

Well, there wasn't a kerfuffle about someone with no ticket, or even the wrong ticket for this train, so I never found out what happened if you did try to trick the system. Perhaps that was the point. The system was so effective that nobody even tried to break it.

The train travelled north as we passed through various suburbs at increasing speed, with scant respect for the locals. I was disappointed I hadn't seen the Mannekin-Pis, which Dwayne or Ben were bound to ask me about, or the Atomium, which Shove was more likely to ask after. Ah well, this wasn't a tourist trip anyway. I was working, wasn't I?

The residential areas petered out and the train sped through swampland. Presumably the railway was on a causeway above the water level. I wondered what had been there before the land was partly flooded, as there were few houses in the swamp, apart from the odd one standing on the top of mounds. They looked like farmhouses, except for the boats they had outside the doors instead of pods or tractors. I wondered whether they used those boats to catch fish or perhaps crabs or other shellfish. Flanders may have a new industry as a result of global warming. It's an ill wind, I thought, but didn't go on, as another thought entered my head. I leaned forward and spoke quietly to Dietrich. 'What happens if the guy gets caught with a gun in his baby's baggage?'

'We will need to look over our shoulders.'

'Does he know who you are?'

'I would imagine so, though I've never actually met him. There aren't so many people travelling from England to Europe as there were before. He was probably on the lookout for a German travelling with an English woman and was a little thrown that the police didn't want to interview you too. I imagine he thought that I would stop while you went through Immigration and we could do any exchange while that was going on before he had to go through himself. Just as a matter of interest, why didn't the border people want to see you?'

'I assume it's because I'm travelling on an up-to-date Anglian pass rather than on an old British one. To be honest, I don't really know.' Suddenly I did know, though. My pass has an official law enforcement stamp, and presumably the system thought I was undercover. Could it be that the computer thought I was shadowing Dietrich, and that it knew him to be a hit man? There was a thought – did the Flemish authorities expect me to bring him in for them? Well, they were going to be a little disappointed if that was the case.

The marshland gave way to an increasingly built up area. We were entering a big metropolis. 'This is Antwerp' he said. 'It was the biggest urban area in Belgium even before the floods came. There was a fair amount of Antwerp in the Netherlands, too. Now, of course, it is all Flanders, so that doesn't matter. Actually, it didn't matter much really since the war. Belgium, the Netherlands and Luxembourg were all grouped together as components of Benelux anyway. The real border was between North Belgium – or in other words Flanders, where they spoke Flemish, their version of Dutch – and South Belgium, called Wallonia, where they spoke their variant of French. Now, those groups really didn't mix at all well together. They still don't.'

'What's the difference between Flemish and German?' I asked.

'Much the same as the difference between English and German. If I hear someone talking Flemish, I have no idea what he's saying. Did you know that there's even a small part of Flanders where they speak German, as opposed to anything else?'

'Have you ever been there?'

'No, but I've heard about it, and I'm told there's a town called Eupen whose town centre looks more like a German town in the nineteen-thirties than any German town ever did, even in the nineteen-thirties.'

The train pulled slowly into Antwerp Central Station and stopped.

Dietrich pulled the bags down from the rack and passed me the handle of mine, then stepped out of the train while I followed. There was a big sign over a large door at the far side of the platform which said simply '*Uit*', and people were heading 'uit' through it. It was simple and effective in any language. If it didn't mean '*out*' then I was wrong, but that was the sign we walked underneath. 'Where to now?' I asked him.

'Well, believe it or not,' Dietrich said, 'we've walked out of the station straight onto *Pelikanstraat*.'

'You mean, this is our destination?' I said, waving an arm at the street in front of us. 'I don't believe it. It's like getting off a train from Edinburgh to London and there you are in Bond Street, in front of the shop you wanted to go to.'

'Quite,' he said. 'Follow me.' He crossed the road and walked a few yards south to a fork in the road, where he nodded at the tall building round the corner past the fork. 'We'll be coming back there in a few minutes. Meanwhile, let's get rid of these bags.' And he crossed the other road and set off down Pelican Street for perhaps fifty yards before turning into a short, rather modern side street. I was very tempted to walk straight into the wonderful looking chocolate café on the corner but Dietrich wasn't stopping. He walked up to a door down the street and put his wristy up to a panel beside it. The door swung open and he stepped through. 'C'mon,' he said. Inside, he went straight up to a panel in front of him, which lit up as he approached it. He tapped a couple of keys and it spat a couple of cards at him. 'Rooms twenty-one and twenty-six, any preference?'

I shrugged and took the top card from his hand. It was twenty-one. He headed towards a door beside the panel, which bore the words 'Lifts' in several languages on it. Sliding his room key into the slot, the door obligingly opened and we both walked in. The lift travelled upwards for a few moments and then stopped and opened. On the wall in front of the lift door was a sign pointing to the right, 'Rooms 21-30'. To the left there was a row of vending machines with various delights to be had, from chocolates and sandwiches to cans of beer and even small bottles of spirits. I turned right. Almost immediately, I reached my room and pushed my card into the slot on the door, which swallowed it. Rather alarmingly, it didn't appear to have any way of giving it back for future use. The light by the door handle did glow green, and the handle worked, so I pushed the door and went in, towing my bag behind me.

'Meet you in the lobby in five minutes,' Dietrich tossed over his shoulder as he stuck his card into his door.

The room was utilitarian, spotlessly clean mind you. There was a door to the right at the far end, which I opened, and there was a loo, basin and a shower. Back in the room itself there was a hip high rack onto which I swung my bag. There was a mirror with a light over the top and a chair and dressing table. Under the dressing table there was what looked like a fridge. I opened it, full of hope, but there was nothing in it. Presumably it was there for me to fill with the merchandise I had bought from the vending machine down the hall but I had a better use for it. I rummaged in my bag and pulled out my bag of miniature Mars Bars. I thought about having a celebratory one straight away but decided against it. We hadn't got anything to celebrate yet, apart from a safe arrival at the Pelican Street Autohotel. I had never actually been inside an Autohotel before. It was quite bizarre, there really wasn't anyone about at all, aside from me and Dietrich of course.

I ran a comb through my hair but, as he had said 'five minutes', then five minutes it was. I went back to the door, taking a moment to bounce on the bed beside it. That would do, it was quite comfortable. As I approached the door, I noticed a light flashing by the handle and there was my key-card. Relieved, I pulled it out and slid it into my pocket. The door opened and I walked back to the lift, where Dietrich was indeed waiting for me.

Chapter 19
In Which Steffy Meets Mr. Jacoby

I was thinking about *A Pluperfect Murder* as we went down in the lift, and remembered how Sue Laking and her sidekick were planning on going into the diamond dealers in disguise. How important was it that we went in character? I asked Dietrich about that as we walked through the front door of the hotel into the little side street.

'Why should we do that? Can you act?' he asked with some acidity.

'Moderately well, actually,' I replied, slightly put out.

'Well done, you,' he replied. 'Me, not so much. However, we are not here to win you an Oscar, we are here to get Adelina's diamonds back, so I think we just play it straight.'

'Have you got the diamond?' I asked as we arrived on Pelican Street proper, once again with that wonderful chocolaty smell on the wind from the right.

'Of course,' he said and pulled the little velvet bag out of his pocket. He tossed it at me, and just for a moment I thought I was going to slip on the snow as I tried, successfully, to catch it. The snow was just as gritty here as it had been in Anglia, needless to say. It had come from the same part of America and brought the same part of America with it. I put the little bag in my pocket and followed him.

He walked as far as the fork in the road. 'This is Vestingstraat,' he said, and proceeded to cross it. There was a door in the tall building near the fork. 'And this is the Diamond Exchange, which I think is where we start.' He walked through the door without looking over his shoulder at me, and I followed him in. Once we were through the door, I took over and walked up to a desk which had a sign advertising 'Assistance' in various languages suspended rather precariously above it. The woman under the sign was obviously used to that thing hanging over her head. If she could cope with it, so could I. She looked up as we approached.

'Does anyone speak English, Français, Deutsch?' I asked.

Before she could reply, Dietrich explained in English that we had a diamond we needed valuing. That was tactful of him – he could just as easily have spoken in German and that would have excluded me from the conversation. I can read a menu and order a meal but that is more or less the extent of my German: the valuation of jewellery is way out of my league.

'Mr. Jacoby speaks English,' she said in slightly accented but idiomatic English. I wondered if she spoke all the other languages suspended over her head as well. 'I'll see if he is free.'

She pressed, presumably, some sort of button on her desk and spoke into a microphone protruding from it, then looked back up at us. 'He is,' she replied, then added 'Door Seven' and pointed at a door down the corridor with a seven on it. She nodded at the desk further down with 'Security' also in several languages over it. Presumably she had shared her conversation with Mr. Jacoby with the Security desk. I wondered whether Dietrich was armed at this moment. I suspected we had already been scanned and if there was anything shaped like a pistol about his person, Security would know all about it. If he had and they did, they weren't reacting.

The room behind the door was small and dominated by a desk in the middle of it. On the far side of the desk was a closed door, and in front of this closed door sat a silver-haired, elderly man wearing bifocal glasses. Either side of the closed door was a rack of books, and on the desk was a telephone almost as elderly as the man himself, even featuring a rotary dial on the front. It was as if we had stepped into a time warp. He gestured to the chairs in front of the desk. They were stackable chairs, and there was a small stack of more chairs in one corner, presumably in case we had come mob handed.

'Yes. What can I do for you?' he asked in a soft voice that certainly didn't show his age.

'I have a diamond here,' I said, rummaging in my pocket for the velvet bag. 'I am looking for its brothers and sisters, which have disappeared.'

'Disappeared?' he asked, cocking a large grey eyebrow. 'You mean they've been stolen?'

'That's how I understand it, yes.'

He clicked his teeth for a moment, 'Oh that's sad, very sad,' he looked up at me. 'May I?' he asked putting a hand out.

I passed him the bag and he tipped our stone out onto the leather on the desk. 'You do know this diamond has been cut, don't you?' he asked. Maybe he thought we were stupid or something. Well, being charitable, maybe he thought we were just poor little foreigners who didn't know how diamonds existed in the wild.

'Of course,' I replied. The stone glinted back at me.

He pulled out an eyepiece from under the desk somewhere and, having removed his spectacles, screwed it into his right eye. He then slid out a pair of white cotton gloves, which he gently pulled on before picking up the diamond and peering at it through the eyepiece. 'Oh, very nice,' he said. 'It's not very big but it is flawless, and has been beautifully cut.'

'So, if its brothers and sisters turn up, you'll be able to recognise them?' asked Dietrich.

'If they were cut by the same artist who cut this one, I would think so. I believe this one was cut by Lorenz van Poeck.'

'How do you know that?' I asked.

'Mr. van Poeck has a quite distinctive style,' he replied.

'So, if some more diamonds cut by this Lorenz van Poeck were to come on the market, you would be able to spot them.'

'I'd like to think so, but I would probably have to check it with the man himself, just to confirm this.'

'So he's still alive?' I asked.

'Oh yes, Mr. van Poeck is still a young man and he works just down the road.'

'So how old would you say this diamond actually is,' I asked, 'just as a matter of interest?'

'Several hundred million years old. It's a common mistake to believe that diamonds date from the Carboniferous era. That is when coal was laid down, but diamonds formed a lot earlier. They may well be from limestone, which was then forced down deep into the earth's mantle to a depth of perhaps a hundred kilometres, which is the only place with the right temperature and pressure to make diamonds.' He chuckled, 'Maybe that diamond is what remains of Jules Verne after he made his *Journey to the Centre of the Earth*.'

I looked at the diamond again; its beauty was quite riveting. 'Poor little chap,' I said. 'It lived all that time underground and unmolested and then suddenly it gets dug up and assaulted.'

Mr. Jacoby smiled the soft smile of a man who has heard it all before. 'Yes, it must have known its number was up as soon as it found out it was being shipped to Lorenz van Poeck in Antwerp. Talking of whom, can I hang on to this for a little while to discuss it with him?'

'If we can have a formal document stating ownership of the diamond,' replied Dietrich drily. 'You can't expect us to leave a valuable jewel here without proof that we have done so and that we have the right to claim it back at any time.'

'No, I imagine the owner would be most upset if you lost this one too.' The little old man in front of us smiled knowingly. He knew the stone wasn't ours without either of us telling him. Once again, he reached under his desk. This time he pulled out a tablet and tapped it to wake it up. He took a picture of the stone with it and then popped it back into its velvet bag and took a picture of that too. Then, far too gently, he took hold of Dietrich's left hand between his index finger and thumb and waved the hitman's wrist over the tablet. I was stunned that Dietrich didn't seem to object to being manhandled that way. The two devices swapped digital ID and he gave Dietrich back his hand.

I grinned at Dietrich, 'You don't lose wristies, do you?' I had no idea what else to say at that moment but I was sure it merited something.

'No, of course I don't,' he replied crossly, but he was aware that I was making sure that he realised he was taking responsibility for Adelina's diamond. But then again, he had had it in his care all the way from Peterborough anyway.

'Even if he does, I will remember it is in his possession,' said the old man with a gentle smile. 'The documentation is only to make sure that, if anything happens to one of us, Head Office knows whose diamond this is.' He slipped it under the desk whence he had got the tablet and the eyepiece. He must have an invisible safe under there.

'When might you have anything to tell us?' I asked.

'Well, if you come in this time tomorrow I will at least have been able to confirm that it was cut by my friend Lorenz. If any other diamonds of the same cut have already come to light, then maybe I will know that too.'

'So, you would know everything there is to know about it by then?' was Dietrich's question, to which the old man replied in the affirmative. 'And we would be able to take it back with us to its owner?'

'Maybe,' he paused, and then added. 'Well, you can always take it away with you,' he reached under his desk and pulled out the velvet bag, 'You can take it now if you like, but we may not be able to answer all your questions if you do so.'

'No, Dietrich,' I interjected. 'Adelina gave us that diamond to find its brothers and there is no point in us taking it back until we've found them.'

He looked at me, knowing that I was right of course. 'Okay,' Mr. Jacoby said and added, 'Do you want me to put your ID on record too, just in case things take longer than we expected?'

'Maybe, yes, why not?' I leaned forward offering him my much smaller arm. He didn't seem to be particularly interested in it but he did the same thing with my wristy and the tablet as he had done with Dietrich's.

'Now if one of you presents your ID and collects the diamond and then the other one turns up also to collect the diamond, we will tell him or her that the other one of you has already collected it. You must be aware of that, just in case you fall out with each other.' He looked at us carefully.

'I can't see that happening,' I said.

'As you have correctly surmised, we aren't a couple, we simply work for the same person, looking for the missing diamonds. We have no particular loyalty to each other,' Dietrich remarked drily. 'We are both, however, very loyal to our boss.'

Mr. Jacoby put the tablet back into his desk, though for the moment he left the bag on the desk. I picked up the bag and felt it, just confirming that we hadn't been the victims of a bit of sleight of hand. There was certainly a stone in the bag, and it was the same size as Adelina's, so as far as I could tell it was the real thing. I took one final look at it, remembering the first time Adelina and I had met a couple of days before, when she poured the fake diamonds on my desk and even I could tell that those were fakes. As far as I could tell, this one looked like a real diamond. I popped the stone back into the bag and returned it to Mr. Jacoby, promising him that we would see him on the morrow.

We stood up and left the room. Walking back out towards the main door, Dietrich asked me, 'What now?'

'Well, I don't know about you, but I'm a bit peckish. A little food and drink?' I suggested thinking of the chocolate-scented coffee shop just down the road by our hotel.

'Why not?' he said, and disappointed and annoyed me by turning right up Vestingstraat away from the chocolate shop. 'I need a drink,' he said firmly and, as I had no idea whether the chocolate café sold alcohol or not, I followed him. There were jewellery shops all the way up Vestingstraat and it was almost a surprise when we came upon a shop that wasn't one. And it was a bar, even better. We walked in and Dietrich parked himself on a chair beside the first empty table while I sat down on the other side of it. The waiter came round from behind the bar and Dietrich asked, this time in German, for a beer and the menu. We were offered a choice of beers and he chose a Grimbergen Dubbel. I really didn't know much about Flemish beer, apart from that they were famous for it – rather like their chocolate, I thought wistfully – so I said that I would have what he was having.

The bar wasn't busy but I would imagine it would be once all the jewellers closed. The beer therefore arrived in about five minutes, each in a glass with a Grimbergen badge painted on it. The glass looked new. I wondered how long it would take to wash the paint off the glass and what they would do with their glass once it faded. I picked up the glass and sniffed it as if it was wine, and was interested to find that the beer had an aroma of its own, a sweetish heady aroma. I looked at Dietrich and nodded approvingly before taking a mouthful. Full of flavour too, it was, not particularly bitter, and it was fairly obvious that it was quite strong. I wouldn't need more than two of those I thought.

'What do you want to eat?' he asked.

'Surprise me with some local speciality,' I replied.

'Well, Antwerp has always been a port, and has been one of the mouths of the Rhine since forever, so I imagine that fish is the main local speciality. I'll see what they're offering. Do you want a starter?'

'Why not? Let's push the boat out.'

He then indulged in a long, complex conversation with the waiter which I couldn't follow, so I sat back and let them get on with it. The waiter tapped his tablet finally and walked off. Dietrich smiled.

'Well?' I asked.

'I have ordered us as a starter a dish called *Tomaat-garnaal* which is a sort of prawn cocktail made from grey shrimp in mayonnaise stuffed into a hollowed-out tomato.'

'Sounds good, and the shrimp is local?'

'So I understand.'

'And as a main course?' I continued.

'Well, what he particularly recommended as a personal favourite is an Antwerp speciality called *Stoverij-Friet*. That is, this version of it is an Antwerp specialty.'

'I can tell you're dying to explain.'

'Well it's very slow-cooked chunks of beef, but instead of cooking them in red wine like the French do in a *Boeuf Bourguignon*, the Belgians stew their beef in the local beer. Stoverij is considered a national dish like *Fish and Chips* is in England or *Bratwurst mit Sauerkraut und Kartoffeln* is in Germany. However, what makes this a local dish is that it is stewed in the local beer made by *De Koninck*.'

'This is De Koninck?' I asked waving a hand at the glass in front of me.

'No, that's a Grimbergen, which was made a few kilometres north of Brussels. We passed through Grimbergen at a quite disrespectful speed in the train to Antwerp. We'll have a De Koninck next if you like. The other thing that comes with the Stoverij is chips.'

'The Flemish eat chips as part of their national dish?'

'They invented chips,' he replied.

'I assumed it was the French, as the Americans call them "French Fries".'

'Yes, as per usual they got that wrong. I understand that the first American ate his first chip when he came over in the First World War. He was obviously billeted somewhere in Wallonia, south of Liège and, being American, he probably thought he was in France at the time and anyway, he couldn't tell the difference. Hence when he went back to the States he took the idea back with him and French Fries were born.'

'I learn something new every day,' I said and, swallowing another mouthful of beer, waited for the banquet to commence.

Chapter 20
In Which Steffy Visits Casualty Before Rush Hour

The next thing I remember is waking up in my room. I was lying on my bed and I had no trousers, shoes or socks on. As far as I could tell, my top half was as dressed as it had been earlier that day. I still had my waterproof pullover on. What had happened? Had I got completely sozzled in the bar? Had Dietrich been a star and brought me home and put me to bed? Or had he had his way with me first? Was that why I wasn't wearing anything below the waist? I put my hand down there – no, that wasn't quite true, I still had my panties on.

Well, whatever had happened I felt foul and it wasn't in the slightest bit post-coital, but it didn't particularly feel like a hangover either. Having been in both those places in my life often enough, after good and bad times, I knew what both felt like. Whatever it was that I was feeling was new and rather unpleasant. Firstly I just felt unwell, then on top of that I felt stressed and rather sweaty. Tell you something else, I felt really hungry. Did I even eat that dinner I had been so looking forward to as the last thing I did remember? Well, at least I had a solution to that – I had put my Mars Bars in the fridge. I always liked Mars Bars slightly chilled – there is something very un-Scottish about me, *nae hen, I dinna like ma Marrs Barrs deep-fried.*

I put my right leg out to the floor and stepped forwards halfway to the fridge. My left leg then followed it. Hot crap! What had I just trodden on? That really hurt. The pain shot through my left foot as though I had been stabbed. Some bloody idiot hadn't left a drawing pin on the floor or something? I lifted the foot up and the pain went away again. I gingerly put it back down and back it came. Well, I was more than halfway to the fridge so, carefully putting my right foot down, I leaned into it. At least the Mars Bars were still there. Out they came, and I made my way back to the bed, carefully putting only the heel of my left foot to the floor. That didn't hurt so much. Once I was on the bed, I put the bag of Mars Bars down and pulled up my left foot to pull out whatever it was that was stabbing it.

There was nothing in the sole at all, moreover there was no sign of any puncture wound either. All I could see was the sweat on the inside of my leg but sweat didn't usually hurt. I pushed at the sole of my foot with a finger. Oh! that was it. Ow! That hurt like a proverbial. So, whatever had happened, it was inside my foot and wasn't a pin or a thumbtack or anything. Had I broken a bone in my foot during the adventure I couldn't remember? I hoped it would come back to me in a moment.

I ate one of my miniature Mars Bars and then I ate another. After the third one I felt a bit better. My heart rate started dropping and I was beginning to feel less famished. The problem was that the improved feeling of well-being didn't last, and within ten minutes or so, I was beginning to feel stressed again. So I popped another Mars Bar. Now I don't usually devour Mars Bars like they're going out of fashion. That's how I have retained the shape that Ben likes so much. Mars Bars are strictly treats, or occasionally things that I eat to make me happier if I've got the blues. By the time I had five empty wrappers sitting beside me on the bed, I was becoming concerned. I hobbled across the room to my bag and got out a clean pair of trousers. Where were the trousers I was wearing yesterday? If I lost this pair I would be stuck with just that short skirt that Ben encouraged me to buy. I also gently pulled on my spare pair of shoes, and then popped a sixth Mars, deciding that I needed some help here. I had no idea what was going on but I was rapidly running out of Mars Bars and I had this feeling that I should be seeking medical assistance before I actually did so.

So, trousers on, shoes on, I found I still had my wristy so I summoned a pod and headed directly for the lift. I pulled a couple of Nuts bars out of the vending machine while I was waiting for the doors in front of me to open. Nuts bars were the European equivalent of Mars Bars, only they had hazelnuts in the soft bit as well, and these of course were full-sized and not the miniature ones like I carried around with me. Did they make miniature Nuts bars? I had no idea and I was still mulling over this conundrum when the lift doors opened, inviting me to get in, and I did so. When they opened again, I got out at the lobby and was just hobbling through the front door of the hotel when a pod pulled up. I would have been even more impressed with the efficiency of the Antwerp transport system had I not realised that it was now quite dark and there didn't seem to be a great many people about. I reckoned I had lost at least six hours. I pulled myself into the absolutely standard pod and tapped its screen. Okay, so the language was different, but I do speak a bit of French, even if the locals refused to, and therefore I knew that a SAMU was the French for a casualty department. That was where I headed.

I had also arrived at a time when the SAMU was fairly quiet. They would get busier later on when people had actually had time to consume the excess alcohol required to attend a SAMU and that, I assumed, was what they were busy doing at that moment.

I was ushered into a triage room, and found myself talking to a Flemish girl who spoke English. She didn't speak French, or at least wouldn't admit to it, so we spoke English. She took a print of my wristy onto her tablet, much in the same way the old diamond man had done earlier that day. What was his name? Jacoby, that's right. There was nothing apparently wrong with my short-term memory.

I peed in the cup she proffered and she did my basic numbers, while explaining to me everything she was going to put me through before she did it. She ran me though a blood-sampling machine and then arranged for a scan to be taken of my left foot. It was all very slick, very efficient. Even the scan man was ready, and his English sounded as if he had been furiously practising it all evening in preparation for my arrival. I was helped onto the table and lay down while both my feet disappeared into a device that looked like a large ring doughnut without the sugar. It clanked around them, then moved slowly, but worryingly noisily, towards my head. To my relief it stopped by the time it reached my pelvis, and then moved away from me again. The technician helped me off the couch and back into the wheelchair and, in next to no time, I was wheeled back to my cubicle. I was beginning to feel unwell again and was contemplating having another Mars Bar when the nurse came back in with some test results on a pad, followed by a tall, rather weary-looking young man behind her. He looked like a doctor, likely one who had been up all day, and I had that feeling I was disturbing his 'feet-up' time.

'Good evening, Mrs. Flack,' he said, still in English, but much more strongly accented than the nurse. 'How long have you been diabetic?'

That was a facer. 'I didn't know I was diabetic.' I replied.

He looked thoughtful for a moment, then asked me what other medication I was taking.

'None,' I said. 'I'm not taking any medication at all.' All that did was make him more thoughtful.

Then he said, 'Well, your blood sugar is very low, which is probably why you feel so unwell and feel you need to eat sweets. Shall we at least sort that out and then we can find out why it's going on?'

'Yes, please,' I said.

He turned to the nurse and asked her for a glucagon syringe. She rummaged in a cupboard over the sink and pulled a long thin device out, which she put in a long, kidney-shaped metal tray and passed it to him. What is it with the medical profession, this obsession with kidney-shaped dishes? I knew they had a thing about stainless steel kidney dishes on the other side of the North Sea but it appeared that the Flemish are similarly obsessed.

'This will bring your blood sugar back up,' he explained, and it felt like he had shot a jet of cold air at my shoulder.

'Thank you,' I muttered, waiting for it to work. It did so fairly quickly. I stopped feeling stressed and my heart stopped feeling it was going to jump out of my chest.

'What was that?' I asked.

'Glucagon, it is a natural hormone to bring your blood sugar back up. We just don't make as much as I've just given you.'

'Oh.'

'Now, Mrs. Flack...'

'I'm not married,' I said. 'Miss, or Miz if you like, but why not call me Steff? It is my name after all.'

'Hokay, Steff.' He rolled it round his mouth as if he was trying it on for size. He seemed satisfied with the effect. 'So, what medications have you been taking?'

'None at all. Honestly,' I added, and wondered why anyone ever used that word. There was absolutely no way it could ever not be a lie, except that just this once, it wasn't. I carried on rapidly and asked what he had found.

'Well, so far there's two things; the first, and it's probably minor, but we have found some benzodiazepine in your urine.'

'Benzo ... what's that?'

'Well, it's a family of drugs which used to be commonly used and abused. They are calmers, tranquillizers and sleeping pills. Sometimes they can also be used as an acute anticonvulsant and, if abused regularly, they can be psychologically addictive. They are not used very often now, apart from within the addict community, but I did notice you had no other drugs you can become addicted to in your urine, so why would you have a tranquillizer?'

'I have no idea. I haven't taken any medicine of any sort for months now, that is apart from caffeine and alcohol.' I grinned to show I was making a joke.

He missed my attempt at frivolity and ploughed on, 'That was unless you had been fed flunitrazepam in your meal somewhere. It is tasteless, so you wouldn't notice it.'

'Flew … What's that?'

'Its old trade name was Rohypnol. It was a date rape drug. That would fit your story of losing consciousness completely.'

'Dietrich, you bastard,' I muttered under my breath. So he had doped me up and raped me. Funny though, I didn't feel as if I had recently been penetrated. He must have a very unimpressive weapon.

'However,' the doctor continued, 'what is far more interesting and important is the amount of insulin in your system.' I don't think he wanted to hear me swearing about someone called Dietrich, and what I was thinking he had done to me.

'Don't we all make insulin?' I asked.

'Ah yes, but this was synthetic insulin.'

'How can you tell?' That was the investigator in me coming out.

He cleared his throat as if he was going to deliver a lecture, then grabbed a chair and sat down. He really was going to give a speech. I hoped it wouldn't take too long. I had no idea how long that glucagon shot would last. 'Well, under normal conditions, the body makes a lot of stuff called pro-insulin, which is completely inert, and it floats around in the blood stream, *en garde*, looking for places where it might be needed. If it spots the blood sugar starting to climb, the body bites the pro-insulin in half, making active insulin and a substance called c-peptide. In normal circumstances, therefore, the level of insulin and c-peptide in the blood are roughly the same. Do you follow that?'

'Yes, I think so,' I replied uncertainly.

'Right, the problem that insulin dependent diabetics have is that they don't make any pro-insulin, so we give them depot insulin, which is still the best we can do. However, if you measure the insulin and the c-peptide levels in an insulin-dependent diabetic, they are wildly different, as their insulin is not made from pro-insulin, and therefore they don't have any c-peptide in their blood. Does that make sense?'

'And you're telling me that I don't have any c-peptide in my blood?'

'Got it in one, well, not a lot anyway, and certainly not enough to explain all the insulin floating around in your blood stream.'

'I understand what you're saying, but I don't understand how it came about.'

At this moment the scan man rolled up with a pad in his hand and showed it to the doctor. They gabbled for a moment in what I guessed was Flemish, and then the doctor turned back to me. 'Well, that, Steff,' he rolled my name round his mouth, 'is even more interesting.'

'Go on, tell me,' I said, trying to sound like an excited six-year-old.

He passed me the pad and pointed to a bone in the middle of the screen. 'That,' he said, 'is your second metatarsal, the bone in your foot that hurts. Well, I must admit, when I examined your foot, I had thought you had fractured it. Look, can you see?'

I couldn't see anything particularly wrong with it but then I'm only a detective so what do I know about these things? I shook my head.

'Quite,' he said. 'No fracture. You are absolutely right. However, look carefully at this.' He pointed to a tiny blob on the edge of the bone, which I must admit I hadn't spotted until he pointed it out.

'Oh, yes,' I said. 'What's that?'

'Well, it looks as if you have fluid under the skin that lies over the bone.'

'So what does that mean?'

'Well, it is that skin, which we doctors call the periosteum, that carries all the nerve fibres from a bone, so when you break a bone it hurts because you tear the nerve fibres in the periosteum.'

'So how did that happen, considering there isn't a fracture?'

'You are a very intelligent woman, Miz Steff. You know all the right questions to ask. You aren't a detective by any chance, are you?' He laughed at his little joke, but he stopped when I replied, 'Well, yes, actually I am.'

He felt gently along the top of my foot; in fact, until he reached the sore spot, I thought he was being a little unprofessional and caressing my foot. 'Ow!' I said. He looked very closely at that spot and shook his head. He then picked up my foot by the big toe and squinted at the space between the big and second toe. He got very close and then suddenly smiled, 'Ach Zo!' he exclaimed. 'There it is.' He looked at me and, having let go of my toe, contorted himself in various unlikely positions. Finally, he looked me directly in the eye again and said, 'No. You would have been twisting yourself into various unlikely bends to do that to yourself.' He smiled for a moment. 'I think we have found out what happened, so perhaps this evening it is me who is the detective.'

'Go on,' I said.

'I think someone injected the insulin between your toes but wasn't quite on target and injected it into the periosteum of your second toe and not into the blood vessels in the web space. I would be willing to bet that if I put a tiny needle under the periosteum and drew out that fluid, two things would happen. Firstly, it would stop hurting, as the periosteum would not be stretched any longer and secondly, when we analysed that fluid, it would be neat insulin.'

'Shall we get on with it then?' I said.

The doctor was a man transformed. From being dour at the beginning of my consultation, he was positively excited. I was wheeled back to the scan room and parked up on the table again. The scan man set everything up and the doctor selected himself a long, very fine needle on the end of a slender syringe. He then watched its progress into my foot, on the scanner screen, while I had my eyes screwed tightly shut. I didn't want to watch this. I wasn't aware I was particularly squeamish but this was my own foot he was sticking a needle into. Ow! That was the spot, I told him. It hurt just like before, where he was putting his needle right now.

Suddenly he made a noise that sounded suspiciously like 'Eureka', and at the same time my foot stopped hurting. 'How is that?' he asked, grinning from ear to ear.

'Bloody magic!' I said.

'What I must do is get this analysed,' he said, putting the syringe into a port on the analyser and pressing a button. We both held our breath. It didn't take long: insulin a very high number, and c-peptide zero.

'Well, Miz detective,' he said, 'we have made you better. The next thing we have to decide is what to do now. I think someone has tried to murder you.'

Whoa there. I had to admit I was rapidly coming to the same conclusion, but a little short of a bedside manner, wasn't he? I grinned at him. 'Well, I'm the detective and you're the doctor, but I'm afraid you may be right.'

'Shall we call the police then?'

'Can you hang on a moment? I think I may know who is responsible and if so, I can sort this out myself.'

He looked alarmed. 'You mean you're telling me that you're going to kill him in exchange?'

'Good lord, no. However, if who I think is responsible actually is, then I can sort this out without involving the police. If I end up under a bus over the next twenty-four hours I was wrong, and please activate the Flemish Police, and can you also contact the Chief of Police in Peterborough, Anglia? She's a friend of mine and she will want to know.'

He looked at me, suddenly rather sadly, 'I shall keep all these tests pending then,' he said.

'Can I have a copy of the relevant tests on my pad to take with me?' I asked.

'I don't see why not – you have, after all, paid for them.'

I asked him, just as a matter of interest of course, how much I had actually paid. The figure he quoted shook me a little. Well, that would be deducted from Adelina's expenses. 'Can I also have a copy of the receipt on my pad too?' I asked.

'On your way out go up to the main desk and sort that out with the nurse there. They should let you have everything you want. Oh, and Steff...'

'Yes?'

'Look after yourself and I hope, for all the right reasons, that we don't meet again.'

I wished the smile I gave him was the sort that would launch ships but I wasn't Helen of Troy. 'Thank you for all your skill,' I replied. 'It was worth every cent.'

He nodded and wandered off to see his next patient or, I rather hoped, to put his feet up. He deserved that. Meanwhile, I made my way to the main desk, where the nurse I met when I arrived was sitting, waiting for action. My bureaucratic needs sorted, I summoned a pod and went out of the entrance door to wait for it. It wasn't long and, after I had climbed in and programmed it to take me back to the Autohotel off Pelikanstraat, I sat back and dialled Adelina.

'Hello,' it was Adelina herself answering her phone. 'How is it going? Have you found my diamonds yet?'

'Not yet, though I have put a local bloodhound on their trail. However, someone tried to kill me this evening. You will be glad to know they didn't succeed.'

'I gathered that, since I'm talking to you. On principle I don't have conversations with ghosts.' Good grief, Adelina had made a joke! I had not imagined she would stoop to a thing like that.

'I was just phoning to tell you that if it was your pet hit-man Dietrich who was responsible, then you need to be aware that one of my best friends is Peterborough's chief of police and if I don't come home from this mission for any reason, she does know who I'm working for, and I imagine they'll be through that door like the Assyrian down like a wolf on the fold.'

'I assume that was a quote from one of your English classics. I do hope you aren't threatening me, Miss Flack.'

'Not particularly, I'm just encouraging you to warn Dietrich off if he was indeed responsible for putting me in hospital.'

'I will have a serious word with him immediately,' she replied and cut the connection, presumably to have a word with Dietrich before I got to him. That wouldn't be too long, as I was travelling in the pod with the curtains open and noted that we had just turned into Pelican Street.

Maybe a minute later we were pulling up outside the Autohotel and I had my key-card out. I was through the front door and into the lift like a rat up a drain. Once the lift spat me out on our floor, I strode along the corridor to Dietrich's room, determined to have it out with him forthwith. Hopefully he would still be half asleep after Adelina's call.

As I approached the door I realised it was ajar, so I wouldn't have to hammer on it for him to open up and let me in. Moreover, his wristy was buzzing. I pushed the door open and walked over to the table and picked his wrist up between my index and thumb, feeling for a pulse at the same time. I let it drop. It said 'Adelina' on the screen. I looked at him on the bed for a moment and then pressed speak.

'Dietrich's wristy,' I replied.

'Who is that?' came the voice I was beginning to recognise quite well over the phone.

'It's Steff here. I was wrong.'

'What do you mean, you were wrong?'

'It wasn't Dietrich.'

'Well, I thought that was probably the case, but why do you say that now?'

'Because he's dead. He has been shot.' I wasn't going to describe how Dietrich appeared as I looked at him. The gun was in his hand and he had been posed as if he had shot himself through the head. There was part of his brain on the wall on the other side of his head. He wasn't going to recover from that. And how did I know he hadn't done it himself? He was holding the gun in his right hand. The killer who had posed him obviously didn't know Dietrich was left-handed. I didn't describe the scene to Adelina, she didn't deserve that. I told her I was going back to the Diamond Exchange as soon as it opened and would explain to Mr. Jacoby what had happened. He would probably decide what he wanted to do with the diamond in his possession, and I would come back to Peterborough with it.

'Are you going to call the police?' she asked.

'Well, when someone comes round to do the room they'll get called anyway. There's a good deal of his head painted over the wall behind him. Even if I was the best cleaner in the land, I'd have difficulty in scrubbing that off.' Poor cleaner, I thought. Perhaps I should pin a warning note on the door, so that he would be aware that the room he was about to see wasn't as pretty as it had been when he left it. I then started wondering what language to write it in and realized the only other language I knew how to say 'brains' in was French and, if he were Flemish, he wouldn't know what that meant on principle.

'Will you leave it like that, then?'

'Okay. I will see you later on today.'

'Thank you for keeping me in the picture,' she said. For the first time, I thought, she sounded human and rather fragile. I disconnected Dietrich's wristy, took it off, and put it in my pocket. Otherwise I touched nothing before I pulled the door to and heard the lock click. As for Dietrich's key-card, it was either on what was left of Dietrich or his killer had taken it. I went back to my room, packed and left the hotel.

As I walked out into Pelican Street, I was disappointed to see that the chocolate café wasn't open yet, so I found an all-night bar and ordered a strong coffee. It was going to be a long night.

Chapter 21
A Scottish Interlude

The gritty snow was continuing to fall but it was possible to believe that dawn was breaking, as the street was becoming more generally lit rather than there just being pools of light clustering round the stems of the street lamps. That being said, for a while there did not appear to be any activity yet in any of the other businesses I could see through the windows of the bar. I was becoming tingly now just from the caffeine consumption which I had been indulging in to keep paying for my right to sit in this bar. It was either coffee or alcohol and I chose to be buzzed rather than drunk, especially as there was someone out there who might still be labouring under the misapprehension that he had killed me. I needed to be wide awake and alert in case he discovered his mistake. I had also eaten a fair number of ham slices, and some delicious buttery croissants. The croissants seriously impressed me, as I hadn't seen any other shops, like a bakery for instance, open and these had that just-baked taste. The waiter didn't appear interested in discussing the provenance of the croissants with me, as I had attempted to talk to him in French. He had claimed to speak English, but it wasn't any kind of English that I recognised. So I had no idea whether the croissants were being baked round the back of the shop while I drank coffee and waited for the diamond merchant across the road to open up for business. I had consumed a great deal of sugary carbohydrate in the previous four hours but the insulin would have fixed a great deal of it somewhere in me. I was under no delusion that Ben's interest was anything more than good old-fashioned lust but, when you came to think of it, that was probably my view of whatever it was that we had together too. I had only ever lived in the same building with three male members of the species in my life: my dad, then my uncle, and much more recently 'Enery Grubbs. I tried to imagine Ben with a little middle-aged spread and my remaining interested. It couldn't be done.

I checked the time on my wristy and thought that Shove would be stirring but wouldn't have left the house yet. I figured that now would be as good a time as any to let her know the situation, so I gave her a call.

'Hi, Hon,' she replied, 'A little early in the morning. Is there a problem?'

I explained what had been happening over the previous twelve hours and asked her what would be best for me to do as far as the Peterborough Constabulary was concerned. I was fairly convinced that if I told the Antwerp cops about the corpse in the hotel I would be stuck here for at least a couple of days 'helping them with their enquiries', maybe longer. And at the same time, there was someone who had tried to kill me out there somewhere, who might take another crack at it if they realised I was still around. Or, I could catch the next train to Brussels and hope to be in a Zipa headed for anywhere in Great Britain before the cleaners wandered into Dietrich's room.

'You're not in any way responsible for this Dietrich's condition?' She asked me with more than a little enquiry of her own in her voice.

'No, of course not,' I replied. 'In fact, when I discovered the body I was on my way to accuse him of trying to kill me, or drug me, or something.' I explained that Dietrich hadn't given me an inkling that he might try to kill me, and I had no evidence one way or another even about his sexual orientation, so I might well be the last person on earth with whom he would want to have had relations. And anyway, rape isn't about desire, it's about power. Feeling suddenly rather foolish, I stopped chuntering at her and said, 'Sorry, I'm much more shaken up by the whole thing than I originally thought.'

'Don't worry, Hon,' she said gently. 'I think you'd be better off here in Anglia, and when you're home I can call my oppo in Antwerp and tell him you had handed yourself in to me when you got back. So, make your way back to Peterborough as soon as possible. May I suggest you get a pod from where you are and go direct to the airport? Get on the next airship to leave the area. You can get a connection to Anglia wherever you end up, even if it's as far away as Stockholm.'

'Will do,' I replied. There was a bit of activity at the diamond dealer's over the road so I said, 'See you very soon,' and disconnected her. I paid my bill at the bar and headed out across the road and into the shop.

'Is Mr. Jacoby in yet?' I asked the woman at *Accueil*.

'I'll check.' She tapped the desk in front of her in different places as if she was playing a steel drum with her hand. 'He's there, but he's expecting someone.'

'I'll take less than a minute,' I said.

She had a quick chat, presumably in Flemish – well, it could have been in Yiddish for all I knew – then, 'Room Seven,' she said, taking my ID from my wristy.

I rushed down to Mr. Jacoby's room and burst through the door. 'Ah, Ms. Flack,' he said from behind his desk. 'You're back so quickly. Don't tell me you want your diamond back so soon?'

'No, not at all. It's just that Dietrich and I have got to go off somewhere this morning and we won't be back for several days. On top of that, he's lost his wristy, so if anyone comes in with it claiming to be him…' You never know, his killer could have cloned Dietrich's device onto his own before leaving Dietrich's in his bedroom for me to find. I couldn't immediately work out why they might do such a thing but it was possible they could have.

'Don't worry,' the old man smiled. 'I may be a little elderly but I'm firing on all cylinders up here.' He tapped the right side of his head, 'I will remember what your Herr Dietrich looks like.'

'That would work if it were you that someone came in to see,' I said. 'But if you weren't here and the person with the wristy came in demanding the diamond back…'

'It wouldn't happen,' he replied. 'It needs my presence to release the stone back into someone else's hands.'

'So,' I began getting down to the nitty gritty, 'what happens if you were to get run over by a bus? Does your company think it can take over ownership of the diamond under these circumstances?'

I was actually concerned that an attempt might be made on his life too. Someone had killed Dietrich, perhaps someone else had failed to kill me with a totally different method and, if I disappeared as I was intending to do very shortly, then perhaps somebody would be after Mr. Jacoby too. I wasn't going to say that then though.

'We have protocols in place that will cover that eventuality,' the old man smiled, 'aside from the fact that there aren't any buses about any more and that nobody has been run over by a pod since the new safety pods were introduced, I see what you are saying. The diamond will only be released to you or Herr Dietrich, I can guarantee that. The problem will be for the owner to prove that he is the owner, if...' he coughed, 'you and Herr Dietrich have similar accidents with buses.'

'He's a she,' I replied, wondering how The Rail would get round that one. Actually, I could see that she probably would have her own solution to that problem. 'I ... or Dietrich,' I added hurriedly, 'will be back in a few days to see what you've found out.'

'I will see you then,' said the old man, still wearing that inscrutable smile. 'I must now ask you to depart, as I have a booked appointment, and diamond people don't like to be kept waiting.'

I stood up and said, 'Thank you so much for fitting me in.'

'My pleasure,' he replied and I left the room, already summoning a pod as I was walking up the hallway to the exit.

The pod's arrival was as brisk as it had always been in Flanders. Mind you, it wasn't quite rush hour yet, and I supposed that most people were still having their breakfast. Hadn't I been lucky that Mr. Jacoby came in to work so early?

I climbed into the pod and drew the curtains. This was for two reasons: aside from my usual weakness that these things scare the crap out of me, I didn't want my face to be seen and photographed by a street camera. If the said camera had already spotted me getting into the pod I was done for anyway. I knew from even my own surveillance work that once you had picked up a face and the number of the pod in the panel above the windscreen you could trace that journey wherever it went. So with crossed fingers I keyed in Zaventem Airport and the pod set off.

My next project was to find out when the next airship to anywhere on the Big Island was leaving the nearest airport. I was relieved to see that an EU shuttle from Paris to Brussels to Edinburgh and Dublin was leaving in an hour. It would, I supposed, be full of bureaucrats in transit from one place to the other. They might be carrying papers, I assumed, but people were the sole commodity that they had yet to work out how to transfer electronically. I was wondering how long it would take for 'Beam me up, Scotty' to become a reality as I booked a seat to take me to Edinburgh, from where I would catch the train south. It wouldn't be long, I hoped, before Norwich, Cardiff and Winchester were included on those bureaucracy cruises.

There were moments when I peered through a crack in the curtains. The land was now quite swampy and suddenly a train rushed past me going in the other direction. They had put the road and the railway on the same causeway, much the same as we had. The reality of how close they were was all the more exciting without good preparation for the experience. I pulled away from the window and sat back in my seat. Maybe the coffee overdose I had consumed during the night was beginning to wear off as I was feeling quite drowsy, my lack of natural REM sleep beginning to win over my previously chemically altered state. My eyelids became heavy and I decided to let them rest for a moment.

'Zaventem Airport,' the pod screamed at me in English. The door was open and if it had the ability to tip me out I was sure that is what it would have done. I pulled my wheelie-bag out and wandered into the terminus. Now would be the moment of truth. I sauntered up to the ticketing desk and waved my left wrist at it. I had formally declared that I was there. My wrist tingled as the desk acknowledged my request, and the receipt of the electronic ticket. It also told anyone who was looking for me exactly where I was at that moment in time. Now would the air suddenly be thick with police, as they were informed of my whereabouts? I glanced around. There was a pair of armed policemen chatting together a little way off but there was nothing about them that suggested that they were on the look-out for an Anglian woman of medium height with short fair hair. One of them even looked straight through me. The only response I got to my signing in was my earpiece telling me to shift my backside to Gate Five smartish as my flight was already in the process of embarking.

There was no police presence at the gate either as this was an all-internal EU flight and it wouldn't make any form of landfall until it reached Scotland. I could imagine it flying up the North Sea side of the English east coast. I would try to get a seat on the left-hand side of the shuttle, just to see if I could see any land at all during the flight, probably not very likely while it was still snowing.

It was a much smaller airship than the big intercontinentals on which I had travelled earlier in the week. I wondered whether it was the same sort of size as the old Hindenburg, famous for being the catastrophe that killed the original series of airship transports when it caught fire at New York over a hundred years ago. Mind you, that was all the Americans' fault. The Hindenburg was designed to be filled with inert helium gas, as are all of today's airships, but the only available source of helium gas in the mid-to-late thirties was the United States and they weren't going to let the Nazi regime in Germany have any of it, even though the airship in question was being used to fly civilian passengers from America to Europe and back again, including Americans. As a result, the airship in question was filled with inflammable hydrogen and the rest, as they say, is history. It's interesting that one of the most iconic photos from the nineteen thirties was that of the Hindenburg crashing and burning.

It was, however, boarded in the same way as the big intercontinental airships, by loading a container with passengers and then picking it up under a skyhook and lowering it through the top of the airship. The container was noticeably more full of people than I remembered at Huntingdon. I did find a seat but there weren't many to spare and there was no storage room for my bag on the container. So, like many others, I pulled it up onto my knees for the upward flight. Well, it was only going to take five minutes or so. Once the container was loaded and the doors opened I eased my way out into the airship proper. I did find a seat on the left hand side but it wasn't a window seat. I could, however, see through the window by looking across a couple of people who were more interested in each other than in what was going on around them. There were a fair few travellers, who just stayed in the container. They had a seat after all and probably already knew they would see absolutely nothing.

The panel above the window said that this airship was called the 'Heinrich Heine', and that he was a nineteenth century German poet and a bit of a celebrity during his lifetime. Various composers who are seriously highly rated nowadays set his poems to music, though it was uncertain whether they were 'hits' at the time. Did they even have the concept of a hit parade in the nineteenth century? I doubted that somehow. However, the plaque went on, he was certainly fêted in

Paris over the last half of his life, where he wrote satirical works. He is, of course, widely admired nowadays, at least partly because the Nazis hated him and publicly burned his books, while at the same time singing *The Loreley*, one of his lyric poems with a tune by Friedrich Silcher, at their boozy knees-up-and-boots-downs. This airship company had a neat sense of irony. I remembered a German acquaintance who predated Dietrich by several years once remarked, 'Who said we Germans have no sense of humour? When we make a joke, people die laughing.' I have never forgotten that, and when I tell it I usually put on a cartoon German accent. Bearing in mind what had just happened in Antwerp, perhaps it wasn't so funny at that moment in time.

The airship started to move and still no one showed the slightest interest in me, all well and good. I was still feeling sleepy and, the snooze in the pod not having proven adequate repose, it was not long before I nodded off in my seat.

It was probably a good thing that I hadn't found a window seat. I slept most of the journey to Edinburgh and if someone who really wanted to hadn't been able to see out of the window, then I wouldn't have been popular. I was woken by a fairly loud recorded voice telling anyone who wished to disembark at Edinburgh Airport to make their way to containers two and three. I found myself back in the same container I had been in when I came aboard. With groggy reluctance to leave my comfy nest, I pulled my case up onto my knees again.

As we started to move upwards to meet the skyhook, the voice with a definite, if soft, Scottish 'Morningside' accent told us that if we were being collected at the airport we'd need to get out of the container at the airport. Those wishing to travel to Edinburgh Waverley Station should remain in the container. Change at Waverley for all destinations beyond the city. And that was what I did. Within a further ten minutes I was out of the train and up on a platform, looking for a train travelling south towards London. Maybe all stations look the same, I don't know, but once again I only had to wander a short distance from the container train I was leaving to the train I wanted to get on to. I climbed aboard a carriage that appeared to be waiting to travel south and found a seat that didn't seem to have been pre-booked and plonked myself down in it. Wearily, I waved my wristy over the scanner beside the seat and it obligingly turned green – the

173

light on the slot that is, not the seat – acknowledging my booking and my payment. I was tempted to settle down and snooze a bit more but apparently I was finally all slept out. I wasn't going to sleep any more for the time being so all I could do was wait for the thing to depart. Once we were actually moving, I would send Shove a text and let her know I was on the last leg of my way home.

Chapter 22
In Which Steffy Crosses the Line

I have always liked the countryside of the Scottish Borders. I remember actually driving a car between Edinburgh and London when I was an articled clerk and the Island was still a single country. I was playing at being second chair to one of the partners, whom we clerks all nicknamed The Slug, on that occasion, would you believe? The Slug would only take an articled clerk with him to nice places if the clerk in question did all the driving so that he could safely fill himself with a rare local spirit. If you looked very carefully, you might also notice that these driving clerks were all young and female. He would expect them to generally arrange his entertainment when he wasn't actually working. If I remember rightly, it was the first criminal case I had been directly involved with, though I never uttered a word in court. My role was to know in advance which bit of paper The Slug would need next and pass it to him when he waved a hand at me. The case was about some well-heeled Scottish nob who had hired the firm to defend the indefensible. Our Slug, much to my shame, persuaded the jury that said nob was not guilty of screwing his secretary against her will and that their coupling had been totally consensual. As an aside, the Caledonian nob in question did get his come-uppance a little while down the line; his wife divorced him very expensively using exactly the same arguments that The Slug had used to get him off the rape charge, as he had proven beyond reasonable doubt that the sex was consensual. Oh, while I'm about it, even further on down the line, The Slug got his too, when the articled clerk of the week took a pistol to him. It was deemed in the subsequent court case to be justifiable homicide in self-defence. Now, why didn't I think of that?

That aside, the countryside around Edinburgh was beautiful and the hills were far more memorable than the objectionable little man for whom I had once worked. Back in the now, as we approached the border itself, it was fascinating to see from the top of the hill we were crossing that a tall wire fence had grown up on either side as far as I

175

could see. The train slowed right down, though it didn't stop until we reached the fence itself. A voice over the loudspeaker announced that all Scottish train crew should disembark now and would be replaced by an English crew. The cheery Scots barman with whom I had been chatting got off the train just in front of me. He caught my eye and grinned, 'Ye're at the mercy of the English now, hen. Good luck!' and he climbed out of the door.

Once the Scots left the train the English got on. Those that got on at our carriage seemed civil enough. The bar steward wore a similar smile as the Scot who had just got off and even had similar reddish hair but the accent that said, 'Good morning,' to us all was pure Geordie. Oh well, I never could understand the Geordie patois so I doubted I would have much of a conversation with him, though I hoped he understood Anglian, so at least my sandwich would contain what I expected when lunchtime came around in an hour or so.

The train started moving again, so presumably all the crews had handed over. The progress, however, was slow. 'Will everybody please return to their allocated seats and have their ID and ticketing available for inspection by UK Immigration Control?' came over the speakers.

'Oh crap,' said a young man in a cockney accent on the other side of the gangway. 'This is going to take for-fucking-ever. Why didn't we take a fucking airship, Boss?'

'Cos you know I don't like flying,' said the grizzled old man in mirror sunglasses sitting opposite him. Sunglasses in this light – what was the old fool thinking of? 'You in a hurry or somefink? It's not as if we've got nuffink to 'ide now, we've done the business, all done and dusted, so don't sweat kiddo, we'll 'ave a drink shortly just to pass the time. What you fancy?'

I couldn't help wondering who they were, a lesser London mobster and his minder no doubt. I just hoped the business didn't involve diamonds stolen from a greater European mobster from Peterborough. When I was using words like 'greater' and 'lesser' it was to describe importance rather than physical size. 'Mirror Shades' had a considerable belly on him, and you already know about The Rail's physical dimensions.

A group of soldiers in uniform, armed with submachine guns hanging lazily from their shoulders, came through the connecting door from the front end of the train. Leading them was a man wearing three stripes on each arm, declaring he was a sergeant. 'ID and tickets, please,' he said loudly, and everyone waved their wrists at him as he reached them. It looked like a bizarre, rather camp form of salute. Once he had looked at each one, and passed his sensor over them, he nodded and, having dealt with a passenger, he took no further notice of them. I wondered what would happen if someone did actually dig into their pocket and pull out a cardboard ticket or one of the old paper passports. Apart from his intermittent bark of 'ID and tickets, please' he never said anything – that was, until he got to me. 'Anglian, eh?' he said.

'Yes, that's right.'

'What were you doing in Scotland?'

'Coming home,' I replied, aware of the Londoners on the other side of the aisle sucking air in between their teeth. Oh joy! I was going to cause a delay.

'Where from?'

'Europe.'

'Europe's a big place.'

'Sure is.'

'Now, don't you start trying to be funny with me, girlie, I'm not in the mood for a pissing contest, especially with some piece of foreign fluff.'

'I'm not foreign, I'm Anglian.'

'Your lot decided to leave the UK so you're now a fucking foreigner as far as I'm concerned.' He turned round to one of the men-at-arms behind him, 'I think this bimbo needs further questioning in the holding area up the front,' he said. He turned back to me. 'You're going to have to follow the officer here down the train, and take some free advice – don't give him no lip, he's just had some very bad news and he isn't in the mood for no bunny from no one.'

He moved across to the Londoners and asked for their ID. Once the mouthpiece had moved on, the squaddie pointed his sub-machine gun at me and jerked it upwards, gesturing towards the front of the train. I got up and asked whether they wanted to see the contents of my bag. He nodded so I pulled it behind me. As I passed a couple of elderly ladies I distinctly heard one say to the other, in a gentle

Morningside accent, 'There's always one on every train, there's always one.' She even looked like how I imagined Jean Brodie would look, when I read Muriel Spark as a teenager, like a bulldog who had swallowed a wasp.

Once we were through the first class compartment, I was led into another carriage that was dressed even better than first class. The squaddie pointed to a single chair with his weapon and barked, 'Sit.'

I sat. Nothing very much happened so I asked the squaddie, affably and sympathetically, 'The officer further back said you'd had some bad news, do you want to talk about it?'

'No,' he replied sharply, and added a staccato. 'Shut it.' Well, I supposed I deserved that. It obviously wasn't going to be him that asked me the next set of questions. I wondered whether the Antwerp police had finally discovered Dietrich's body. If that was the case, it was an interesting observation that the English police had been contacted first rather than the Scots. I tapped my wristy, and was about to dial Shove, when the soldier said from behind my ear, and so close to it that I could feel the breath, 'Put that away or I'll confiscate it.' I did as I was told, as I could have sworn that it was the business end of his gun that had just flicked the back of my right ear.

Then there was silence. I could at least look out of the window at the countryside. It wasn't advisable for me to rummage around in my bag for my tablet to try to pick up on the news. I had no idea what the squaddie would do with that weapon slung round his neck if he was provoked, but the politest way I could think of describing his expression was 'grumpy'.

When he had no doubt explored the whole train, and without sending anyone else to join me down in his private first-class carriage, the original NCO reappeared and suggested to the surly squaddie that he should go and find himself a drink. How the conversation went after the squaddie left was surprising to say the least.

'May I apologise for the way I addressed you up there in the public area of the train?' he said. He sounded almost obsequious. 'I needed to make a bit of a show of moving you here like you were in trouble. We can't have everyone wanting to be upgraded now, can we? There simply isn't enough room for everyone in here, is there?'

My response was a simple, 'Huh?' What was he on about? 'I don't follow.'

'You're on my list here as one of Colonel Osborne's VIPs, and if your name crops up in England anywhere, you are to be assisted in any way possible; for me, that meant moving you into the Officers' Compartment. If an officer wants to travel on this train, he travels in here. Gotta do that, haven't I? Look,' he added showing me his pad, which had my face and the official page of my pass staring back out. I remembered having that picture taken, it was the only moment in the whole of that shoot that I was wearing even vaguely a straight face, and it was certainly the least flattering of the lot. Memo to everyone, don't take your best friend with you when you're going to have the photo for your pass taken, it can only end in giggles.

'Look,' I said, 'this is very flattering and everything, but I don't think I know anyone called Colonel Osborne. I know that that mugshot you've got is mine, but I would be very interested in knowing how you got it. And who, please, is this Colonel Osborne?'

The NCO looked at me with a very puzzled expression on his face. It had obviously never occurred before that someone he was upgrading wanted to know why they were being upgraded and then denied the reason he gave for doing so. Well, beyond the training manual, that was. 'Well, it's all here, shall we try to work it out?' he asked. 'Shall we at the very least order a drink or something? Tea? Coffee? Champagne? A cocktail perhaps?'

I decided on a coffee. The caffeine overdose to which I had subjected myself a few hours before appeared to have worn off but I asked for a decaf just in case. He spoke into his phone and then asked me if I objected if he sat down opposite me. 'I don't usually get to sit down in the Officers' Compartment,' he grinned. I told him I didn't mind and so he did.

For the time being I was amused by what was going on. I wondered whether this was a gag that Ben had put into the system. I had no doubt he had had access to my wristy. A mere forty-eight hours ago we had been completely naked together. I had taken my wristy off and completely silenced it before I wrapped it round the magazine of the Lee-Enfield I had just been firing. I didn't want anybody, and I did mean anybody, to disturb what was next going to happen.

However, if Ben had been the reason why my picture had ended up on the sergeant's pad, why had he blamed it on this Colonel Osborne? Ben outranked the sergeant in spades. Mind you, so did this mythical Colonel, even more so, if he existed at all.

'Before I start explaining who Colonel Osborne is, can I just explain to myself who exactly you are?' he asked. He said this without any threat so I didn't feel uncomfortable with my reply.

'Of course,'

'Shall we start at the beginning?' he asked smiling at me. 'Why were you in Scotland?'

'I was coming back from Europe, and it seemed to be as good a way in as possible at the time.' I decided to give him another piece of his jigsaw. 'There was an airship from Brussels to Edinburgh and a train from Edinburgh to Peterborough. That was the quickest route available this morning.'

'The Peterborough Marshalling Yard,' he said. 'The train stops at the Marshalling Yard, not in Peterborough itself.' Oh really? That was a facer. Still, it was only ten minutes across the border and I was sure I could summon a pod to the Marshalling Yard to pick me up. 'Anyway, I am sure that won't be a problem, so the next question is, why were you in Brussels?'

'On a job,' I replied. 'You will know from my passport that I am a licensed private investigator...'

'Ye-e-s,' he replied slowly.

'Well that's what I was doing in Antwerp, investigating.' Oh, that was a mistake, Antwerp had never come up in the conversation so far. Rule 101 of being a private eye – never give anyone more information than they ask for unless they're the client.

'Ant-werp?' he asked, separating the syllables as if he had never heard the word before, and raising his eyebrows as if he had hit on the nub of the problem. 'Who mentioned anything about Ant-werp? I didn't.'

'Antwerp is a seaport not far from Brussels, and the nearest airport is outside Brussels itself.'

'Really?' he asked and tapped his pad. 'It says here there's a place called 'Anverse' just north of 'Bruxelles',' and he pronounced the x as a very hard x. 'Are they the same thing?'

I explained that they were the French names for Antwerp and Brussels, and he mused, 'Why have I got French names in this?' and glared balefully at his pad.

I shrugged, 'Your guess is as good as mine as far as that's concerned.'

'So what were you doing in Ant-werp then?' he asked, not giving up yet.

'I have to say that that is confidential...'

He interrupted, 'That's not an answer.'

'It's the one you're going to get,' I replied drily. 'If I was doing a job for you, one of the things you would be paying me for would be my discretion.' At that point I had an idea, 'and if I was working for your Colonel Osborne, then I think it might just be the last thing he would be wanting me to do to be talking about it to all and sundry. Think, he had employed someone from the other side of the border to do his discreet investigating for him.'

'Oh yeah, no, quite, I get it,' he was obviously very flustered that I might be working for this elusive colonel of his, and I might be able to make things very difficult for him.

At this point a young man in a white jacket walked through the door at the engine end of the compartment, carrying a tray. 'One lattay, decaf, and one pint of Newkie Brown, Sarge,' he said. And put the tray down on the table, saluted, which looked vaguely ridiculous as he wasn't in any sort of military uniform, and walked away towards the back of the train.

I tasted the coffee. It was pretty ropy, to be honest, and tasted as if it had been made using instant coffee powder, but then he wasn't to know that I drank stuff made from freshly ground beans. I would drink it just to keep the NCO happy. I really hoped that he wasn't going to pick up on my sudden apparent knowledge of Colonel Osborne. The train pulled up in Newcastle station just as the NCO took a long pull on its most famous product. He sat back with a satisfied sigh and muttered, 'God, I needed that. 'Ere, don't you go telling no-one I was drinking on duty.'

I pulled an imaginary zip-fastener across my mouth and reassured him that my lips were sealed. I was now in control of this conversation and was wondering how I could persuade him to tell me about Colonel Osborne while not letting on that I had never heard of the man before

181

five minutes ago. Perhaps Ben was responsible for my being in the English system anyway, and this Colonel Osborne was the executive officer for the whole of North Mercia, and to put someone's name on a database required the approval of the local XO. That seemed reasonable logic. As you can see, I had learned quite a lot about how the local quasi-military police operated north of the border.

I looked out of the window at Newcastle station. It was tatty and I doubted that it had ever had any sort of facelift, maybe hadn't even been swept, since England bought itself out of the European Union with large sums of money that it never had in the first place. Whoever it was that owned Newcastle certainly didn't give a damn about what it looked like. Maybe they had made an effort with the city centre, who knows? I certainly wouldn't have any idea, at least on this trip. I decided to keep on the lookout for a job in Newcastle at some time in the future.

'Gotta just get out and stretch my legs on the platform,' he said. 'I'll be back before we leave Newcastle and if there haven't been any officers got in here at Newcastle, we'll carry on where we left off talking about the colonel.'

'And if one has?'

He shrugged, 'Maybe he'll talk about the colonel. If we're really lucky, he may even be the colonel.'

Chapter 23
In Which Steffy Reads a Real Book

'Gotta go walk the train again,' said the sergeant as we pulled out of Newcastle, having noted happily that we hadn't been joined by a junior subaltern in Newcastle and still had the compartment to ourselves. 'Do you need anything?'

'Can I use my wristy?' I asked.

'May I ask what for?' he replied

'I want to text my office to tell them where I am.'

'Feel free,' he replied and, with a 'see you soon,' he walked out the door. Yes, I thought, and someone's going to listen in on any conversation I might have, so I sent Shove a simple text to her private line which went, 'Leaving Newcastle Station, arriving Peterborough Marshalling Yard about three hours. Retxt when passing thru Newark for better ETA.' Newark was after the train's final stop at Doncaster so I supposed that at that point I would be about half an hour out. I opened my bag and got my tablet out to have a look at any news that was being broadcast officially. I wondered whether the news was different in England than we got in Anglia. If it wasn't, the whole island was having a really dull day. I looked at the sport just out of interest to see what was going on. The cricket news on the sport page told me that the Test Match at Trent Bridge in Nottingham had been snowed off, much to the amusement of one of the Australian commentators. There wasn't any comment on, or explanation as to the cause of, the unseasonal snowfall. There wasn't any real speculation either which suggested to me, cynic that I am, that the press was being muzzled. I tried to find the *Anglian Times* but that didn't seem to be available. Oh, well. Fortunate I had had a decaf, maybe I could try to have another zizz. That didn't work either so I got up and looked around the compartment to see if there was anything else to read in there. A short story would be ideal as, with a bit of luck, I would have it finished by the time I got to Peterborough. Fortune smiled on me, for in a locker between the windows, I found some real old-fashioned books made of card and paper. See how bored I was getting? I pulled out one of the older ones, just to feel it. It was so long since I had touched a real book; I'd only looked at the spines of Volffy's old volumes at home – it must have been ages since I had actually freed one from the bookcase. I riffled through the pages; yes, text only, no pictures, and it was in English. It also felt fragile and that if I wasn't careful it would come apart in my hands. I looked at the frontispiece, which informed me that the book was called *The Twentieth of July*, that someone called H. H. Kirst had written it, and someone called Maxwell Brownjohn had translated it from the German. I had no idea what it was about but, as I was so worried that it would come apart in my hands, I put it back. I flicked along the spines in the cupboard. Oh, there was one I knew, *The Daughter of Time* by Josephine Tey. It looked fairly recent, as it still had a dust jacket on it, and yet the book had been written in the nineteen fifties. I flicked to the information page and it told me that this copy was a reprint from 1992. Presumably they did hardback reprints of old classics in the nineties for the libraries. I continued scanning the spines of the books. Oh, hang on a minute, there was a book that didn't have a title on its spine. The dust jacket, however, looked new. I pulled it out and found that on the front of the dust jacket it read that it was a pre-publication proof copy. Opening it, the spine creaked as I looked inside – had anyone ever opened this book? And another question also occurred to me, 'Who is still publishing stuff on paper?' I know, I know, I should have guessed what it was as soon as I saw the dust jacket. It just had to be a copy of *A Pluperfect Murder*. It couldn't have been anything else, could it? I turned to the frontispiece and my guess was confirmed. There it was, *A Pluperfect Murder*, in the only format of the book that simply wouldn't vanish into the ether if summoned. It would have to be physically burnt to destroy it.

Once I opened the book I saw an *ex-libris* sticker, which told me it is the property of one Colonel Osborne and is a restricted document. I grinned slightly wolfishly and told myself that the sticker had got its tenses wrong. Sorry Osby, but this book is now mine. I reorganised the books so that it wouldn't appear that there was one missing and then pulled out *The Daughter of Time*. That would suit my needs perfectly. It was one of those books that I had read and reread on a number of occasions. It explained very honestly the old adage that 'history is written by the victors.' It asserted that yes, Richard, Duke of Gloucester and Prince Regent to Edward V, the boy king, did die at the Battle of Bosworth Field in 1485, but Tey's book went on to state that was the only true fact in the accepted story of the Tudor accession and that the 'Princes in the Tower' survived until they reached the age of majority, well into Henry VII's reign when, as an embarrassment to the Tudor rule, they disappeared, presumably on the orders of the Tudor king. I could almost argue her case off the cuff. I wrapped *The Daughter of Time*'s dust jacket around *A Pluperfect Murder* and placed Josephine Tey's masterpiece back on the shelf in the Landry book's plain cover.

So, I tucked into the story again, once more fascinated to discover whether I had been right as to whether Constable Gold would be collateral damage at 14% of the book. It would be more difficult to assess whether it was at exactly 14% by reading it in a physical book, although that could be done with the use of the calculator function on my wristy. But you could gauge easily enough whether it was early, in the middle of or late in the book when the deed was done. Then I would need to find out why this book was so restricted and how on earth it came to be secreted on the train, so get reading, that detective.

Well, I certainly wasn't far off with my prediction that Gold was a disposable character in the book. Certainly, in none of the DS Laking books that I had read had she ever worked with a partner and this was obviously to be no exception. Now that's a spoiler, but really only a little one, as anybody who has ever read any of her books will know that Melissa Landry really isn't very good at male heroes. She was one of those authors who wanted her heroines to be strong and empowered, and, in Laking's case, be seriously beautiful as well as whip smart. I wondered whether that was why I hated the character so much. At no time had she ever needed a man to support her, apart from to satisfy her urges and so often, as in this case, to be an early casualty in the novel to cause her some concern and temporary regret for something she might have done slightly differently.

I read on; okay, so Laking did stay on to discuss the case with the local Flemish police, and I chickened out, and that wasn't going to endear her to me either. Moreover, she explained that she was an

English police officer on a case, which the author explained, promptly made her an ally to the Belgians. I doubted that somehow. No one I'd met seemed to be particularly friendly towards the English at the moment, which was why I kept having to explain to everyone that I was Anglian, even to get a minimum of service in a bar. I checked to see if this declared itself to be a 'historical novel', you know, set in the early twenty-first century before the Brits threw all their toys out of their pram and told the Europeans they didn't want to play friendly games together any more. No, it didn't look like that. I would have to see how they got about, whether it was by pod or by car with someone formally driving it, and maybe the story of how Laking got back to Manchester might give us the answer. Was it a global warming-friendly way or not?

I went back to the book. Certainly the book was about a diamond theft, but that was really just a topic of conversation. She hadn't seen a diamond yet, even when she and Gold went to the Diamond Exchange just like Dietrich and I had. And then Gold had had his 'fatal accident', which transpired to have been a little more painful than Dietrich's, in that he had had the thumb and fingers of his right hand removed whereas, apart from having had his brains blown out, as far as I could remember Dietrich's body was intact. I found myself wondering why he had his right hand mutilated. Probably someone wanted his finger and thumbprints to access something that belonged to the Earl of Flint. There was a twist. Did the character Gold was playing actually exist in the world of the novel, or was he a fake character Laking had made up? Anyway, when the killer tried to use Gold's prints to get in somewhere he must presumably fail and that would put Laking in jeopardy too, which made it extremely similar to my own case. In fact, it more or less declared it was contemporaneous, as it stated that diamonds were a much more stable currency than any 'paper' money. The value of sterling, according to Landry, was all over the shop, and wouldn't pass as an international currency any more. It was interesting that she declared much the same for the Euro and the US Dollar. Well, she was an author from the province of the Duchy of Lancaster, so I supposed she had to show some loyalty.

How was Gold killed? He had appeared to have died of natural causes, the loss of his extremities weren't fatal, just very painful, and yet Gold was dead; only, of course, Laking didn't believe that. I was beginning to wonder whether Melissa Landry had written a poisoning with insulin into her book. There was this odd, nagging idea that she had actually described her own death. Was she killed by insulin poisoning? I sent Shove another text, suggesting that she ask Dr. Clark to check for fatal traces of insulin. I hoped she would understand 'Clark insulin OD?' which was the sum total of my text, and that whoever was spying on me, and I was sure there had to be someone, wouldn't make the connection.

I returned to the book, still uncertain why the novel that was a textbook on Melissa's own murder should be so officially proscribed. And also, why English officers were permitted to read it and, as far as I could tell, we Anglians weren't. That is, if the Anglian police services were permitted to read the thing, then Shove would surely have told me about it, wouldn't she? I read on, increasingly puzzled. I could understand them banning the book on the grounds of taste – it really was a badly-written pile of drivel and it was obviously popular because of the horny heroine, though at the same time the book wasn't in the slightest bit erotic, not that it was intended to be, as any sexual adventures she did have in the books I had actually read were 'off the page'.

I couldn't even judge whether any part of the book was geographically accurate, apart from Antwerp, but at least she appeared to have done her research there. As far as Manchester was concerned, well, your guess was as good as mine. Yes, I had been there, but it is a very big and cluttered place, and I have to say, I had no idea whether the streets she was talking about were where she said they were.

I stopped myself in mid rant and went back to just hating Sue Laking for being much prettier than I am and so insufferably tall. One other point that I found interesting was that diamonds seemed to have a much greater value in Manchester than they appeared to have in Peterborough or Antwerp. I wondered whether that was actually true. I supposed it was possible that they had some sort of rarity value I pondered, as the train pulled into York station and I closed the book displaying *The Daughter of Time* dust jacket to anybody who might look in. Just in time too, as only a few seconds later the sergeant walked through the door. 'Just popped in to see how you were doing,' he said.

'Fine,' I said, 'I've been reading.'

'Anything interesting?' he asked.

'Oh, it's an old detective story that claims that Richard the Third wasn't such a crook after all.'

'Oh, *The Daughter of Time*,' he said, 'Yeah, I've read that one too. Quite an entertaining read, provided you aren't expected to believe any of it. Do you need anything?'

I thought for a moment and then shook my head, 'Nope,' I said.

'See you shortly, and I'll come and talk to you about the colonel,' he said and clambered out of the train, walking off down the platform while I ducked as a piece of snow-covered rubbish flew past my window.

Chapter 24
Earworms and Memories

Various tunes from Volffy's record collection rolled round my head as the train made its way south. It hadn't been very long ago that Shove had produced the Bachman Turner Overdrive's LP 'Not Fragile' as our record of the night and I found the track 'Rolling Down The Highway' ridiculously catchy, even if it wasn't their biggest hit, which Shove assured me was 'You Ain't Seen Nothing Yet'. 'Highway', however, was the earworm for that journey. The problem was not really the earworm, it was more the quality of the book I was trying to read, and that was where the whole enterprise almost failed. I even wondered whether I should just say 'sod it' and read the Josephine Tey anyway. But, I reminded myself, I wasn't reading *A Pluperfect Murder* for pleasure, I was reading it for clues. The author had been murdered and I had taken on the job of solving that murder. It was part of the job I was being paid to do – finding the solution to a diamond heist.

A lieutenant had got into the compartment in York and my pet sergeant raised his eyes to the ceiling for a moment before he went and introduced himself to the young subaltern with, 'I'm the commander of the train, sir. Can I get you anything?'

The young officer didn't want anything, apart from knowing who the hell the popsy in mufti over there was. The sergeant explained that I was Colonel Osborne's personal guest and surely he didn't want to upset the colonel? The young man assured the sergeant that he didn't, but would he keep her away from him, as he didn't want accusations of any sort to be flying his way. The sergeant glanced at me to make sure I had heard, and I acknowledged him.

Somewhere between York and Doncaster I must have nodded off, as I was next aware of my surroundings when the train stopped at Doncaster. The lieutenant had obviously got off there – whether I had frightened him off, I had no idea. 'Well, that's that,' said the sergeant as he sat down again, just as the train started moving off. 'Next stop Peterborough Marshalling Yard.' He grinned at me and somehow I felt that it was the least friendly expression he had given me throughout our journey. Even when I thought he was arresting me on the far side of Newcastle, his expression hadn't felt so vulpine. It wasn't a smirk – those were just grubby – this expression somehow felt like 'lunch!'

I thought I might test this out and asked, 'Any objection if I text my chum at home and give her an ETA so she knows when to put the kettle on.'

He shook his head, 'I wouldn't bother,' he replied.

I gave him the dismayed look of surprise, 'Oh? And why not?'

'Well, before you get back home, you've got an appointment and I have no idea how long that is going to take.'

'Oh! And why don't I know anything about this appointment?' That was true. I really didn't know anything about the appointment either. My surprise wasn't an act.

'Because I haven't told you about it yet. I decided to wait until after we left Doncaster.'

'Why did you do that?'

'Because you looked so content sitting there and reading your book. I didn't want to spoil it for you.'

'So, who is it that I have an appointment with, then?'

'The garrison commander at Market Deeping has instructed me to bring you to see him when we get to Peterborough.'

I suppressed a giggle. So it was Ben all along! He was winding everyone up now, me included. And no, he was right, neither of us had any idea how long that one would take. Mind you, the thought of an imminent session with Ben made my being able to concentrate on Melissa Landry's disasterpiece even more difficult.

'I assume you know the garrison commander,' said the NCO.

'Yes, unless they've changed the commander over the last couple of days, I know him. What I wouldn't mind knowing is how he actually knows I'm on this train.'

'I told him, of course.'

'And how would you know that he might be interested? I wouldn't mind betting you didn't send him the details of everyone else on the train.'

'He hasn't got an APB out on other passengers on this train, only you.'

'Why has he got an all-points bulletin out on me?'

'I really don't know the answer to that one. It's going to be something for you to ask him yourself when you get to see him,' he consulted his wristwatch, how quaint, 'and that's going to be in about thirty-five minutes time. Incidentally, you've worked for him too, I gather.'

Well, that was one way to put it. 'Sure have,' I replied. Actually, it wasn't so far from the truth, we had first met when I was working on a job across both sides of the border and, being a civilian investigator, it was easier for me to potter backwards and forwards from one country to the other than members of the official police. I never quite worked out why Ben or Shove never put mufti on and crossed the border themselves. They wore civilian clothes at work often enough. Still, why should I complain, I got paid, didn't I? Moreover, I met up with a man who has given me a good deal of fun since we met. In fact, I would probably say that Ben has been the most fun since James, if in a completely different way.

James? I haven't mentioned him before, have I? James was the one man I ever loved. And yes, I was going to marry him. I was twenty-four at the time, still a clerk, articled to The Slug in London, and James – never Jim – was the kindest, gentlest human being on the planet. He even wanted to keep our relationship chaste till our wedding night. How sweet was that? I felt a little guilty about that, as I'd had my virginity taken from me at least ten years earlier, and had been less than chaste on a regular basis ever since. In fact, I may well have actually been engaged to James when I accompanied The Slug to Edinburgh to that fateful second chair episode. But James wanted our first night together to be our wedding night. I never found out whether that was going to be his first time ever with a woman or not, as someone else's wedding night finally brought the whole thing out into the open. He had been best man when one of his friends got married. The reception was at some stately home somewhere near the Forest of Dean on the Welsh borders, miles away from anywhere, and certainly neither of us were in any fit state to drive back to London. The problem was that he, as the best man, already had a room booked, and every other room in the place was booked solid. It was a magical night and romance was in the air or something, maybe someone had put an aphrodisiac in the punch, I don't know. One thing led to another, and if the best man wasn't going to sleep with the maid of honour, as I gather sometimes happens, thus freeing up her room for me to stay in, then his only other option was to sleep with his fiancée, which was going to happen soon enough anyway.

All went swimmingly until yours sincerely found herself with no clothes on and the scar on my tummy was visible for all, well, James anyway, to see. And needless to say, he asked, 'What's that?' His response was rather different to most people who had asked me that before. Most men I had been with were really rather relieved that I wasn't at all likely to end up pregnant following a night's physical activity. For James it was a disaster. I hadn't really realised that his idea of a marriage included a cottage on the South Downs with a white picket fence and three kids. The eldest would be called James Junior, the second would be a delightful girl called Rosalind and the third might be of either gender but, given the choice, it would be a spare boy, in case James Junior turned out to be of an arty frame of mind. It was, however, vitally important to him that he should have contributed to the gene pool from which these kids would appear, but what I hadn't fully understood was that his chosen mate should also have donated her fifty per cent to the concoction and no amount of harvesting my eggs, which I assumed I was still making in the one ovary I had left, and cooking them up in a surrogate, was an acceptable alternative. Once he realised that his great plan wasn't going to happen, sadly he lost interest, both that night in the activity that had found me naked to begin with, and after that night, in me. Six months later he had married someone else, who appeared still to be fertile, which she rapidly proved to be true. The children came along just as he required, with the exception that the spare boy turned out to be a spare girl, but James Junior, fortunately, is indeed intending to study law.

I was devastated. He was the only man I had ever considered living with as a couple my whole life. I don't consider living under the same roof as Mr. Grubbs as 'living with him'. Ever since James I have lived with women, and for the last ten years I have been living with Siobhan Flynn, whom I love dearly. I often wondered what might have happened if I had had any gay tendencies in my being but no, for my sexual gratification I require a man to be doing the gratifying. I have known that from the get go. Ben is ideal for that, I love the way he does sex, and there is no chance one of us is still going to be there as late as lunchtime the following day, but at the same time, we know it won't be too long before we get together again. It is the ideal 'friends with benefits' relationship.

The NCO said, 'So it was all about the major in Deeping then?' with a smile. 'Do you still want to know about Colonel Osborne?'

'I would always be interested in knowing something I don't out of principle but I'm not hugely concerned any more. Does that make sense?'

'It does.' He replied. He gave me five minutes on Osborne being in command of MI3, which was European Intelligence, and what they got up to in England.

'Includes Scotland and Ireland?' I asked.

'I would imagine so, and when your lot becomes a member of the EU again I imagine it would involve you too. I wouldn't worry too much about it. From what I understand, your lot and our lot are pretty friendly.'

I went back to the supposed *The Daughter of Time* once the NCO got bored with looking at me, having finished discussing spies and stuff, and wandered off to 'walk the train' again. I couldn't help thinking that the English citizenry were being really quite closely watched by their powers that be. His continual prowling round the train did not smack much of trust. Unable to conjure up too much interest in *A Pluperfect Murder*, I had a quick look at my tablet, just to check the news channel. I have no idea why I did it, call it a sixth sense if you like, but I did and there it was, in big capital letters, Yellowstone Explosion. And, in slightly smaller letters underneath, it read, 'possible extinction event'. Well, I'd known all that for the best part of a week and had rather assumed that it was because of the potential for unrest that it was being kept quiet. Now here it was, out in the open, with the big terror immediately in the headline. The censor was obviously asleep – either that or the poor soul had shat himself and didn't have any idea what to do with the news so he just threw it out there in terror. I had a quick look down the rest of the article to see what it actually said, but there wasn't really much else. It didn't say, for example, that the last extinction event caused by a volcanic eruption was the one at the end of the Permian epoch, and that one heralded the age of the dinosaurs some two hundred and twenty five million years ago. That particular event took several thousand years to wipe out the number of species that it did. A mere blink of an eye it may appear now, given that we're looking back as far as we are, but it really isn't going to shorten the lives of many people currently alive. It may change their standard of living a little perhaps, but for the moment, that's your lot. The other thing was that the brightest animal around at the time was probably the Dimetrodon, whose sole ability as far as controlling the climate was deploying its sail, through which it was thought to lose heat on a really hot day. It probably had the problem-solving ability of a house brick. We, however, might actually be able to turn the Yellowstone event off completely, which would be the first time an extinction event had been stopped by the resident fauna. I thought about that for a moment and then asked myself, how would we ever know? An 'extinction event that never happened' by definition never happened. Hell's teeth, the Gunpowder Plot is only remembered because the English really like to celebrate their failures, and a failed revolution is a far better reason to have a party rather than the successful one forty-odd years later.

I sent Shove an e-mail suggesting that she cast an eye over the e-news that they're slinging around north of the border, and that she might consider contacting the Senior Lecturer to warn him. I didn't disguise that one. It was more important that she got that message in clear language. Maybe it was also not a bad idea that the English realised that the Anglians were aware of the crap their press was dishing up to their populace.

At this time, you're probably concerned that you are listening to a middle-aged woman who knows all about dinosaurs. Well, a little bit anyway. A good private eye has got to be able to follow a conversation despite the roundabout way it is travelling. And there are men who used to be boys who were into dinosaurs before they got into girls. And there's an alarming thought for all of us. Boys got into dinosaurs before they got into girls. Though I seemed to remember there were girls in my class at school who could pronounce 'Ornithomimus' correctly too. I wasn't a hundred per cent happy with knowing that one of my predecessors in James's heart had very sharp teeth and weighed thirty tons. Sod it, they're welcome to each other.

The NCO wandered back into the compartment and said, 'Do you want another quick coffee before we come to rest at Peterborough, there's just about enough time?'

'Go for it,' I said, knowing that it would also give him an excuse for another swift Newkie Brown, and I felt more comfortable thinking his judgement might be slightly more impaired in the run-up to this meeting with Ben.

Chapter 25
Lionel, Richard and Ben

I stepped down from the train at the Marshalling Yard. They hadn't got round to building such mundane things as platforms at the MY, even for the first class carriages. Probably Anglia and North Mercia each thought the responsibility for such a construction should belong to the other. I could understand Anglia's point of view, they had a perfectly serviceable station two miles south with all sorts of platforms and everything if the Mercians wanted to use it. 'Follow me,' said the NCO in my ear, in a voice that would not tolerate my putting up a fuss. Not that I was going to, I was quite interested to see what was going on and anyway, I wasn't afraid of Ben so why should I be afraid of one of his sidekicks? He led me over to a rather tatty looking pod that had seen better days. It was interesting to see that this one had chipped paintwork. The pods in Anglia, and come to think of it in Flanders too, had never been painted in the first place. They were made out of duck egg blue glass fibre. This one had been painted, but I bet you'll never guess what colour? Got it in one, duck egg blue! And then it had been allowed to chip, which surely defeated the object of painting the poor little thing in the first place.

He dialled in the police station in Market Deeping and pressed the off button, as in 'off we go'. It appeared that not all the sensors on this pod were working either; one or two brown-coated labourers had to jump smartly out of our way, as the pod was showing no signs of slowing down, let alone stopping, as we approached them. 'Silly pillock,' said the amused NCO, 'should be looking where he's going.'

The pod drew up at the front end of the police station and he said, 'This is where we get out.'

'Aren't we going round the back to park in the car park?' I asked, remembering that we could get directly into the building from there rather than having to pass the bureaucracy of the front desk.

He knew what I was on about, as he reassured me that he would be able to take me straight through to the back, and 'besides,' he added, 'the car park is full of all sorts of other stuff; we'd never get in.'

So up through the main entrance we went, and the desk sergeant touched his cap to the NCO as he led me straight through into the back. No problem whatever. As we wandered down the corridor I saw the universal pictogram on a door that signified 'ladies'. 'Mind if I get rid of that coffee I've been filling up with since Edinburgh?' I asked. 'If I'm going to be grilled by the major, I might at least be comfortable while he's doing it.'

'Be quick about it,' he said, 'we don't want to keep him waiting, do we?' and that was definitely a leer he threw at me as I nipped through the door, pulling my wheelie case in with me. I was going to have a quick pee while I was about it but the real reason for my visit to the ablution block was a bit of a costume change, and also a surreptitious look out of the window at what was filling the car park below. That I did first. Oh, what! As the alien in that TV show might say, 'Fascinating!' The car park was full of three very large battle tanks, each with a very long gun coming out of the front of the turret. Was that what they called a naval gun? I wondered, as I removed my slacks to have a pee and, having performed to nature's requirements, folded them into my case, wrapping them round *The Daughter of Time*, err, *A Pluperfect Murder*. Out of the case came the short skirt, which had travelled all over Europe with me waiting for its moment to come, and I exchanged my sneakers for a rather natty pair of slush boots I had bought before I left in case the snow actually started lying. They covered my ankles and the bottom of my calves and had an imitation fur lining that poked perkily out of the top. I hadn't got any stockings or tights with me so I would have to go bare legged. If that was a problem, I had seriously misread the situation. There wasn't a full-length mirror in the loo, so I just had to hope that the effect was okay. I ran a comb through my hair, snapped the case shut, and sauntered out. As the NCO was already wearing a leer when I went into the loo, I had no idea whether the costume change met with his approval or not. There was no discernible change in his expression. To be honest, I really didn't give a damn what he thought. The only approval I wanted was from the man on the other side of that door.

'I've got Miss Flack here for you, sir,' the NCO said loudly into the intercom following his application of a sharp rap on the door.

'Send her in,' came from the speaker, 'and thank you for your efficiency, Corporal.' That was tantamount to a dismissal. There was nothing in Ben's tone that suggested that the NCO was invited in too.

'Sergeant,' he muttered glumly. 'I'm a fucking sergeant.' It was not said loud enough for Ben to hear. At least I imagine that was what he hoped. His mouth wasn't far from the microphone when he swore. He turned on his heel without looking back at me while I slipped through the door, shutting it behind me.

'Steffi! Poppet!' came a shout from the desk. 'You changed! When did you have time to do that? Come here, you gorgeous thing, and let me look at you properly.' He wasn't in uniform today and looked all the better for that. It was definitely a civilian pale blue shirt he was wearing and, from the way it clung to him, he wasn't wearing a lot underneath. Not a man for string vests is our Ben.

Of course, I didn't stop when I got to the position where he could 'look at me properly', I continued on in to the full contact position and we settled down to some in-depth osculatory exercises. He grabbed me by my waist and swung me up so that I was sitting on the edge of his desk, with my legs dangling down, swinging gently.

'Lionel! Richard!' he addressed my knees. 'Great to see you again, guys, I haven't seen you dressed like that since forever.' He kissed both of them in turn most appreciatively. 'So, luscious lady, what have you been doing since we last met?'

'I have a feeling you know the answer to that,' I replied drily, 'you seemed to know that I have just done a costume change. And why do you call them Lionel and Richard?' I was all breathy and excited-girly; he usually liked that.

'Well the left one is Lionel with all the L's, and the right one is Richard with its R's. Simple really.'

'Look, in case you hadn't spotted it, I'm a woman so why not call them Louella and Rosa?'

'Cos you didn't name them and I did.' He kissed them again just to make sure I wasn't cross or anything. 'And talking about the costume change, I have been watching out for you since you came through the front door and then you appeared at my door looking completely different.'

I would probably have been relieved that they didn't appear to have a camera in the ladies' loo if I had bothered to think about it. I also wasn't sure I would care to mention the tanks I had seen out back, not yet anyway. So I told him that I had avoided death at the hands of a Flemish murderer during the past couple of days. He looked adorably aghast. 'Oh, my poor little Poppet, what would I have done without you and those beautiful knees?'

'I'll leave them to you in my will if you like,' I cracked.

He shuddered, as if thinking about receiving just my disconnected knees in a package from my lawyers, then shook his head to clear it and said, 'Follow me,' opening the door behind the desk. 'I have an on-call ready room back here,' he added with a gentle smile. I followed him. The room didn't have a lot in it, but what it had was functional. There was a large bed with a bedside table on either side and an old-fashioned telephone with a dial on the right hand one.

'Does that still work?' I jerked a thumb at the phone.

'I haven't the faintest idea,' he replied, 'I always have my wristy with me if I'm sleeping here.'

I grinned at him and said, 'And how many women have you brought in here to have your wicked way with then, hmm?'

'Believe it or not, sweet thing, you're the first. What my predecessor got up to in here I have no idea, but you're the first during my time. I think the room thinks I'm not interested in that sort of thing. Sorry room, prepare yourself for a bit of a shock,' he said, unbuttoning my top. Of course, he was close enough for me to do the same to him, so I took the opportunity.

For a while, time seemed to be deliciously irrelevant, and I had no idea how long it was before he started stretching. I wasn't sure if he was going to work up to a repeat performance. We had been there before but no, on this occasion he didn't. Instead he walked over to the chest of drawers beside the window. 'Steff,' he said in a tone of voice that I hadn't heard often from him before, sombre and serious. He tossed a diamond at me. 'What do you think of that?'

It was huge. Certainly it would have impressed Mr. Jacoby and would probably have impressed The Rail. Colour me impressed, anyway. Hang on a moment, I thought, The Rail? Was this one of her diamonds?

'What's this?' I asked.

'It's a diamond, what does it look like?'

'Oh, it looks like a diamond, but then I have been shown recently that, just because a stone looks to Mr. Average like a diamond, doesn't actually mean it is one.'

'Take it from me, that's a diamond, and if my information is correct, rather a good one.'

'Where did it come from?'

'You're asking me where I got it?'

'Uhuh.'

'I don't think I want to tell you that, certainly not yet anyway. What I do want to ask you is what you would do with a stone like that?'

'Well I understand that they're a very stable form of currency at the moment, certainly much more stable even than the US Dollar or the Euro. Local businesses from my side of the border trade with The Rest-Of-England in diamonds rather than Sterling for example.' I hoped he didn't hear the hyphens and the rather contemptuous way we Anglians sometimes talk about what was left of the 'United Kingdom'.

'Yes, we know that Sterling has declined steadily in value over the past few years…'

'It's not its steady decline that's the problem,' I said firmly. 'It's the fact that it's so unstable. We don't know from day-to-day what the damn thing is worth. Because of that nobody will trade in it, and thus its value drops even further.'

'So what do you use in Anglia? Oh, that's right you use Anglian Credits, and they follow the Euro.'

'We use all sorts of things, including Bitcoins and, bringing the whole conversation round in a full circle, diamonds. The local Asians also use Pakistani Rupees.'

'So you do use diamonds?'

'Personally I don't – the sort of business that is transacted using diamonds is usually of high value. People don't usually want to talk about hiring a private eye, so don't want to spend loads of money doing it.'

'So you don't use diamonds then?'

'Not often, no.'

'So what would you do if I offered you that one then?'

'I would ask you what on earth you wanted me to do for it.'

He took the stone back off me and continued, 'I know this guy up in Sheffield who's a goldsmith. If I were to ask him to set this stone in a gold band, would you consider wearing it for me?' I suddenly realised that this ludicrous naked man was on one knee with a precious stone in his hand and was proposing to me. I had always imagined that most women had some sort of inkling that a proposal was on the way long before it actually happens. I know, when it finally arrived, I had been expecting James's proposal for some considerable time – in fact, I was worried I had sort of willed it out of him by some kind of mystic telepathic force. This one, only the second proposal I had ever received from a man who was still sober, I hadn't been expecting at all. And to be honest, it wasn't a proposal I particularly wanted. It suggested to me that he wanted more out of this relationship than I did. At least it wasn't about kids; he knew well enough that I no longer had the equipment still on board that was required for the construction of sprogs.

'Whoa,' I spluttered, 'that's a bit of a facer. Can I think about that one?'

'You mean you don't want to?'

'No,' I said and quickly added, 'No, that's not what I am saying. It's just that I had never really thought about it. I had got kind of used to us popping in and out of each other's lives when the mood took us. You know it will change the nature of our relationship quite considerably if we get married. For example, one of us is going to have to change our nationality, can you still be an English major if you hold an Anglian passport?'

'I haven't the faintest idea,' he replied. 'I was rather thinking that it might be you who might change your nationality,' he was beginning to sound uncertain, 'after all, you have been English before,' he looked me up and down, 'and it doesn't seem to have done you a lot of harm.'

I pointed to the rather scrappy emergency midline scar on my lower abdomen and gave him a dry, 'Oh yeah? That happened when I was English.'

A noise of rotors whirring came from outside the window. He walked over to it and peered out. 'Oh, come and look at this,' he said. 'I'm sure you'll find it interesting.' I could see through the window a skyhook coming in from the north, though I didn't recognise the cylindrical looking thing suspended underneath it. I walked closer to the window, wrapping myself in the curtain to hide my nakedness from anyone who might be outside looking up. Ben wasn't that bothered. Men! Always boasting. The long, slender cylinder slung underneath the skyhook was slowly lowering into the car park. 'What is that thing it's carrying?' I asked.

'It's a fuel container,' he said, 'for the tanks.'

'Huh?'

'They're diesel-powered,' he said, 'That's what's in that cylinder, diesel fuel.'

'Diesel?' I may even have spluttered, 'but that's illegal.'

'Listen, Poppet, the people who make the laws for this little patch of the Earth also own those tanks so I guess they feel they have a right to waive the regulations if they find them inconvenient.'

The skyhook had now lowered the cylinder into the car park, where a number of squaddies helped it nestle into a rack between two of the parked tanks. That was a really impressive piece of flying by the skyhook pilot. The gap between the tanks was hardly greater than the diameter of the cylinder, and yet the pilot plopped it between the tanks without it making contact with either. Nicely done. The opportunity had come to ask him about the tanks. 'What are these tanks all about, then?' I asked.

He grinned at me, 'The name's Ben, not Then.' But he continued without a pause. 'They're here on exercise.'

'Oh?' The question mark was louder than the word that preceded it.

'The English government is concerned that there may be a little, shall we say, unpleasantness on the way with the Europeans, something I imagine caused by that stroppy American volcano, and they want to be prepared.'

I thought about that for a moment. 'Surely if anyone was thinking of invading then the first history lesson at school will tell them that the place to do it is the Home Counties' south coast.'

203

'The Danes didn't, a thousand years ago and change. They even succeeded in their conquest. England ended up with a Dane on the throne who then used the East Anglian coast as an exercise to see if he could drive back the sea by sheer willpower alone.'

'Oh, Canute, you mean?'

'Clever girl, you remembered your schoolwork. Now, supposing there is a Dane who thinks he has got the pushing back the sea problem licked, where better to try it out than along the shoreline of The Wash? I suppose the Vikings could also be getting stroppy too, although they tended to invade North Yorkshire and Northumbria. But let's look at the Danes for a moment. Have you Anglians got any of those tanks down there?'

'Not that I know of.'

'So how are you likely to see off a marauding Scandi looking for cheap plunder?'

'I imagine Norwich and London have some sort of trade agreement in place about us continuing to provide you with energy and food in exchange for you protecting us from wild and woolly barbarians.'

'No doubt. However, the last uninvited invasion the island ever had to put up with was when the Normans arrived on the south coast at Hastings.'

'Uninvited?' I asked, realising he obviously knew something I didn't.

'Well, William of Orange invaded in 1688, but the general consensus was that the British government invited him to try his luck doing so. He and James II then had a very peculiar battle during the course of which, from what I understand, both of them tried to surrender to the other. In the end Parliament told William to stop shilly-shallying about and to get his b.t.m. up on that throne or else there would be real trouble. Anyway, that's why I only got three tanks. It's just possible that the Europeans might get tricky and try to fool us. It's our job to hold them off in the saltmarshes until the tanks can be brought back from Hastings or wherever. So these babies are out on exercise today. I've got to learn how to command them.'

'Is that difficult, commanding a tank?'

'The trick is, like everything in the Army, not to let on to the squaddies that you haven't the faintest idea what you're doing. If the men get that from you, you haven't a hope.'

I giggled, 'That's why you're showing those private soldiers down there that you've got privates too.' I walked back to the bed. 'So where did this diamond come from, then?' I asked.

'It is taxation revenue,' he said and I knew that wasn't true.

'It was stolen, wasn't it?' I said firmly.

'There are people who say that all taxation is theft, that's what the American Revolution was about in 1776. Remember the Boston Tea Party?'

'"No taxation without representation," yes, I know that one but I am going to squeeze you a little harder here – who was "taxed" for this payment in diamonds?'

'You mean you think it might have been one of your clients?'

'The job I have been working on the past few days has involved stolen diamonds and they were taken from Peterborough, which is in Anglia not North Mercia, so any taxation that might accrue from their value would not come to this side of the border.'

'Is that an accusation, my favourite doll?'

'I don't know, is it? What I am asking you is, do you have some papers of provenance for that diamond? Did it belong to someone called Adelina Paravilyenko?' See? I did remember her name.

'Doesn't sound like an Anglian name.'

'She was originally Slovakian,' I explained.

'Doesn't sound Slovakian either,' he mused. 'Sounds Ukrainian to me.' He was reminding me that he wasn't some sort of numbskull, but a rather attractive pongo officer, who was a more than competent detective in his own right.

'Her husband was Ukrainian, and she took his name.'

'Was?' Detective Ben continued.

'Yes, he's dead and no, she didn't kill him, he died of old age some time ago.'

'So this Adelina Whatshername is an old lady then?'

'Not especially, about my age I would think, there or thereabouts.'

'Should I be thinking eww?' he asked. 'Old man with child bride, icky stuff?'

'I would think it was none of anyone else's business. Having met the woman, I am convinced that nobody would make her do anything she didn't want to do. Are you trying to avoid my original question? Is this Adelina's diamond?'

He looked at me and shrugged. 'It could be,' he replied. 'Is that a problem?'

I didn't know. Was it? 'Well if it is, then I will have to explain the situation to her and return her retainer. If I have to do that, I suspect that your government owes me my expenses at the very least.'

'Let me know how much we owe you and I'll discuss it with Colonel Osborne.'

'Colonel Osborne? That name keeps cropping up today, who exactly is he?'

'He's the head of MI3.'

'MI3? Does that still exist? Nobody has talked about any of the MIs apart from five and six since forever.'

'Three was set up during the Second World War to deal with European intelligence, and most of it was subsumed into MI6. However, it was only mothballed, and when Britain pulled out of the EU, and bits kept falling off the edge of the country, it was revived with Colonel Osborne in command.'

'Should you be telling me all this?' I asked carefully.

'I've asked you to marry me, I don't think we should have secrets do you?'

'And this Colonel Osborne organised the theft of Adelina's diamonds.' That was definitely a statement and not a question.

'If this diamond is one of hers then yes, it would have been collected by one of Colonel Osborne's men,' he paused, 'or women. There are some very dangerous women working for MI3. You might even be one of them soon.'

This whole conversation had been carrying on without either of us wearing a stitch of clothing. It was about as erotic as cold porridge and my nakedness was beginning to feel awkward. I walked back into the office and wheeled my bag into the ready room. I took out my slacks and wriggled into them. He didn't stop me.

'Where are you going?' he asked.

'I have to go back and clear things up with her before I do anything else, don't you think?' I tossed the diamond back at him, which he deftly caught despite being halfway through pulling up his trousers. 'Satisfy my curiosity – why does your Colonel Osborne have copies of Melissa Landry's *A Pluperfect Murder* when, as far as Anglia is concerned, it never existed.'

'Simple,' he replied, 'It was the textbook he used for all the diamond "collections" he has been doing around Britain.'

'And was it also the textbook for all the various hits during those thefts, for example the hits using insulin?' I asked.

'Quite possibly,' he said. Maybe he was shuffling his feet out of awkwardness as to where the conversation was going or maybe he was just trying to get his shoes back on.

'Including the failed hit on me?'

Ben turned round crossly to face me. 'Look, woman, it's quite possible that you were on Osborne's hit list, yes. And I really want you not to be on his list. I want you to be safe and the safest place for you right now is here with me. At the same time, I'm not going to force you to do anything that you don't want to do. I do think, however, that you probably haven't got very long to come to a decision.'

I nodded at him. 'I take your point. I promise I'll think about it very seriously. Meanwhile, I do have to go back to Peterborough to clear things up with Adelina and also to sort things out at the office. The kids haven't seen me for the last couple of days and I need to touch base with them. How about we reconvene the day after tomorrow to discuss this further?'

He gave me one of those melting looks that usually result in my whipping off all of my clothes and falling on him like a rabid hyena. It didn't have that effect this time, and he said solemnly, 'I'll summon you a pod.'

Chapter 26
Steff, Shove and Dwayne Work It Out

The pod that pulled up outside the police station looked just like the tatty little pod that I had travelled in a couple of hours previously, right down to the peeling paint. As it was taking me to the border point at the Maxey Cut, at least it wasn't scaring the brown-coated Happy Harries in the railway yard this time.

'May I check the pod?' asked the border guard on the Anglian side of the Cut. 'We've had one or two of these come through here which are not in a fit state to be allowed on the road on our side of the border,' he explained with an apologetic smile on his face. He wandered round the pod with some sort of electronic sensor on a stick, the like of which I'd not seen before. When he finished he came back to the window. 'I'm afraid I'm going to have to ask you to step out of the pod, madam,' he said. 'As I suspected, this pod is not fit for Anglian roads. If you wait in my cabin, we'll summon an Anglian pod to take you on from here.' I climbed out and went into his little cabin from where I saw him climb into the pod and take it back across the border. He then got out, had a cheerful word with the border guard on the North Mercian side, and sauntered back over the bridge into Anglia.

He walked into the cabin. 'Sorry about that,' he said. 'About half of its proximity sensors were not working. I could practically have guaranteed you an accident by the time you had got to the town centre if you had carried on in that ruin.'

'Why do they allow it on the road on their side of the border, then?'

'Well, they've got much less traffic on the roads over there, and most of what they do have are manually driven container trucks anyway, so the chances of two of them actually wanting to occupy the same piece of real estate at the same time are not that high. We have so many pods in Anglia that, without properly working proximity sensors, there would be mayhem on our roads, as they would be forever crashing into one another. That would cause an increase in hospital bills, and the rest, so we don't allow substandard pods on our roads.'

'Why do they?' I asked again.

'I guess, like everything else, even life is cheaper over there,' he mused for a moment and continued. 'I suppose it's something to do with the priorities of how they spend what little money they do have,' he paused again. 'Coffee?' he asked.

'Is it going to take that long coming?' I asked.

'I'm a great believer in Sod's Law,' he said, and continued in explanation, 'If I make you a really nice cup of coffee, then a pod will be along before you have a chance to drink it. If I don't, then the pod will take ages to come and we're going to spend some really awkward time trying to find something to talk about, and wishing we'd had that cup of coffee all along.'

'I'd love one then,' I replied with a chuckle and introduced myself. 'Steff Flack,' I said, offering him my hand.

He took it. 'Constable Daniel Whitton, Anglia Border Police,' he replied.

'Via Widdecombe Fair,' I chuckled, remembering the old Wessex folksong. He looked perplexed at that so I let it go. I liked this chap. It wasn't much of a life being a border guard here. It was a solitary job, though I couldn't help thinking that if any trouble were to happen at that post, the guards on both sides of the bridge would band together and sort it out between them. Maybe one of them was even called Tom Cobbleigh, and maybe he was someone's uncle, who knows? After all, I had seen the quick amiable chat they'd had when he returned the pod to them just now. There hadn't been any tension there at all. I wondered whether their rifles took the same size of ammunition. That would be handy.

Actually, I had half finished the best cup of coffee I'd had since Antwerp when the pod drew up outside the cabin, and Constable Whitton put his head round the cabin's door. 'Your chariot awaits, Madame,' he said with a little bow.

The pod that awaited me was clean and comfortable, and Anglian through to the last stud in its leatherette seat. I could even imagine my wheelie-bag letting out a satisfied 'ah' as it settled into the luggage rack behind my seat. My first stop was home, just to unload the bag and to give Mrs. Grubbs a 'Hi, I'm home,' before I pottered round to my office to see the kids.

I had been away the best part of two days, and yet Dwayne and Sabrina didn't appear to have moved a muscle since I last saw them. He was still perched on the edge of her desk looking into her eyes when I walked through the door. He scrabbled to the floor, jerking upright as if I had caught him he doing something he shouldn't have been doing. Heck, I had no problem with Dwayne and Sabrina having a thing, though I wasn't sure what her family would think, him not having a drop of Muslim or even Asian blood in his body, that is unless he had become a vampire and had started drinking from Sabrina's neck.

'So, Boss,' he said with a cheerful and rather forced grin, 'how did it go?'

I pulled over a chair from the wall and sat on it in the middle of the floor. 'Well, I know where the diamonds have gone and I know what happened to *A Pluperfect Murder*– I've even got a copy,' I gave them the expurgated version of my travels, but did include my trip to the Antwerp Hospital in my narrative.

'See, I told you you should have taken me with you,' remarked Dwayne. 'You need looking after, Boss, and Duh-wayne's your man if you need looking after.'

'I'm sure you're both glad that I didn't. You will notice that Dietrich didn't come home with me. I now have to telephone Shove and tell her I'm home before going to see Adelina and giving her the bad news.'

I walked into my office and closed the door. 'Hi Shove, it's me,' I said into my wristy.

'Where the hell are you? I've been waiting forever for your call.'

'I'm now in my office in Cathedral Square,' I said and explained that I had become delayed in Market Deeping but, once again, I didn't go into unnecessary details as to what I had got up to. 'Have the Flemish police been on to you yet?' I asked.

'Surprisingly enough, no, I haven't heard a cheep out of them.'

I proceeded to give her a moderately expanded version of my adventures and asked her whether she would rather I went to see Adelina first or formally reported in to her, so that we could at least report Dietrich's demise officially.

'Can you come here on your way to Adelina's?' she asked. 'That way I will have your story straight if I do suddenly get large quantities of phlegm landing on me from a great height.'

Eww! I thought. 'On my way,' I said. I was summoning a pod as I walked through the waiting room when I noticed that Dwayne was once again perched on the edge of Sabrina's desk. He was, however, staring at me this time. 'Do you want me to come along too, Boss?' he asked.

'Why not?' I replied. 'I could use the company.' I turned to Sabrina, 'When you've finished, Sabrina, why don't you potter off home? After Dwayne and I have been to Thorpe Wood, we'll be off to The Borscht to see Adelina and then we'll close down for the night. I'm beginning to feel quite tired myself.'

I could see Dwayne and Sabrina exchange a smile as we walked through the door and I realised that I might have to solve something there with her family. I had come to some sort of agreement with them when I took her on. Offhand I couldn't remember exactly what its terms actually said but I was fairly convinced that it would have included ensuring that she didn't become emotionally involved with anybody while in my employ and, while it wasn't actually specified, I was certain that that would have included my sidekick if they had found out.

Crossing town out to Thorpe Wood took about ten minutes, and the pod pulled up in front of the police station, where we walked up the steps and presented ourselves to the desk sergeant. 'Stephanie Flack for chief Superintendent Flynn. We're expected.'

The sergeant glared at Dwayne. 'And he is?'

An Irish brogue came from out of nowhere, 'My present'. That was the chief of police's voice.

The desk sergeant snapped to attention with almost military precision, And that wasn't a 'Sah!' that came out of his mouth, was it? Maybe I was just getting too used to police playing at little boy soldiers from my recent experiences across the border.

'Come on through, you two,' and she led us into the bowels of the building. 'By the way, Dwayne,' she added, 'Your PI licence will need renewing shortly so, if you've got your wristy on, I can do it while you're here.'

'As if it's likely that I won't be wearing my wristy,' he said, and I could almost feel the grin on his face while he said it, though I wasn't even looking at him.

She led us though into a small interview room. Interesting, not her office, and it had a one-way mirror in the wall behind her. Was this a formal interview – were we being watched? 'Tell me about this Dietrich?' she started, once she had stopped fiddling with Dwayne's wristy and returned it to him. 'Where did he come into the picture?' She obviously sensed that I, for one, was feeling a little uncomfortable. 'Oh look, I'm sorry about this but if the Belgians do get difficult, at least I will have something on video to refer to.'

'Are they likely to get difficult?' I asked.

'You tell me, you're the one who was recently in Belgium...'

'Flanders...'

'Flanders, quite, and you're the person who abandoned a dead German in one of their hotels.'

'Boss!' It was Dwayne's turn to sound shocked.

'Guilty as charged, as far as leaving the scene of the crime, but I had nothing to do with the killing.'

'Oh, I know that, but we're still going to need to have something for them to look at in case. Do you mind?'

No, I didn't mind. After all, she wasn't going to hand me over to an angry sprout any time soon, so we went through my adventures in Antwerp and what led up to them, starting at the meeting with Dietrich at The Borscht café on Lincoln Road and finishing with us sitting here in the interview room. It even included the train journey south from Scotland and my introduction to the tanks in Market Deeping. The only bit I left out was the slice of horizontal activity in Ben's ready room.

'And your thoughts as to who might be responsible for it all?' she asked.

'I suspect that Colonel Osborne has a squad out there following me. Does that sound paranoid? Just because you're paranoid,' I began.

'It doesn't mean they aren't out to get you,' she completed. 'Go on.'

'I appreciate he didn't start out by following me. He started out chasing the diamonds. I got involved very early though. When Adelina came to see me...'

'Adelina?'

'Adelina Paravilyenko. When she asked me to find her diamonds, then I was involved too.'

'Satisfy my curiosity, as I have an open murder case on my desk, that of Farrukh Ahmed.'

'Ruke?'

'Now I appreciate you will have very little interest in what happened to him, and in all probability hope that it hurt, but he is part of an open case.'

'I don't particularly want for him to have died in pain,' I replied for the camera. 'Though I can't say that I'm particularly sad that he's dead.' I was aware that Dwayne was watching both of us with his mouth flapping open, not believing what he was hearing. 'He was Adelina's courier, so if he was carrying the diamonds at the time when Colonel Osborne's man took possession of them, then it's a reasonable assumption that that was when he was hit.'

Shove nodded. 'That's how I read it too. Do you have any evidence to support that?'

'None whatever, apart from Occam's razor.'

'The simplest solution is usually the right one,' chipped in Dwayne to show he was listening.

'Pretty much,' I agreed.

'I think I should come with you when you go and see this "Rail" friend of yours,' Shove remarked.

'If you go there dressed like that, you can't expect me to be responsible for your safety.' I replied drily.

'Huh?'

'In uniform,' I clarified. I know that the police had dropped in from time to time when it was still Lev's café. They got a lot of street scuttlebutt from the old man. I wasn't quite so sure about how things stood now his widow and Shove were running things on either side of the fence.

'That's something I can alter in an instant,' she replied. 'Wait here.' She disappeared out of the door.

'So what happens now?' asked Dwayne.

'I think we're taking the chief of police to The Borscht, and once we walk through Adelina's front door, your guess is as good as mine. Stay alert.

'We lerts always do,' it was an old joke but one that always seemed to give Dwayne pleasure, so I let it fly.

It took Shove about two minutes flat to do a complete change of outfit, most impressive. I wondered whether she had ever done revue when she was at cop school. That was the sort of show that taught you the art of speedy costume changes. 'What do you think?' she asked.

'Do you keep a complete wardrobe here in your office?' I asked.

'Pretty much, you never know when you're going to need to look completely different, especially if you're the plod in charge. There are times when I need the authority of a uniform and times when I need the discretion of mufti. And then again, there are times when I am going out to an event straight from work and I need a ball gown.'

'You keep a ball gown in your office here?' I asked.

'Sure do. Volffy was forever dropping surprise dinner dates on me when I was still fairly low in the pecking order, so I always kept something fairly swish in my locker in the girls' changing room, just in case. Come kids, let's go and beard this Adelina in her den.'

So, while she summoned a pod to the front door of Thorpe Wood, I phoned Adelina to tell her I was on my way with news, though I didn't explain what it was.

Chapter 27
In Which Adelina Faces the Truth, and Tells Some Truths of Her Own

A pod was waiting for us when we got to the steps in front of the main entrance so, if it wasn't our pod, then the person who had buzzed it would have to wait for the one Shove had summoned, and who was going to argue with the chief of police on the front steps of the Thorpe Wood cop shop? It didn't take the three of us long to cross town, and as I was outvoted two to one as far as the curtains thing was concerned, I had to lump it and just screw my eyes shut as we did so.

The door of The Borscht was ajar and we walked straight in. Adelina was sitting at the table two thirds to the back of the room and Yuri and the waitress-on-display were watchfully present.

Adelina obviously knew exactly who Shove was, so the costume change had been a pointless exercise. 'You have brought her here exactly why?' I was acidly asked.

I chipped in, 'Shove is my friend and she has come with me to help me tell you some bad news.'

'I did not hire you to have friends in the police,' she replied acidly.

'No, my friends in the police, like my taste in music, predate my being taken on by you. You hired me much more recently to find your missing diamonds and who killed your courier.'

'And have you?'

'Up to a point.'

'In other words, no, so you bring a policeman here to my café as a present instead.' The tension in the room was ramping up at a rate of several degrees a minute.

'I didn't bring her as a present, she came as my friend to tell you what I found out and also to offer her assistance.'

'So she's your friend, you say?'

'Yes.'

'Prove it.'

At this point, I felt I needed to defuse a situation that was threatening to detonate. The waitress was inscrutable but Yuri seemed ready for action, and I felt he was probably going to be handier than Dwayne if it came to a fight. I turned round to Shove, pulled her close to me and kissed her full on the mouth. I had never actually kissed a woman before, not like that, anyway, and it felt different. She was softer than Ben, not flabby or anything like that, but she was firm rather than hard. What she was going to do now remained to be seen. Was she going to hit me, or ask me fiercely what the fuck I thought I was doing? To my relief, she kissed me back. For a moment we remained locked together, then she pulled gently away, and turned and faced Adelina. 'That sort of friends,' she said. 'We care.'

Adelina looked up at Yuri and nodded at him, and he sat down beside her at the table. 'So!' she said and nodded at the girl. 'Vodka,' she said. She looked at Dwayne for a moment and asked with a grin, 'He is old enough?' Yes, Shove had been accepted.

'He's a big boy,' said Shove.

'Vodka for everybody,' commanded Adelina, and continued, 'so tell me what you know.'

'Dietrich's dead,' was my opener.

Adelina didn't show any particular surprise, just asked, 'How?'

'Well, I didn't take Dietrich for someone who was likely to commit suicide, so I guess someone else shot him through his head and then put the gun in his hand.'

'Where was this?'

'In the hotel in Antwerp.'

'The hotel I booked for you?'

'Yes.'

'What a waste,' she said, 'he was a good man.'

'I thought so too,' I said and, while it wasn't strictly true, I was certainly willing to admit that I had no reason to believe that he wasn't a good man.

'So what happened to the diamond?'

'It's still in the Diamond Exchange on Pelican Street, waiting for one of its brothers to turn up.'

'Do you think that's likely?'

'Not now,' I replied and told her about the big rock I had been offered a few hours before. I did say that I had been shown it rather than suggested that I had been offered possession.

'And the others?'

'I didn't see them.'

'The others are a little different from those two,' she said quietly.

'How do you mean?'

'Well, the big one and the one I gave you to take with you are real cut diamonds that were originally mined from the Earth. The others were sort of industrial diamonds.'

'Not so valuable, then,' said Dwayne, swallowing his mouthful of vodka.

'Exactly the opposite, they were even more valuable, it's just that they weren't mine.'

'Go on,' said Shove.

'They were what are going to become known as "battery diamonds".'

'What are they?' I asked.

'They're made up of almost pure carbon-14.'

'You mean, they're radioactive?' was Dwayne's question.

'Exactly. Apparently, so I was told, they were made of pure C-14 and then compressed into a diamond. They have quite a slow rate of decay and are a very good way of storing energy over a long time. They break down to C-13, which is stable by flinging out a neutron, which then breaks down into a proton and an electron. That may remain as hydrogen gas, or it might fuse with a neighbouring C-14 atom to make an equally stable nitrogen-15 atom, which is also a gas. After a while the diamond will become porous, I suppose, but the reorganisation of the two atoms will release energy, and the amount of energy released compared with the size of the diamond means they will be a very efficient way of storing energy.'

'Will be?'

'Yes, it's still very experimental at the moment.'

'I hate to ask, but how did you get hold of them?' That was Shove's question.

'I am involved in the funding side of some very big business,' she replied. 'I didn't steal them. They were given to me by their owner for safekeeping.' She laughed coldly and added. 'Fat lot of good that was.'

'So their value at this moment in time?' Shove again.

'Incalculable,' she replied.

'Would the English government have any idea how to make use of them?'

'I have no idea. I don't know how to use them myself. I was, as you say, looking after them for someone else.'

'I thought you were going to trade them in for a supply of cocaine,' I observed drily.

'No, I was going to show them to Sigmund to prove I had actually got them. There really wasn't any cocaine involved, that's just feeding you information that you would understand.'

'Can you make an atom bomb with them?' Dwayne chipped in worriedly.

'No,' she said, 'at least, I don't think so; they won't form a chain reaction once they have achieved a critical mass or anything.'

'But the owner?'

'Is going to be profoundly upset. They trusted me.'

'Did Ruke know they were, what did you call them, battery diamonds?' That was me asking that one.

'Well I didn't tell him. As far as I know all he thought was that they were industrial diamonds for cutting stuff. He wouldn't even have known they were radioactive unless he had a Geiger counter of his own, and even if he had one, why would he think of studying my little bag of diamonds with it? He was given the diamonds to bring directly to me for storage, but none of them got here.'

'I said you should have sent me to go and pick them up,' muttered Yuri sadly.

'If I'd thought there was going to be a problem, I'd have gone to collect the bloody things myself,' was her reply. 'So where do we go from here?'

'Are you asking me as a police officer?' asked Shove.

'Why not?' replied Adelina, 'I'm not committing any crime by harbouring radioactive diamonds am I?'

'I don't suppose anyone had ever considered that diamonds might be radioactive,' Shove smiled back. 'It's like drugs, they can only be pronounced "illegal" and "class A" once they have been proven to exist in the first place.'

'And would they be made illegal if the government knew about them?'

Shove contemplated for a while. Personally, I thought our Witan in Norwich was a fairly liberal operation and didn't like making anything illegal unless, firstly, there was a point to it, and secondly, if they could enforce the ban. The concept of battery diamonds seemed to me to be such a very useful idea that I thought our government would positively encourage their creation and exploitation. The only problem might be if some clown tried to turn them into weapons of mass destruction, and from what Adelina had just said, that wouldn't be possible. Shove came to much the same conclusions, and then wondered why the English government had been so aggressive about getting their hands on them.

'Probably because that's where they came from,' Adelina replied.

'You mean you nicked them from England?' Dwayne asked. 'Neat,' was his opinion.

'I didn't nick them at all, and I don't think the owners who passed them on to me for safe keeping had any deed of provenance.'

The conversation went on for a while and, by the end of it, I'm sure that the tiny gangster with the huge eyes and the local chief of police were firm friends, having decided that they were going to find the diamonds and return them to their rightful owners who were, interestingly enough, based in Oxford in South Mercia. Me, well, I had to work out how I was going to get Adelina's stone back from Ben without marrying him in order to do so. There, I had at least made that decision. Were we still going to remain friends with benefits?

The three of us were fairly quiet as we went back to Thorpe Lea Road, where we left the pod with Dwayne to take him home. I suspected the ramifications of that kiss would remain unaddressed for a while, and I was still thinking about what had been left unsaid when I went up to bed that night.

Chapter 28
A Sort of Coda

'Do you want eggs, Steff?' asked Mrs. Grubbs at breakfast. 'I don't know why, but the chickens have got carried away with their laying this morning.' I had already been fantasising about scrambled eggs on toast for breakfast that day, so how was that for a coincidence? She bustled off to do the egg-scrambling and the bread-toasting when Shove walked in. She was still wearing civilian clothes, though not the same ones as the evening before.

'I think we should go over to the station in Market Deeping, once we've broken our fast. I want you to introduce me to Adelina's diamond this morning.'

'And you're not going in uniform?'

'No, I thought mufti was more casual, and it would be less assertive if I was dressed like a tourist.'

'But your passport states exactly who you are.'

'There are more people in and around Market Deeping than just the border guards and the police. I think, at least at the moment, it would be better if we went low profile.'

'Why?' I asked. 'Are you going to arrest him or something?'

'No, but I might be suggesting that the person directly responsible for the murder of Farrukh Ahmed would have an arrest warrant waiting for him if he ever crossed the border.'

Fair enough, I thought. It would be fairly obvious to anyone who was actually looking that we came from south of the border; our pod would be the only one that wasn't falling apart at the seams.

Plans established, an oppressive silence fell between us. I hoped that Mrs. Grubbs wouldn't notice it, or if she did, that she would put a different spin on it, like us having been so busy yesterday evening that we were still too sleepy to have a conversation at breakfast. Maybe that was true – neither of us were ever the most chirpy over breakfast anyway. If the silence had anything to do with that kiss, then what we had done meant more to both of us than either of us was willing to admit to ourselves.

The fresh scrambled eggs were wonderful. The toast made from the homemade bread was wonderful, and a second piece of toast, this time covered with marmalade made from the bitter oranges that had, at least until very recently, grown in our back garden was also wonderful. The coffee was wonderful too. Yes, I was concentrating far too deeply on the content of my breakfast, and how it was, yes, wonderful, and not enough on the company I was keeping round the table.

In the end, Mrs. Grubbs wandered out to start the washing up or something, and maybe Shove got fed up with the silence. She announced, 'Come on, let's go over to Market Deeping and sort this all out. There was an Anglian citizen called Farrukh Ahmed who has been murdered here in Anglia. We know who was responsible for it, even if he didn't physically pull the trigger himself. However, if this Colonel Osborne has a number of professional killers operating on our side of the border, at the very least they need rounding up and sending back to him, preferably parcelled up. Am I right or what?'

I agreed with her. At least she wasn't blaming Ben for the hit on Ruke, even indirectly. But then she didn't know about what Ben and I got up to. That set me thinking about how much Ben knew about me. He knew about my operation, and what triggered it, but I had never mentioned any names, partly because they didn't mean anything, really, to me either. For most of my life Ruke had been behind bars, and not for destroying my ability to be a mother. By the time they had caught up with him, he had been responsible for abducting other even younger white girls and forcing them into prostitution. I was never in court as a witness at his trial or anything. Shove had kept me out of that in her role as my family worker. From what she'd said, they had enough on him to put him away for a very long time without anyone even mentioning my name. So, at that point, I got better, got back into doing my schoolwork and headed off to university. I was given some 'counselling', if that's what you called it. My personal thought was that, actually, I would rather have been allowed to forget all about it, rather than having had it brought up again each week. Especially as, when they let me out of hospital, I found my predatory uncle had ceased to exist. Apparently he had had a skinful and had fallen over, hitting his head on the hearth in his front room, and no one had found him 'til it was too late. It was an ill wind indeed that blew no good. Even now I can't help pondering why James was the only man I had ever considered living with. I wondered what had happened to James that made him the same as me, someone to whom sex and love were mutually exclusive? Maybe it was now that I should be having counselling, rather than when I was just fifteen, and already seriously damaged. My parents were not there any more so I went to live with my mother's sister, whose husband abused me regularly. Two years after that I got raped by Ruke's gang and they nearly killed me. It was only then that anyone thought of offering me counselling. What was the point in that? I had already worked out what I was going to do with my life – the administration of justice – and, while the fine tuning of how I administered justice had changed a bit in my twenties, my life was still part of actively being one of the good guys.

'Come on, kiddo,' said Shove. 'Our chariot awaits outside.' I followed her out to the front door, where a pristine pod was waiting for us with its doors open wide. Was it me, or was the snow actually settling? There was certainly a chill in the air that I didn't much care for. Shove too put her hand out, palm upwards, looked up at the sky and grimaced. I even noticed at that moment that I thought her expression was pretty. No, that was nothing new, I remembered right from when we first met when I was fifteen, I thought she was pretty, it's just that now I thought, oh well, I don't know what I thought now I had kissed her, it was only now that I felt she was pretty or something. And then I was wondering whether it was still possible to be 'pretty' when you were our age. Look, Steff, plug your brain in, you only kissed her to show Adelina that you cared, geddit?

The pod moved out, heading north over the Crescent Bridge, and left past the railway station where the train had refused to come the previous day. Why was that? I turned to Shove and asked her if she minded if I called Allo to tell him I had got a physical copy of the book now.

'No, not at all. Oh, I didn't ask, what was it like?'

'Pretty ordinary,' I replied, 'but I'll read it from cover to cover over the next few days and get a better feel of it. Do you want to read it after I've finished with it?'

'Only if you think I might want to. Right now, just going on what you've already said about it already, I'd just as soon not bother. What you might consider doing would be to ask that Sabrina of yours to make a 3D copy of it. She can make functional 3D copies of old physical books, I presume?'

'I haven't the faintest idea,' I replied. 'But she'll know. If she can't, I'm sure we still have the wherewithal to make a straight photocopy of it. It'll be a little laborious and take time, but still …' I left the rest of the sentence unfinished.

Past the station, we then headed north up Bourges Boulevard and on up through Werrington. On the right was the township and on the left, even though there were industrial areas between the road and the yard, which included the local pod assembly and servicing plant, the presence of the Marshalling Yard was all-pervasive.

By the time we had reached the bottom of the Marshalling Yard, I was actually talking to Allo and explaining to him that I had got my hands on a physical copy of the book. 'Tell you something, if you can get me a paper copy of it, even just a paper photocopy, I can upload that into my system. At the very least I can then get a copy of that to the readers who were royally fucked off about losing their copy they had already paid for. That would be seriously good PR for my little bookshop, even if I could provide that sort of service to just a few punters.' That would have been another use for one of Sabrina's copies. I put a knot in my hanky to remind her to make two copies.

The Marshalling Yard was probably the only place on the whole Island where two separate governments had joint control. In most places there were bits of No-Man's-Land between borders, here the borders overlapped. There were moments when I wondered how the police were selected, as both forces patrolled the Yards. Mind you, they were the only people apart from the brown-suited 'Happy-Harries' who were allowed to walk about freely. The lorry drivers had to stay in their cabs. The men who monitored the trains had to stay in their control rooms. The men and women who operated the cranes which lifted the containers off the trucks onto the trains, and vice versa, were all Happy-Harries. I wondered how you got a job as a Harry? Must ask Shove some time, but now would be inappropriate. She was concentrating.

We turned left at the Werrington Parkway junction. If we had gone straight on, we would have gone into the fenced-up village of Glinton. It was then that there came an extraordinary whistling sound over our heads. We turned to each other, our faces wearing identical question marks. A moment later, there was an explosion in the industrial area somewhere to our left, and the line to Allo went dead. I tapped my wristy, 'Allo? Allo?' Shove and I both actually said, 'What the fuck?'

We followed the road as it bore right on its way to the Maxey Cut border. That's when we both realised what the fuck it was. Shove flicked the pod to manual and it stopped. The border, some half a mile ahead of us, wasn't there any more. The 'steel topiary' that had been there the previous evening had been brought down and was draped over the monster that had caused its collapse. The cabin where I had had my decent cup of coffee was now matchwood, and in its place was a Chieftain tank. I had seen that tank just yesterday and its owner hadn't mentioned that it was going to be coming our way the following morning. If he'd even dropped the slightest hint, I'd probably have got that. The leading tank was certainly on the Anglian side of the border. It wasn't moving. Behind it were the other two tanks, with their barrels elevated, so as not to point directly into the turret in front of it, but they were conspicuously pointing into Anglia. The barrel on the tank at the back had a wisp of smoke coming out of its barrel: it was the rear tank that had fired.

Shove pressed the slow forward button on the pod and it eased ahead. The second tank belched a shot of flame from its big gun. Again, there was the terrifying whistle over our heads and then, after a moment, there was an explosion somewhere behind us in the North Bretton township.

The one thing that I noticed immediately was that the gun on the lead tank, which had not been fired yet, was not elevated like the two behind it. It was pointed straight at us. At that moment, the hatch on the top of the turret of the front tank opened and a head, wearing a peaked cap and goggles, popped up. The head looked behind him, presumably at the tanks in the rear, and he waved his hand forward. The whole area behind the tanks was covered in clouds of dark smoke.

'Oh fuck!' said Shove, 'We're being invaded.'

I had the feeling that the future of Anglia would probably depend entirely on our actions in the next few minutes. I took off my shoes and followed that with the removal of my trousers. The shoes went back on and I opened the door.

'What do you think you're doing?' asked Shove.

'The local CO likes my knees,' I said. 'He's even got names for them,' I told her as I got out of the pod.

'What?'

'They're called Richard and Lionel,' I told her, looking at the gun, which was swaying with the movement of the tank as it rolled towards me. With Richard and Lionel both taking on a rather cold blue tinge, I walked steadily forward, looking straight down the barrel of that gun which, from where I was walking, was a perfect circle with a black centre. Was this my own Tiananmen Square? *Okay Ben, you say you love me, what are you going to do next?*

The figure in the cupola raised his hand as I reached the front of the tank, or perhaps it was more correct to say the tank reached me. I looked into the eyes of the driver which were visible through the slit in front of me, ignoring the man pretending to be Rommel in the cupola. I climbed up onto the tank, acutely aware its steel was distinctly cold on my knees. When I had got as far as the turret, Ben climbed out of the cupola, and waved a hand at one of the soldiers behind the third tank. He said first to the soldier, 'Please take Miss Flack to Headquarters, and put her in a cell. We will process her when this is over.' He then turned to me, and said, 'Now run along with the nice soldier, Poppity, and we'll have a little chat when I've finished with this.'

Shit, I thought, *I'm a prisoner of war.*

About the Author

Following a highly successful career as a GP, R.M. Cartmel returned to his first love, and took up writing again. He is now the author of five novels, with a sixth coming out in Spring 2019.

He writes two very different series. The first, The Inspector Truchaud Mystery Series, features a French policeman based in Paris but closely involved in the family vineyard in Burgundy. Cartmel, a lifelong wine buff, introduces fascinating details of viticulture and wine-making alongside his well-plotted, charming crime cosies.

The first three novels in the Truchaud series are set in the small Burgundy village of Nuits-Saint-Georges. The fourth takes the French Inspector to the Rhineland vineyards of Boppard, to investigate the murder of a colleague.

The second of R.M. Cartmel's series, North Sea Noir, is a long way from Truchaud's 'wine and crime', both in tone and geographically. The first book in the North Sea Noir mystery series is *50 Miles from Anywhere* (first published under the name Michael Cayzer), which describes in harrowing detail the dark underbelly of contemporary Peterborough over the course of four days. *North Sea Rising* is the second in the series.

Books by R.M. Cartmel

The Richebourg Affair (2014)
The Charlemagne Connection (2015)
The Romanée Vintage (2017)

50 Miles from Anywhere (2017)
North Sea Rising (2018)

Dear reader,

There are a number of people who need to be thanked for the creation of a story. The creative process is a somewhat lonely affair, and I for one find it impossible to write in anything but a state of total silence. I can't even have music on in the background when I am attacking my laptop, it is either distracting or irritating. I have even found I have written the words I was hearing down on the page, a little worrying when I had an Italian Opera on in the background! However, music is deeply involved in the creative process, so I would particularly like to thank Ludwig van Beethoven, Charles Valentin Alkan, The Grateful Dead, The Who and The Rainmakers to name but a few, whose music has been part of the thought processes over the years.

Obviously the most important people responsible for the creation of what you are holding are my publishers, Crime Scene Books, and my label-mates, who have been very supportive.

To Sarah, my editor and publisher, may I offer my [insert hyperbole here] gratitude. Without you none of this would have happened.

To Kelly, congratulations on your recent marriage and collection of even more consonants as a result. This book in particular thanks you for your input.

To Katharine May, who has copy-edited this book, I have no idea how you manage to do this and keep sane.

To Dan Harding, our publicity czar, thanks for being and doing.

For my family who keeps me fed and watered while I am hiding in my study, 'Dad's "writing".'

To Maggs for getting me out of my cave sometimes to go to the pictures.

To my reading gang who never say nice things to me because they think I might like to hear it. Their criticism is always on target, even if I don't respond in the right way.

To my 'label-mates'. Never having been published by any other firm, I have no idea whether other authors get such support as I do. I really hope so. But Rosie, Candy, SW, Stuart and Leye, thank you for being there. It feels good.

And finally to you, dear readers. Thank you for reading this, and if you didn't like it, you do know who to blame: the half-witted politicians whose idiocy created the scenario posited in this book. I actually wanted to dedicate the whole shebang to them, but Sarah wasn't having it.

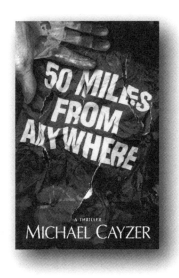

50 Miles from Anywhere

by R.M. Cartmel
(previously Michael Cayzer)

North Sea Noir mystery series 1

It could never happen here – or could it?

Ever wondered what really goes on in the place where you live?

When questions come bubbling to the surface of a seemingly quiet little English town, no-one's happy with the answers.

RM Cartmel's new thriller was originally published under the name of Michael Cayzer.

It is a book which chills from the very first page as it takes the reader on a desperate journey through failed lives, lost hopes and last chances.

The Inspector Truchaud mystery series

by R.M. Cartmel

The Richebourg Affair – The first in a series following the acute if rumpled Inspector Truchaud of the French police as he pursues fraudsters, murderers and gangsters over the course of a winemaking year in the vineyards of Burgundy.

The Charlemagne Connection – The second in the Inspector Truchaud series finds the diffident policeman unravelling yet another mystery in the little Burgundy village of Nuits-Saint-Georges. A young German tourist seems to have gone missing. But what at first appears quite a straightforward affair soon turns dark when a decomposing body is found in the woods.

The Romanée Vintage – The third in the Inspector Truchaud series set in the vineyards of Burgundy, which sees Truchaud following up a mysterious phone call, with explosive results.

The Amy Lane mystery series

by Rosie Claverton

Binary Witness – As clubbers in Cardiff are targeted by a brutal murderer, the police turn to unconventional means to catch the killer. Amy Lane, a desperately agoraphobic grey-hat hacker, only at peace with her fingers on a keyboard and her eyes on a screen, can peek into virtual corners in ways DI Bryn Hesketh would rather not know about. But he needs her skills, and turns to her for help. Jason, an ex-con looking to go straight, starts as Amy's cleaner, but soon becomes much more.

Code Runner – Ex-con Jason Carr thought he had faced the toughest challenges when in prison, but nothing had prepared him to be the assistant to an agoraphobic hacker. They make quite a team though and are able to hack the cases even the police struggle with. But when a corpse washes up on the beach, the duo might be in over their head. Jason can't resist searching for clues and when he gets framed for murder, Amy feels her life crumbling around her. She's the only one who can prove his innocence and when his time in prison threatens to claim his life, she knows she has to solve the case fast.

Captcha Thief – Agoraphobic hacker Amy Lane and her sidekick ex-con Jason Carr are caught in a tortuous and increasingly dangerous adventure as Amy seeks to help track an art thief and Jason seeks to impress the National Crime Agency investigator Frieda Haas sent to recover the missing painting – and its abductor. As the evidence leads Amy and the police in circles, Jason finds himself taking more and more risks in his hunt for the thief. Nothing is as it seems. Are Amy and Jason merely playthings for a vicious murderer? Can they survive the game?

Terror 404 – In the fourth in the Amy Lane mysteries series, Amy Lane, agoraphobic grey-hat hacker, has been isolated in a private psychiatric hospital, away from friends, associates and every form of connection to the web. Jason, her trusted companion and co-conspirator, is in hiding and on the run. When a fellow hospital patient is mysteriously murdered, Amy and Jason must find a way to join forces to solve the murder and save themselves.

The Jocasta Hughes mystery series

by Candy Denman

Dead Pretty – Dr Jocasta (Jo) Hughes, thirty two years old, a willowy blonde with a wicked sense of humour and an unsatisfactory love life, works part time as a GP in Hastings, a small English fishing town, and is on call as a Forensic Medical Practitioner for the local police. As it becomes clear that there is a serial killer on the loose in the town, Jo finds herself increasingly at risk.

Body Heat – The second in the Dr Jocasta Hughes sees the Forensic Medical Practitioner faced with a gruesome series of murders which leave the remains of the victims twisted and charred. The hunt heats up for the arsonist, and so does Jo's relationship with the exasperating DI Miller. A chilling mystery with lead characters you want to spend more time with, and a murderer you definitely want to avoid.

Small Deaths

by S.W. Williams

A serial killer is loose behind the lines on the Western Front during the First World War. As the armies mass against each other readying for battle, someone is kidnapping and killing small boys. The military is indifferent – civilian problems are not their affair. The police are powerless – the military will not allow civilians to investigate in a war zone. Set against the build-up to the battle of Cambrai in November 1917, this historical thriller builds to an unexpected, heartbreaking finale.